THE BOOK BOYFRIEND

JEANNA LOUISE SKINNER

To Jess

Happy reading!

love

Jeanna Louise Skinner

x

For Charlie and Jesse. Write all the books; sing all the songs; shoot for the moon, my Superstars! There aren't sufficient words in the universe to tell you how proud you make me and how much I love you.

For Kieron, whom no book boyfriend could ever replace.

And for Phillip, who—just like Emmy—deserves to find his own "Happily Ever After".

CONTENTS

CONTENT GUIDANCE

Even though this story is a romance, filled with magic, hope and an uplifting conclusion, please be advised that the narrative deals with a number of sensitive and potentially triggering issues, which are listed below. I hope I have given these the care and consideration they deserve.

Main character with schizoaffective disorder and anxiety

On page panic attacks

Grief

Anecdotal emotional/psychological abuse and gaslighting by ex

Reference to historical cheating by ex

On page medication taking

References to therapy and psychiatric appointments

Reference to historical suicide attempt

Reference to historical sectioning

Reference to historical body image issues

Historical misogyny on page, which is later addressed in the narrative

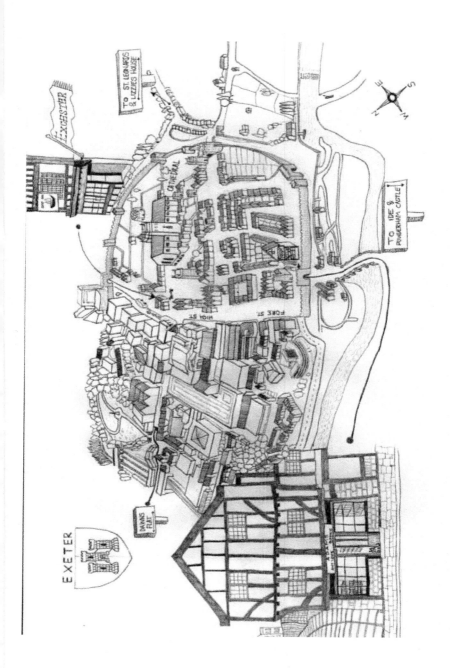

"And yet, to me, what is this quintessence of dust?"

William Shakespeare

"It should be me; I should be the person who saves you.
Not because you need saving, you probably don't, but I do and
in the process of saving you, I would finally be free from the
trappings of loneliness."

James McInerny

CHAPTER 1

2008

*T*he old bell over the door tinkled.

"Maggie!" A girl of maybe sixteen called into the dust-imbued gloom. She browsed familiar, untidy shelves, trailing a fingernail along the spines. Retrieving a battered copy of Vanity Fair from one towering bookcase, she made for the burgundy leather armchair in the window where the light was good.

A thud behind her sent a shockwave to her heart and she whirled to find its source.

"Breone!" She crouched to scratch the cat's ears, palm to chest. "Did you fall off the top shelf again? You don't fit, silly." He purred into her hand; the only sound inside Adams' Antique Books besides an authoritative ticking from the grandfather clock in one dim corner. Except...there was another noise: an undeniably masculine timbre, floating into earshot as if borne by the dust motes. The girl frowned, straining to make out the words, but they were muffled by haphazard battalions of books lining the shelves; dog-eared casualties of war in the battle for territory in the cramped shop.

"Maggie?"

The clock stopped, Breone fell silent and for the second time in minutes the girl's chest quivered. The perennial dust bloomed, like billions of tiny iridescent fireworks. Then Maggie Adams' wizened form emerged from behind a bookcase; blue eyes - lately scudded with cataract clouds - now sparkling like far-off stars. For a split second, the girl fancied there was another figure lurking in the shadows behind Maggie. A taller, broader figure. But then her eyes adjusted to the dimness and the apparition was gone.

"Who were you talking to? I thought I saw-" The teen stooped to kiss the old woman's crepe paper cheek. She chased imaginary wraiths around the walls, nostrils flaring in the musky, vanilla-soaked air.

"Talkin' to?" Maggie removed a duster from her apron pocket and began wiping one caked shelf. "T'aint no one 'ere but me and the people in the books, my lovely. You knows tha'."

2017

"You're imagining things again, Em. Listen to my words, *my* voice. Trust me."

2018

LEFT ARM ALOFT, as if hailing a Saturday night taxi, Emmy stood on tiptoes to deposit the thick volume on top of the tallest shelf. With her right hand she shielded her eyes, nose wrinkling in anticipation of the inevitable dust cloud. Digging in her pocket for a tissue, her fingers instead closed around the letter. The last letter she'd received from Maggie Adams. It shouldn't have been a shock, she'd been carrying the tear-stained note around for weeks, after all. But her heart still plummeted to her stomach, as if she'd missed a step going downstairs or blundered blindly into an empty lift shaft.

The unwelcome voice sounded inside her head; words jumbled but cloaked with the scorn of a crow cawing. She squeezed her eyelids shut; instant tautness in her chest robbing her of breath, like a too-tight corset. *Maybe this is what drowning feels like?* Lungs over-spilling. Saltwater tears. She gasped, grasping for a memory, a lifeline before the riptide voice could drag her under. *There!* A phrase Maggie used to always whisper: "Let us find solace in the quiet moments. Let us be peaceful in pauses, find stillness in silence. Wisdom is caring yet remaining immovable with our words."

Still. Be still…

When she finally eased the sheet of notepaper from the small, crumpled envelope, Emmy's hand did not shake.

My Darling Emmeline,

I know things must seem insurmountable right now, but I have faith in you. You are much stronger than you give yourself credit for and YOU WILL get through this. I only wish I could visit, but my health isn't what it used to be. Alas, I fear we shall have to forgo our trip to The Globe this year. I hope you do not mind too much.

Breone sends his love. Have you considered coming back here? Or adopting a cat? They can be wonderful company. I do worry about you all on your own in London. I wanted to ask you how your writing is coming on. I don't suppose you get much chance at the moment, but maybe it will actually help to write about how you feel about Dan and everything else? Forgive me for interfering. You must do what is best for you. Ignore an old woman and her sentimental fancies.

Before I go, I must tell you about my friend Jonathan, but there's so much to say and I don't know where to begin. He'll be visiting again soon; I do hope you get to meet him. I know you will love him as much as I do. Also, there's a book in the shop you simply MUST read. I'll show you when you next come to stay. It's my absolute favourite!

I'll say goodbye now, but I want you to remember something: It is a truth universally acknowledged that a single woman in possession of neither good nor bad fortune, must be in want of nothing but belief in herself.

All my love,

Maggie

P.S. Deeds Not Words

Emmy had read it numerous times, hoping to find refuge in the old lady's fragile, spidery handwriting and archetypical cryptic messages, but she was still none the wiser even now. When their mutual friend, Lizzie, called last month with news of Maggie's passing, Emmy hadn't hesitated, allowing her comfort blanket of memories to soften the three-hour train ride back to Devon: the over-powering sweetness of lavender soap; the funny little glasses Maggie wore on a chain around her neck; the older woman's surprisingly girlish laughter, which filled the tatty shop with unbridled warmth. The omnipresent dust. Still, Emmy couldn't help but fill some of the journey praying Lizzie was mistaken. Maggie Adams could not be dead. She was as much a part of Exeter as the topsy-turvy Tudor buildings or the centuries old Cathedral.

Now, as she read the letter again, Emmy massaged the ache in her sternum; a newly acquired habit, one she wasn't sure was due to stress or the half dozen tablets she swallowed each day. Probably a combination of both. Wandering over to a tired, olive-green sofa she'd picked up second-hand, she dropped down onto it, and was surprised when Breone, Maggie's cantankerous ginger cat, joined her. He pressed his battle-scarred face into her neck, and she scratched at his lopsided ears with her other hand, her mind overrun with memories.

She thought she'd been coping, but grief had crept up on her. At first, it had curled up in her lap, allowing her to pet it, giving and receiving comfort in turn. But the ache burrowed deeper into her chest, settling in her heart. Stubborn and immoveable; a wounded animal hiber-nating in the ribcage of a skeleton long since deceased.

Emmy's fingers came to the same sudden halt they always did. As sure as spring follows winter, her mind insisted on returning to the questions posed by Maggie's final communication. What was all this nonsense about adopting a cat and returning home to Exeter? How would that answer all Emmy's problems? Had Maggie been trying to warn Emmy about her impending death after all? And who was Jonathan and, if he and Maggie were so close, why hadn't she mentioned him before? Was he even aware of Maggie's death? Emmy had asked around Maggie's customers and friends, but no one had heard of him. Finally, there was this mysterious book that Maggie proclaimed to be her favourite. Such was Maggie's obsession with Shakespeare, she and Emmy had undertaken an annual pilgrimage to The Globe every autumn. Curious to discover what literary masterpiece could replace *The Tempest* in Maggie's heart, Emmy had spent her first few days back in Exeter hunting for the elusive volume.

The buzzing of her phone broke her reverie and she stashed the letter back inside her pocket and brought out her mobile. Leticia. Editor-extraordinaire, Emmy's former boss and one of her few London friends.

"Hi, lovely." Emmy smiled.

"Hey Em. I just want to say good luck for tomorrow and remind you that my door is always open. No one can read and edit a manuscript as fast as you." Leticia's voice was filled with its typical mother hen warmth. "Oh, and if you ever do write that book, it's mine, remember?"

"Thanks. I'll remember. At least I've still got plenty of reading material."

There was an uncharacteristic silence before Leticia continued and Emmy's mouth twisted in concern as she waited. Why was everyone so obsessed with the idea of her writing? It was the last thing she felt like doing right now.

"I don't want to interfere, but you know me. Can never keep my mouth shut. Are you managing, financially?

And…are you okay? About Maggie, I mean… and… you know?"

Emmy hesitated, her gaze falling on the shelf opposite. *The Complete Works of Shakespeare* swam into focus as her eyes adjusted camera-like between her near and peripheral vision. She knew what Leticia was really asking. The same question everyone asked since her break up with Dan–and her recent diagnosis.

"I've got my savings so we're okay for now, and I should be getting my share of the deposit on the house back soon. We need to sell at least ten books a day to keep the bailiffs from the door, but we'll muddle through."

Emmy spoke fast, sure Leticia would understand the subtext in her choice of pronoun and secure enough in the closeness of their friendship that she wouldn't push her further. If there was one thing Emmy didn't need today, it was questions about her health. *And selling ten ink and paper books a day would be a lot easier if everyone was as interested in the kind of old and dusty tomes that Adams' Antique Books offered as they were with downloading the latest fast fiction fix.* But Emmy wasn't about to mention that. Leticia was the head of digital at Happy Ever After Publishing.

"And… Maggie?"

"There's a memorial service in October. Maybe ask me again then." Emmy squeezed her eyes tight to ward off the inevitable tears, her voice a cracked whisper.

"Oh Ems. I'm so sorry, Hun. Me and my big gob. I'll let you go. You must be busy… I didn't mean to upset you."

"It's okay. You didn't." Emmy smiled despite herself, picturing her former boss now wearing what Emmy and her colleagues liked to call 'Leticia's Worried Look'. "I'll be back to see you all again soon, promise."

They said their goodbyes and Emmy swiped the screen to finish the call. She'd adored her job at HEA. Publishing books had been her childhood dream. Well, that and writing them. It seemed like only yesterday that her parents, indulging in their only child's obsession with reading and writing, had taken the then ten-year-old Emmy to Adams Antique Books. That was the first time she had met Maggie Adams - *'a much-loved family friend'* - and when the older woman held a finger to her lips, eyes twinkling with mischief as she pressed a battered copy of *Practical Magic* into Emmy's hands, Emmy knew instantly she'd made a bond for life. That night, she'd devoured Alice Hoffman's dreamy, breathtaking tale about the Owens sisters, finding in them the siblings she didn't have and so desperately craved. Was it any wonder she'd found the family she coveted first in the stories she read and wrote, and later in those she helped to publish?

Her heart rattled like a rollercoaster car as she glanced around, now a bookseller of a different kind. Fingers trembling, she stroked the spine of that same edition of *Practical Magic*, unable to believe the old store and flat above it belonged to her. Then a balloon of guilt rose in her throat like nausea, which she swallowed back, closing her eyes again. It's what Maggie wanted. So why did she feel like she was right at the top now, being whipped by the wind and dangling over the edge, waiting for the world to tilt and swoop as she plummeted to Earth?

Still. Be still.

"Em? Where do you want this one?"

The voice came from the mass of black curls snaking

from behind an enormous box. Emmy ran the short space across the store to help her best friend, Lizzie, heave it on to the counter.

"Thanks. What you got in there? A ton of books?"

"Funny." Emmy swatted her on the upper arm. "Is that the last one?"

"Yep, all done. And now I have my spare room back again. It looks great in here!" Lizzie scanned the store, grinning.

Antique bookcases ran throughout the shop, along three walls and twisted around hidden corners. Maggie's battered, oxblood leather armchair still took pride of place in the picture window, but now the green Gumtree sofa sat opposite, with a small, reclaimed pine coffee table in between. Daylight flooded through the sparkling glass and seeped into nooks and crannies. It had taken two weeks of shifting, lifting and cleaning, but thanks to Lizzie (and her spare room) and their mutual friend Dawn, the shop was finally ready for tomorrow's reopening. The hard work was worth it. They'd salvaged everything they could, from the glitzy chandelier, splashing rainbow-filled sun arrows across the walls and the soft lamps dotted here and there, to the antique telephone in its original red box, which had once stood on the cobbled pavement outside like a sentinel before being rescued by a strident Maggie two decades earlier. Now a quirky reading nook, complete with book-laden shelves and cosy seat, it was Emmy's favourite spot in the whole store. No longer dim and dingy, Adams' Antique Books was filled with warmth, light and wonder, and was–to Emmy's mind at least–the perfect place to read and buy books.

"Yeah, it does. Now all we need," Emmy held up her hands to show her crossed fingers, "are customers."

"They'll come, don't worry."

"I *do* worry, but I've got to try." Emmy caught a glimpse of herself in the cracked, gilded mirror behind the counter. Her face was a badly drawn caricature, distorted and gurning like her reflection in the funfair hall of mirrors she'd visited with her ex last year. She rearranged the frown etched on her gamine features into a smile, but there was nothing she could do about the haunted look in her dark eyes.

"Maggie would be proud of you, Ems," Lizzie said, meeting Emmy's gaze in the mirror.

"I hope so," Emmy whispered.

Lizzie rested her dark head against Emmy's blonde one. This *should* have been a difficult feat, given their five-inch height difference, but Lizzie's love of heels was legendary. Even her own mother had once joked that she should have been christened wearing Louboutins rather than baby booties. The disparity between the two best friends' height wasn't the only notable distinction in their appearances. Where Lizzie was brunette and pocket-sized petite, Emmy's strawberry blonde waves topped the kind of body that fashion sites liked to market as "plus". Emmy was nowhere near as reticent and preferred to think of herself simply as fat–and there was absolutely nothing wrong with that, thank you very much.

But loving her looks hadn't always come easy. There was a time in her teens when Emmy would have given anything to not stand out in every class photo, to not tower head and shoulders over most people in a room. But learning to not only accept her body, but to also rejoice in her showstopping-from-every-angle knockout curves, was just one of the many wonderful life lessons Maggie Adams had imparted about being a young woman growing up in a patriarchal society. Of course, the medication she'd recently started taking had made Emmy bigger than ever, but that was a pattern she'd settled to with relative ease. These days, her greatest bugbear about her size was that those same websites didn't seem to cater for her tallness as well as her fatness, and she often ended up wearing so-called men's clothes. But this wasn't such a sacrifice. Emmy was fat and– haunted expression aside–she looked just as fabulous as any other woman, including her tiny-proportioned bestie Lizzie, who she now flung one long arm around to squeeze closer.

"*I know so.*" Lizzie affirmed. "Now, you know, I'm not into all these 'Book Boyfriends' like you, but if I was, *this* would be the first place I'd come to buy *my* smut. What could be more romantic?" She spun, arms flung out wide, like a euphoric Julie Andrews on a mountaintop.

"It is *not* smut! Austen is not smut, the Brontës are not smut!" Emmy knew Lizzie was trying to distract her but she couldn't help reacting all the same.

"Whatever, but you and I both know that even Maggie's reluctance in the face of modernity gave way for more and more bodice rippers over the years. Even Breone agrees with me." Lizzie nodded towards the ginger cat, who was attempting to curl his fat furry body onto a pile of vintage romance novels with limited success. Emmy sighed and grabbed the moggy before he could topple the stack and deposited him on the flagstone floor. The cat turned his squished face away in disgust and somehow slinked into a narrow gap between a book-case and the wall, orange tail swishing in rebellion.

"Romance novels can be super feminist, which you'd know if you'd read my dissertation. And, as I've pointed out multiple times, bodice ripper is an outdated term that doesn't help shift stock," Emmy said, pouting as she turned back to Lizzie. "Plus, it sells, so maybe Maggie was on to something."

"Let's hope she was right." Lizzie's tone was a curious cocktail of doubt and delight as she picked up the book on the top of the pile. "Enchanted Paradise by Johanna Hailey," she smirked, holding the book up for Emmy to see.

The cover was your standard 1980s romance novel affair: an impossibly beautiful heterosexual couple in a passionate clinch, the woman's nudity barely covered by a whisper-thin diaphanous veil, the man—all torso and rippling back muscles—gripping her bare flesh in his hands. What set this particular cover apart, however, was its inclusion of a male and female deer, a unicorn and a rainbow in the pastel toned, other-worldly background. And Emmy loved every inch of it. She snatched it from her best friend's hand with an exasperated tut and set it back on top of the stack as if it were as precious as a first edition Austen.

"Don't yuck someone else's yum."

"Whatevs," Lizzie was unperturbed. She whipped her head to the door, dark curls bouncing. "I think I've left something in the car. I'll be back." She tripped out of the shop before Emmy could respond.

With Lizzie out of sight, Emmy read the letter again, pacing the floor with slow, unthinking steps. It would make more sense to sell, but Emmy couldn't bear to part with Maggie's pride and joy, especially not when Maggie's last wish was that *"Emmy keeps the shop open—no matter what."*

She smiled as her mind flashed upon the chaos she'd found the store in last month. Old tomes had towered like skyscrapers on every surface, lending the gloomy space the alien visage of a cityscape in miniature. The storeroom had been even worse, and the accounts were nothing short of a nightmare. Grimacing, Emmy had rolled up her sleeves and dived headfirst into the task of rescuing Adams' Antique Books with a cast-iron resolve and a lot of TLC.

"Oh, Maggie. I promise, I'll make this work, and find the book. And Jonathan." Her voice was nothing more than a murmur but the particles now glistening in a shaft of light from the chandelier overhead seemed to dance in the current her breath made. Not one to hold sway with superstition, Emmy's mouth fell open at how this small, everyday enchantment could fill her heart with hope and she wiped at a tear trickling down her cheek before it could fall on to the old-fashioned paper Maggie had favoured.

"Talking to yourself again, sweetie?" Lizzie reappeared in the doorway with a bunch of helium balloons in one hand, and the largest bottle of Prosecco Emmy had ever seen and two champagne flutes in the other. Then, the beaming smile on her freckled countenance faltered and to Emmy's alarm, she looked as if she might cry. "Oh Ems, I'm so sorry. I didn't mean... you know? Anyway—surprise!"

Emmy had grown accustomed to people walking on

eggshells around her these days; all delicate words and hushed conversations that ended with furtive glances when she entered a room. *Please, not Lizzie too.* Stuffing the letter away, she fixed what she hoped was a reassuring smile on her face and crossed the store in three long-limbed strides to give her best friend one of her trade-mark, bone-crushing hugs.

IT WAS GONE midnight when Emmy stood in the doorway of the old shop waving goodnight to Lizzie. She laughed as her friend blew extravagant kisses, leaning dangerously out of the taxi window. Ever the party animal, Elizabeth Sorenson was the best friend equivalent of a girls' weekend in Vegas: shotgun wedding and three-day annulment, optional extras. Of course, Lizzie had insisted on cocktails at Dr Ink's after they'd finished off the Prosecco and throwing caution to the wind, Emmy had accepted.

Now she fumbled with the keys as she leaned on the inside of the door for support, but the combination of her weight and inebriated condition caused it to swing shut with a bang. She jumped and swayed, the keys slipping from her grasp and her legs giving way, like a house of cards collapsing from the bottom up. Hiccupping, she reached out, desperate for something to cling to, and her fingers rapped on the nearest bookshelf, brushing against something cold, hard, and out of place. She took out her phone and squinted in the dim screen light at a small, wrought-iron lever, half-hidden in the elaborately carved woodwork.

Mystified, Emmy tucked her mobile under her chin

and grasped the lever with both hands; the metal was cold and unyielding against her palms, and she grunted, pressing down hard. There was a loud *clunk* and she fell backwards, the echo that ran through the darkened shop matched by the pounding of her heart. She crawled forward, one hand now holding her phone like a shield, and peered into the secret drawer which had popped out of the bottom of the bookcase. Inside lay a large, leather-bound book, front cover blank. No title, no author's name. *Nothing.* The spine and back cover were exactly the same. With curious, grabby fingers, Emmy opened it up, breathing in the familiar intoxicating sweetness of old vanilla that only old books possess. Where there would usually be a page of printer's information and dates of editions, there was simply a handwritten note.

My absolute favourite. Enjoy x

Emmy's breath quickened at the sight of Maggie's spiky scrawl. *I've found it!* Her fingers rifled through the pages and only halted when she caught a glimpse of a name: Lord Jonathan Dalgliesh.

Jonathan?

A whispered breath skimmed the back of her neck; gentle as a puff of air from a turned page and she whirled around. Not a good decision. She clung to the shelf again, waiting for her head to stop spinning. There was nothing to see, but as her eyes fell on the half-glazed door, she remembered she hadn't yet locked it. Muttering under her breath about security, Emmy located the key on the flag-stones, got shakily to her feet, and scrabbled with it in the lock until she heard the satisfying *click.* Then she drove the deadbolt home before turning to the stairs, the book now clutched to her chest like unearthed treasure. The air held that tranquil stillness peculiar to late summer and for the first time since moving in the prickle of fear along her scalp at being alone in the old store was almost a caress. Shrugging it off, she climbed the wrought iron spiral staircase, careful to plant her feet on each step.

The next time Lizzie suggests Prosecco cocktails, she can bloody well stay the night and navigate these bloody stairs too. Her laugh sounded nervous and too loud in the dark. Breone brushed against her legs as he followed Emmy into the flat. She made quick detours to the bathroom and then the kitchen to check on his food and water before collapsing on her bed. Her eyes fell upon the blister packs scattered across her bedside table, and she grimaced at the memory of the one and only time she'd been foolish enough to mix the strong anti-hallucinogenics and alcohol. Oh well, one night without meds couldn't hurt. *I promise, I'll never drink again.* She giggled, holding up three fingers like the girl guide she'd once been. Then she sat bolt upright. Her whispered oath to Maggie! How could she have forgotten?

That's not going to work, an unhelpful and all too familiar voice said as she shook her head in a fruitless attempt to induce sobriety. Emmy stiffened, fingers gripping the duvet, knuckles taut. *Not now, please!* Snapping her eyelids shut, she inhaled and exhaled like she'd been taught, counting to ten, then twenty, grounding herself in reality by stroking different textures around her: the soft cotton duvet cover, Breone's warm, shaggy fur, the leathery surface of Maggie's mystery book. Only when she was satisfied the voice was silent did she dare open her eyes again.

Emmy was determined to keep at least part of her

promise that night and nothing was going to stop her. Mentally sticking two fingers up to the voices, she settled back into the cushions propped up behind her. She might not have found Maggie's Jonathan yet, but she had "The Book". Would he be anything like Lord Jonathan Dalgliesh, and could Dalgliesh match up to her own literary heroes, Fitzwilliam Darcy and Henry DeTamble? She smiled as she turned to page one. As if anyone ever could?

∿

1565

I SURVEY THE BATTLEFIELD; *a writhing, grotesque mass. Disembodied cries rend the air as sharpened daggers. The stench of death is overpowering—it rises to greet my senses like a fetid being. I choke back bile and step away from the field upon which I ran as a boy; the once lush meadow, now crimson stained, trampled, and awash with the blood of my brothers, comrades, foes, and fools. If this were to be a victory, then it would be a hollow one. Too many lives have been lost to justify this folly. Yet, who am I to defy my Queen? I have sworn an oath, and my allegiance, like my sword, lies at the Queen's hand.*

I am Lord Jonathan Dalgliesh, a nobleman of Devonshire, though the acts I have committed this day cause me to dispute that nobility. That I will do my duty is unquestioned, but I cannot shake my misgivings. How can it be just to massacre in the name of religion?

A soft weeping at my feet. The prone figure is little more than a child. What is she doing here? This is no place for a female, especially not one so young. A gaping wound on her chest sucks for air as her lungs fill with blood. I take a knee and lean toward the girl, clasping her cold, clammy hands in my own. Her eyes devour me whole and I make a silent vow to remove her from this stinking place, to give her the dignity of a good death. A small salve to my conscience, yes, but it is both the least and best I have to offer.

"H-h- help me! Y- You must help me."

She clutches at my leg, her grip, weak and ineffective. I reach out to haul her on to my back but my hands halt, grasping nothing but fresh air as I spy the speckled marking on her neck. A witch! I know I don't have much time, so do what I must.

$\sim$

2018

EMMY RACED to open the door. How could she have overslept today of all days? Just one drink, Lizzie promised. When was it ever just one drink? She should have known better the moment Lizzie breezed in with the Prosecco and balloons. Emmy eyed the bunch of helium and foil suspiciously, as if *they* were somehow to blame for her wretched hangover, and not her woeful alcohol intolerance. Smiling at her foolishness, she turned the "Sorry, We're Closed" sign over to the reverse with a flourish, so it now proclaimed Adams' Antique Books was, once again, open for business.

Then she switched on the lights and computer, which hummed into life, and waited. The local paper was sending someone over later and Lizzie said she would pop by during her lunch hour, but Emmy had no idea what else to expect. What if no one comes?

What if no one ever comes?

Desperate to avoid a rat run of self-doubt and intro-spection, she turned to the computer (her one big purchase) and updated the store's social media accounts and blog and scrolled through her personal Twitter account–fast becoming a bad habit. Keeping her mind busy helped, and she loved writing. At least she had a small band of readers in cyberspace. Now if her followers' likes and comments would only transfer into the ringing of cash through the till, she could stop fretting. She side-eyed Breone, hoping for a smidgen of moral support, but the cat was asleep in Maggie's armchair, purring as if he didn't have a care in the world.

"Some help you are," she said, wandering over to stroke the top of his head. Then the bell above the door rang and Emmy smiled what felt like her first real smile since she'd returned to Devon.

By five, Emmy's head was spinning, and she rubbed her temples with a weary groan. *Damn Prosecco cocktails.* Between the journalist's visit, Lizzie's hasty gossip-laden lunch call, two telephone conversations from her parents wishing her good luck (although Emmy suspected they were using the store opening as an excuse to check up on her), and a healthy number of actual paying customers through the door, Emmy was overwhelmed from her first day. Several people commented on how wonderfully inviting the shop looked–like a cross between a cosy lounge, an old-fashioned tearoom, and a library–and many others told her they'd known Maggie Adams well.

"It's simply marvellous you've taken over the shop," old Mrs Bath proclaimed at least five times.

But no matter how busy she was, her thoughts kept returning to Maggie's mystery book, and what little she could recall reading last night. It appeared to be a work of fiction, set in Tudor times and the hero was called Sir Jonathan Dalgliesh. She remembered something about the aftermath of a battle and someone's desperate plea for help, but whoever said it, and to whom they said it, evaded her. She couldn't even recollect putting it down and going to sleep, and having overslept this morning, meant she didn't have time to re-read. Now at the end of the day, all Emmy wanted was to lock up, organise for tomorrow, order a budget-stretching takeaway, and curl up with The Book. She rapped on her forehead with the knuckles of her right hand.

And woe betide anyone *who disturbs me.*

She was about to turn the sign on the door again when a stranger almost as tall as Emmy herself walked in. Whether this was his natural stature, Emmy couldn't say because he was wearing a knight's full battle armour, including a helmet and visor. He carried a broadsword and appeared to be covered in mud and–alarmingly–what looked like spatters of blood. Emmy smiled in welcome but darted back to relative safety behind the counter all the same.

"Hi, I... err–I didn't know there was a re-enactment on. Looks like you *really* got into it. Is there... something you were looking for?"

"Forgive me, my lady, for my appearance. I would not have planned to meet you this way, but I don't have much time." The stranger's voice, though distorted by the visor, was deep and smooth. "You *must* help me, Lady Emmeline."

"*What?* H-how do you know my name?" Adrenaline whooshed through Emmy's system, sending synapses into overdrive all over her body. She clawed under the counter for the phone. *Scream, run or fight? Scream, run or fight?* She followed his hands, now busy on the helmet, keeping one eye on the sword. Then she gasped, as the stranger raised the visor and she saw his face for the first time.

CHAPTER 2

2018

*E*mmy couldn't ever recall seeing a more beautiful man.

His hair, though flattened by the helmet, was a mass of dark brown curls. They framed a curiously yin-yang face; bone structure that was strong yet delicate, fragile and masculine, youthful and mature, all at the same time. Polished alabaster skin. Brow smooth, broadening at the eye-line to glass-edged cheekbones that slashed downwards to a sturdy, square jaw, complete with cleft chin. His lips were sculpted but not too full. A broken nose was the only blot on the otherwise impossibly symmetrical landscape of his face, although even this could not detract from his agreeable appearance. Something about him didn't seem real.

He almost shimmered, like a mirage.

It was his eyes that Emmy found most beguiling, however. They were a vivid, clear blue, soft in expression, yet intense in both depth and colour. They put her in mind of the first time she'd seen an icicle– five years old, spellbound by her first winter in the UK after her Mum's job as a university lecturer saw them upping sticks from New Zealand to settle in Devon. She'd held the frozen stake to the pale sun, squinting at it like a bird, watching the colours play a spectrum on her hand. The beauty of December spiked with danger.

Who was this unworldly stranger and what did he want? Not even his devastating good looks could silence the clanging alarm bells in Emmy's head, and she shivered despite the heat. Yanking her gaze from him, she took the opportunity to locate her phone. She held it up for the young man to see.

"I want you to leave." She aimed for her natural voice and was rewarded with a confidence boosting rush of pride when she got it.

"My lady, Emmeline," the stranger replied, bowing his head once more and taking an encouraging step towards the door. "I mean you no harm. I bid you an apology a thousand times over. It was never my intention to alarm you, but I see I have failed, and thus hope for just one measure of your forgiveness. I will leave, as you have requested, but I *cannot* promise not to return. Only you can help me."

Emmy's eyes trailed his broad back as he left and marched past the window. She sprinted outside, her lips on the edge of a scream in case he returned, but there was no sign of him. The Tudor edifices cast magical shadows upon the cobbles, thanks to a warm, late summer sun glowing high over the rooftops of the old city. The omnipresent tourists milled around, capturing everything with their phones, cameras and selfie sticks, but no one seemed to have noticed the ridiculously handsome knight who'd just exited her shop.

How could he have disappeared so fast? What did he mean by being unable to promise not to return? Will he come back? Why does he need my help? And how in the chuffing hell does he know my name?

Something half-forgotten tugged at the elastic of her mind. *"You must help me"* and *"I don't have much time".* She'd heard those phrases recently, but where? It was rather moot considering everything else about him. *He had a sword!* Shivering again, she took one final glance around before locking the shop and calling Lizzie. If ever there was a time she needed a Prosecco cocktail, *this* was definitely it.

Lizzie's breathy, high-pitched voice broke the silence.

"Okay. Tell us again what this guy said."

"He sounded old fashioned, like he'd stepped out of a Philippa Gregory novel or something. He kept calling me 'my lady'. *And* he knew my name. He said he was sorry for how he looked and for alarming me, but that I must help him, that only I could help him. It was nonsense." Even to Emmy, the words sounded hollow and ridiculous. She picked at an invisible spot on her skirt to avoid her friends' worried faces.

In the absence of Prosecco, Lizzie had opened a bottle of cheap white and Emmy's second glass was going down better than the first, the buzz already helping blur the memory of her encounter with the oddly dressed and spoken stranger. She shouldn't be drinking again, especially after last night's cocktails, but for now the alcohol was helping to repair her fractured nerves.

"I don't know, Em. Maybe you should report it," said Dawn, gesticulating as she always did, her every movement expressive and exaggerated.

Never one to turn down an invitation to rally the troops, Dawn was already in situ on Lizzie's grey sofa when Emmy arrived. Friends since that first nail-biting day at secondary school, Emmy, Lizzie and Dawn had shared everything from first crushes and periods, through breakups and breakdowns, to Lizzie losing her mum when she was just sixteen and Dawn coming out as Bi to them both just a year later. The Bookworm, The Party Girl and The Academic.

By the time they were in their teens, Lizzie and Dawn had joined Emmy in working part-time at Adams' Antique Books and those hazy weekends together in Maggie's shop, listening to Maggie as she enthralled them with tales about The Resistance and the Women's Suffrage, were some of the best memories of Emmy's life. The three girls were enchanted by Maggie's storytelling skills. She had a way with words that Emmy could only aspire to. It didn't matter whether they believed in all of Maggie's stories, for stories were all they could be. Maggie was old, sure, but not old enough to have been a suffragette. Still, it was during these fictions that Emmy remembered that neither she, nor Lizzie or Dawn–or anyone else that she knew of–had any inkling of how old Maggie truly was. She always seemed to avoid any discussion of her true age.

When seventeen-year-old Lizzie announced she was

leaving to study local history, it had been the worst day ever. It wasn't much later, however, when Emmy departed for Durham University to read English Classics and Dawn started the first of two degrees at Oxford in Photography, before switching to Cambridge for a Masters in Law. Dawn was an ace at keeping her options open. Now Lizzie was a moderately successful author and historian—she'd even been on television a couple of times, much to Maggie's delight—and post-graduate Dawn was studying remotely for her Bar Exam and saving for her big move to California.

As she'd hovered on the threshold of Lizzie's St Leonard's home, Emmy had allowed herself a precise thirty seconds speculation about what Lizzie and Dawn's conversation might have been about before she arrived, but decided she was better off not knowing. It wasn't as if she'd told Lizzie anything to be alarmed about over the phone. Nothing too alarming at least. Now she bit the inside of her lip as she mulled over Dawn's suggestion.

"And say what?" Emmy took a swig of wine, as she looked at her friend. "A man in fancy dress came into my shop today and asked for my help? I don't think they'd take me seriously, even *I* don't take me seriously!"

"Yeah," Dawn gave a vigorous shake of her head, her cropped blue hair lending such a contrast to her dark brown skin. "But, how did he know your name?"

"It's not too hard to find out. I'm mentioned in that god-awful ad I got on Heart. You know? Where the woman with the worst-attempt-at-a-Devon-accent-ever says, 'Call Emmy on…'? He probably heard it on the radio." Emmy's only lie was one of omission, for she hadn't yet divulged how the stranger had used her full name: Emmeline.

"Yeah, who could forget, 'Adem's Anteek Beks of Wes' Strit?'" Lizzie laughed and refilled her and Dawn's glasses, before disappearing into the kitchen.

"Don't remind me." Emmy nestled back into her chair, cuddling a knitted grey cushion to her chest. She raised her voice slightly, so Lizzie would hear. "Anyway, there's no harm done, and apart from that, it was a great first day."

"Oh no. You're not getting away with that!" Lizzie reappeared wagging her hot-pink manicure in Emmy's direction. She placed a jug of water and fresh glass on the table with a pointed look.

"What?" Emmy ran a finger around the top of her wine glass, studying its perfect curve.

"Don't *what* me with that innocent tone! We haven't finished discussing your mystery man yet. Have we, Dawn?" Lizzie turned to the other woman, but Dawn remained silent, miming pulling a zip closed across her mouth instead.

"He's not *my* mystery man. There's nothing to discuss. Conversation over." Emmy pressed her lips together.

"This conversation is most definitely *not* over, Emmy Walker! What did he look like? Spill–and no convenient memory loss."

Emmy sighed. Lizzie was always able to see through her. Truth was, she'd thought of almost nothing but the stranger's looks since the moment he'd removed his helmet. Since when had she become so superficial? Looks mattered little to her in real life, but something about this man and his undeniably attractive appearance, had her swooning like a Bridgerton sister. Swallowing the last of her wine, she opened her mouth to describe him, and then closed it again. Did she even have the words to express such beauty, when even the faultless and unrealistic men of her favourite books could not compete? Some writer, huh?

"Well," she began, playing with a tendril of her shoulder length honeycomb hair, "he was tall, and he was wearing armour."

"We know that part." Dawn tucked her legs beneath her, dark eyes sparkling. "Tell us what he looked like!"

"He was… he was… I don't know. He was the most beautiful man alive! Are you happy?" Emmy helped herself to water and poked her tongue at her friends, knowing exactly what Lizzie's reaction to this intelligence would be.

Lizzie pouted. "The most beautiful man alive? *Ems, come on!* Surely your slushy romances are more original than that?"

"I knew you wouldn't understand, but if you'd *seen* him. It doesn't matter anyway because he's obviously not all there. Ha! That's a laugh. *And* he has a rather large sword."

"Oh, I bet he does. 'She whimpered as he impaled her with his mighty weapon.'" Dawn threw a dainty hand against her forehead and fell back against the sofa in a mock swoon, causing Lizzie's dozing twin tuxedo kittens, Netflix and Chill, to leap up, fur on end, black tails now bearskin hat bushy.

"Stop!" Emmy laughed, launching the cushion in Dawn's direction, but then she became serious. "Are you two sure you don't mind that Maggie left me the store? You both worked there too."

Dawn barked a laugh. "God, no. I've already told you, the last thing I need is more debt, and it's not like Maggie gave me nothing." She held out her right hand where an ornate gold ring sparkled on her third finger, the three brilliant clear and deep-blue gemstones glinting wickedly. It was probably paste, but Emmy knew that Dawn had always adored Maggie's jewellery collection. "Besides, it was never really my thing, you know that. You'll make a much better go of it than me. Than *anyone*."

Lizzie nodded and came to join the other two on the sofa, wrapping both Emmy and Dawn in a hug.

"Will one of you come back with me?" Emmy sniffed. "I need to cash up for tomorrow. I didn't even set the alarm."

Dawn shook her head again. "Sorry. I've got to-"

"Study, yes we know," Lizzie said with an impish smile. Dawn's attitude to the books was legendary. She was the kind of person who crossed every T and dotted every I, except she used tiny hearts in place of dots–the barest of concessions to her more artistic side. Lizzie had to duck as Dawn whacked her with the cushion. Shrieking, she turned to Emmy again, "I'll go with you. You wanna stay here tonight? Or I can kip at yours?"

"No, it's okay, but thanks. Once I know I've locked up and the alarm is set, I'll be fine. I just spent six years in London, remember?"

"How could we forget? You left us in this backwater for the bright lights of the big city without ever looking back." Dawn swooned theatrically again.

"Backwater? I asked you both to come and live with me! You were too busy conquering Oxford and then Cambridge, and Miss I-Don't-Believe-In-Romance here became the most famous person to come from Exeter after Chris Martin, fell in love with the local gentry and married young. Where is Thomas anyway?" Emmy added, looking at Lizzie.

"I never said I didn't believe in romance, just not in Happily Ever After. Thom's playing cricket with some blokes from work. He won't be home for hours. I can call and tell him I'm staying at yours. He won't mind." Lizzie was already on her feet.

"No, but *I* do. You two have only been married five minutes. Never let it be said that I ruined marital bliss."

"Em, you really ought to stop reading those romances. Book Boyfriends don't exist. Thom and I exchanged vows five years ago." Lizzie held up her right hand, as if taking an oath,

"*'I take you, Elizabeth Jane Burrows, to be my wife from this time onward. To love you and cherish you and to share all that is mine with you.'* That night he farted in bed and dunked me under the covers. Hardly the behaviour one would expect from a member of "the gentry"." She winked. It was a constant source of amusement to them that Lizzie's husband Thom could trace his old-Devonian family seat almost three hundred years. He even had a grandfather called Fitzwilliam.

"Five years is nothing! You're still in the 'Honeymoon Phase'!" Emmy's eyes bored into her friend's hazel ones, "You two are going to be together forever. Leaping into each other's arms the moment he walks through the door. Not even making it to the bedroom. Thom whispering how he can't get enough of you, how the very sight of you drives him wild with desire. You, whimpering as he impales you with his–"

"After everything you've been through, I'd have thought that you'd have given up on all this romance stuff, but there's no hope for you, is there? Or maybe that's what gives you hope. You're a testament to perseverance, Emmeline Walker, just like your namesake." With an exasperated, yet affectionate sigh, Lizzie held out a hand to help her friend up.

"Drink up your water, Sweetie, and let's grab a Chinese on the way to yours. My treat," she added before Emmy could protest. "I'm starving!"

EMMY CLEARED the last of the sweet and sour chicken away and made a final check on the alarm. Only then did she remember The Book and the stranger's voice from earlier echoed inside her head, *'You must help me, Emmy'.* Snatching it from floor by the bed, she leafed through the delicate pages until she found the passage she wanted:

"H-h- help me! Y- You must help me."

Scanning the rest of the chapter, she reacquainted herself with Lord Jonathan Dalgliesh, the aftermath of the battle and Lord Jonathan's meeting with the young witch. *How drunk was I last night? I don't remember any of this.* Okay, so it wasn't exactly the same, but what an odd coincidence.

Putting all thoughts of the handsome stranger on the back burner of her mind, she turned the page to find out more about the enigmatic Tudor knight. No matter what Lizzie and Dawn said, men in books were so much better than the real thing. Strong, handsome and dependable, Emmy's book boyfriends had never let her down. No, real life was far too complicated. Especially when some of the things you see and hear inside your head aren't real, your ex-fiancé cheated not just once but multiple times, and the only man you're attracted to now is a cosplaying *Game of Thrones* fanboy, with a face like an Adonis and a penchant for dangerous weapons. A little escapism seemed more realistic somehow.

CHAPTER 3

1567

The Dread Sweate has returned. The fireplaces burn strong and the court stifles in the cloying summer heat. It is said that death is swift, with few surviving once the sickness takes hold. We must endure the furnaces to prevent further spread.

Miss Caroline Godwin is the youngest daughter of Sir Godfrey Godwin, chief physician to the Queen. She is lovely. At once come-hither, yet aloof. Her smile is radiant with the kiss of youth and her eyes reflect the waxing and waning of the flames. Her pretence is strong, yet the sharp rise and fall of her chest gives her away. Why else would she have agreed to accompany me to a private chamber? She is uncharacteristically unsure of herself. I watch as she takes a coquettish sip of wine and wonder if she will be like her older sister in bed.

"This blessed fire becomes unbearable, my lord. Might we not open a window?" She fans at her cheeks, rosy-stained

and delicious. An apple ripe for picking and I am the very man to shake the tree.

"Ahh, my Lady, I apologise, but surely you understood your father's instruction? We must do whatever we can to work up a clean and natural sweat."

"There is nothing clean about cooking oneself. I feel like a goose dressed for Christmas dinner in July."

I ignore the obvious invitation to compliment and instead make my move. "I hear you are quite the sportswoman. Maybe if you changed into something more suitable, you would partake in a game with me?" I hold up the dice for her to see.

"And why would my lord think I be unsuitably dressed for a game of tables?"

Time to roll the dice. I cross the room in two strides and lean toward her right ear.

"Because, my Lady, I would take great pleasure in licking the sweat from your bosom, as I lay your delectable body across my table."

Her breath hitches and I lean out again to assess her reaction. The fire in her eyes is scorching, and I know I should be grateful if the good Doctor remains ignorant of exactly how we plan to interpret his wisdom.

...

2018

"Your change and receipt. Thank you." Emmy gave a winning smile, but the man swept up his copy of 'Shakespeare's Sonnets' and left without a word. Shrugging, she made for the labyrinth of shelves at the back of the shop and began to tidy up. At least *he'd* bought something, unlike the rest of today's picky patronage. She turned to the very last bank of shelves, the ones hidden from the front of the shop, and dropped the books she was cradling with a startled yelp. Someone was there! But *how*, when 'Mister Not-So-Sweet Silent Thought' had been the only person to come through the door within the last hour?

"*Oh!* I didn't see you there." She bent to retrieve the old volumes, cursing under her breath as she rubbed at a bruised toe.

The stranger turned, and the book Emmy had just picked up almost slipped from her grasp again. It was yesterday's knight-in-less-than-shining-armour, this time sporting a frilled collar, a kind of ruby coloured velvet blouson, and what appeared to be matching tights. *This guy is weird,* she thought without charity, hissing at the tiny, treacherous part of her that was delighted to see him again.

"Allow me, my lady." He knelt to help, and in the scramble to pick up the books, their fingers brushed. Emmy jumped as a crackle of static bounced between them; dust motes sizzling and swirling in tiny eddies. She shook her head, sure she was imagining things and allowed herself a rueful smile. It wouldn't be the first time.

"Thank you. Now you've left the sword at home, is there something *I* can help *you* with?" The whispers in her head were growing and her big toe throbbed. She wasn't in the mood for chivalry.

"I would take great pleasure in accepting your kindness, my lady. Your tone, however, suggests I hath offended again. I should leave you in peace. I will not risk your ire further by rolling the dice today."

He rose and headed for the door.

"What? *Wait!* You can't keep barging into my shop like this, looking like you do, talking in riddles, and then flouncing off! How do you know my name? What do you want?" Emmy was on her feet, anxiety now piqued with anger. She balled her fists at her sides and stood up as tall and straight as her six feet two inches allowed, but it was more a self-defence mechanism than the action of an aggressor.

The stranger faced her again, blue eyes blazing with an emotion that cut through Emmy's temper, weakening her resolve.

I just want to understand him, that's all. Nothing more than that.

"What do I want? My freedom. Good day, my lady."

Then he was gone. Again. Stymied, Emmy watched as he strode past the window and out of sight. She uncurled her hands, wincing at the nail marks she'd dug into her palms, which were now red and sweaty. *What on earth? Why does he need my help, no, my assistance? 'I would take great pleasure in accepting your kindness', yeah and I would take great pleasure in...in–*

Her eyes widened at the preposterous turn her thoughts were taking. "It couldn't be," she breathed. "'*I would take great pleasure in licking the sweat from your bosom, as I lay your delectable body across my table.*'" Then she remembered his comment about not rolling the dice and, with her heart hammering a piano concerto, quickly locked the shop door before tearing up the stairs. Her hands trembled and the skin on the nape of her neck prickled. She tried to tell herself to stop, that she was over-imagining things. She needed to start her relaxation techniques. *You're stressed. You're taking too much on. You're grieving about Maggie. And you stupidly didn't take your meds again last night!*

Thinking about Maggie was a sobering slap to the face, and she paused, resting her riotous head on a low beam and panting as if winded. But Maggie reminded her of the letter, and the letter reminded her of Jonathan and The Book, and round and round her thoughts went until, with a deep breath, she looked down at the old volume and opened it.

The familiar smell of lignin drifted up to meet her nostrils and she inhaled it like smelling salts, allowing its comforting scent to strengthen her spine and bind her resolve. The Book was heavy, but her hands were now steady, and she remembered childhood swimming lessons, diving to the bottom of the pool to lift the dead weight. She shivered, sweat beading on her top lip and trickling down her back. *'A clean and natural sweat'*. With fevered eyes, she read the random page she'd opened the book at:

I remove my doublet and shirt, affording me small, sweet relief from the stifling heat.

With creeping foolishness spreading through her veins and heating her cheeks, Emmy closed her eyes and waited. When nothing happened, one eyelid crept up like a roller blind. Nothing. She threw The Book back on the bed, as if its surface scalded, dashing away the treacherous sting of tears on the back of her hand. *Jesus, Emmeline! What did you think was going to happen? Your mystery man*

*was going to pop up out of a book as if by magic? Keep taking
the tablets, Em.*

Laughing through her tears, she made her way down
to the shop, glancing over her shoulder as a familiar voice
called her name. *Maggie?* She was halfway up the stairs
again, heart almost exploding with relief before reality
kicked her hard in the shins. Another hallucination. She
sank on to the cold metal steps, one hand gripping the
railing, the other at her chest. After several minutes, she
stood, straightening her clothes, her face set. She kept her
eyes on each step as she headed back down the spiral
staircase, daring herself not to cry. Then the wind was
knocked clean out of her and she almost went sprawling
as she collided with something as hard as oak. Her head
snapped up and Emmy found herself face to face with the
very real–and very near-naked–handsome stranger.

What the?

Ignoring voices and visions was difficult, but ratio-
nally she knew they weren't real, even if sometimes they
got the better of her. She could cope with them most of
the time. This was different. Reasoning with herself that it
wasn't possible, that things like this couldn't happen,
Emmy couldn't deny the very solidity of him in the air.
The way his ribcage rose and fell, the sound of his shallow
breathing, his spicy scent spiked with old vanilla and
musk. Swallowing her fear along with the key to an imaginary chastity belt, Emmy didn't step away. Instead, she
lifted her chin and spoke clear and strong.

"Okay, Mister, I've had enough! You're going to tell me
what the hells going on. Right now!" She punctuated with
precise jabs of one pointed finger in the centre of the
dense, dark hair on the man's torso. Her breathing quick-

ened, indignation sending tiny thrills pulsing between her chest and belly. This would be so much easier if he didn't have a marble chest, alabaster abs, and eyes like lost galaxies. Emmy scrambled to pull herself together, imagining how Lizzie would scoff at how easily Emmy's mind had run to typical romance hero descriptors. Seeking neutral territory, she cast her eyes downwards and started when she saw he was still wearing the ruby tights. Or were they called hose? Either way, they were *very tight* tights.

CHAPTER 4

2018

*J*onathan had lost count of the number of times he'd been in this position: disrobed in the presence of a beautiful young woman. But never had he met one so forthright, so tall and well built–in *every* sense of the term. Or so fascinating.

"Well?" Her dark eyes bored into his.

He opened his mouth and closed it again, unsure how to begin.

"My Lady Emmeline. Forgive me again. Once more you find me unprepared. My name is Lord Jonathan Dalgliesh, son of Lord William Dalgliesh, First Earl of Devonshire." He paused and the ticking from the grandfather clock filled the silence, matched by the thumping of his heart. Each tick, each beat, echoed in his ears with the portent of execution drums. This might be his only chance. He must not fail. "I am the man you have been reading about, the man in your book. Centuries gone by, a witch placed upon me a curse to exist as a character within the book, and thus, I have been waiting for someone to free me. I do not understand the magic completely, but I need your help, my good lady. Please, I beg you believe me."

Emmeline withdrew her hand and visibly shrank away.

"Funny. How about you try the truth this time?" Her words dripped with scorn, but there was another edge to them. It was a few moments before he understood what. Fear. A gallery of faces quickly embroidered themselves upon the tapestry of his thoughts; mostly female, some male, yet the single unifying thread through them all was fear. He would never forget their expressions; the wild-eyed bewilderment as they or their family members were accused. The very thought that he could instill those same emotions in another even now, centuries later, was a source of never-ending shame which would haunt him to his grave. Lady Emmeline was afraid of him and that would simply not do.

It was imperative that she believe him, that she understood there was nothing to fear. Not for her, at least. If only he could have kept the same care for himself. But he couldn't afford to worry about his potential fate now and pushed the unwelcome darkness from his mind. Focusing on the immediate problem again, he attempted to diminish his stature, doing everything he could to make his six-foot frame appear less threatening. But the woman's height bested his own by at least a clear inch and the dawning realisation of this unexpected and unusual occurrence jolted his thoughts sideways once more.

How could this unworldly female be taller than him?

He'd heard tales of giant warrior woman from far off lands, but he'd dismissed them as myth. Perchance she was related to these women. Or perhaps the females of Emmeline's time were all like this and Maggie was the outlier. Either way, the young woman's exceptionally agreeable size and stature was as every bit disconcerting as the beauty of her face.

He had to shake himself to snap out of the reverie. She was staring at him, waiting for him to speak. All too easily had he allowed himself to be distracted by her looks and the irony of this realisation wasn't lost on him. It was the reason, or at least one of them, that he found himself in this predicament–his fate in her hands–in the first place. Swallowing a sudden bitter wave of bile, he composed himself and tried again. "Please, I know this will not be easy for you to hear, but I must explain: Maggie assured me I would have your assistance."

It was the wrong thing to say. Her mouth which had been open–presumably to chastise him further–snapped shut. She marched to the door, yanking so hard it hit the wall behind and the glass in the panel trembled.

"I don't know what kind of sick game you're playing, but I want you out. *Now!*"

Jonathan sighed, holding up his palms in what he hoped was a non-threatening fashion. It was folly, perhaps, to have expected differently. Yet the growing realisation that he must so soon play his only remaining hand in order to gain her trust punctured his nerve. He was prepared for the pain. The physical aspect of tearing his flesh and blood from reality and transforming back into his paper and ink self was never pleasant, but he would cope if it meant there was a chance. It was the possibility of what came after that he hadn't been ready to face. He thought he would have more time. And now here he was, after hundreds of years of nothing *but* time, standing on the precipice of life itself, knowing that the clock had finally run out and he was about to dive off the edge into the unknown. If it wasn't so hideous to consider the alternative it would almost be funny. *Almost.*

This was it. The most important game of tables he'd ever played, and he closed his eyes briefly, knowing his fate hung on this, his last throw of the dice. If she did not believe or refused to help, everything was lost.

Time was up, the game done.

The End.

He took a deep breath and dove headfirst into time and space.

"I implore you to understand. You have nothing to fear from me, my Lady, but I understand your apprehension. Please do not be alarmed at what I am about to do."

FOR A MOMENT, nothing happened, and Emmy's already paper-thin patience was about to tear in two. Then the man before her dissolved into a dust-cloud of tiny, glowing particles, as if it was the most natural thing in the world for him to do. Gasping in disbelief, Emmy stumbled backwards. She reached out to catch a handful of the sparkly dust, but then her mouth fell open as her brain caught up with what her eyes were really seeing. Thousands upon thousands of miniscule, barely-there letters; the alphabet in a galaxy. Blinking as if she'd just woken from a fantastical dream, Emmy's adrenaline spiked. Her earlier fear now shot with drunken excitement, a heady cocktail coursing through her veins.

"Wh-where did you go? What's happening? Come back!"

Silence.

The glistening letters hovered in mid-air, as if time was standing still. Emmy did nothing of the sort. She charged up the staircase, two steps at a time, almost tripping over a startled Breone who wailed in reproach and was in and out of her room in a flash. Breathless, she returned to the shop, her heart leaping with relief when she saw the sparkling particles still swirling in the air. Shaking with almost uncontrollable excitement, she opened The Book and re-read the passage from a few moments ago:

"I remove my doublet and shirt, affording me small, sweet relief from the stifling heat."

She tried to keep her voice a natural monotone, but her thoughts flashed on how hard his chest had felt beneath the soft curls and how lovingly those tights clung to his muscular thighs. Her eyes squeezed shut, but whether it was to block out the memories or keep them in, she couldn't say. When she opened them again, he was there, and she let out an involuntary, audible sigh. *Pull yourself together woman!* Exasperated, she straightened her shoulders and forced herself to look into the stranger's, no–*Jonathan's*–eyes.

"Thank you, Lady Emmeline." He performed a small bow and with a slight incline of his head, gestured to her hand, "May I?"

"You may, I guess." Emmy's capacity for staggered disbelief increased further as he took it in his own and raised it to his lips, placing a chaste kiss on it. Synapses jumping, she heard herself talking as if from far away, "I'm not saying I believe you, but you're welcome. Now, what's all this about Maggie? The truth."

A MILLION RESPONSES shuffled through Jonathan's mind, battling for supremacy with one overriding emotion: relief. How much could he tell her without losing her trust? Maggie had sworn that Emmeline would be the one to break the curse, but Maggie had been wrong before. He eyed the sturdily built young woman with the honey-coloured hair and eyes as intense as stormy night skies with renewed doubt. Her attire consisted of a type of deep blue hose, which enhanced the shapeliness of wonderful hips and thighs. The hose was dotted with metallic studs and small, shallow pockets that appeared to be worthless additions; they would house barely a handful of coin. On her torso she wore a tight-fitting white tunic with the incomprehensible legend "Girl Boss" printed across the front in large, stylised pink letters. Finally, a yellow woven item that was a cross between a doublet and a cape was slung around her shoulders, sleeves pushed up to her elbows.

A cloth merchant by trade, he found the fabrics of her clothing fascinating, but jarring. Appearances could deceive, as he knew only too well. She might not resemble any witch he'd ever known, but if Maggie was right, Lady Emmeline was powerful, and he should be more careful. What on earth had possessed him to kiss her hand?

"Maggie was my friend. She discovered The Book

years ago and for a long time, she has been my only window into your world. She was confident we would find the answer. We searched for years, but to no avail and yes, perhaps as time passed, we became resigned to my fate. She was easy company; fun and well-read, as I'm sure you know. She taught me so much about your world and we would spend hours talking about the books we'd read. What else is there to do here?" He held up his hands and glanced around, grinning. "Then she told me about her plans for you and the shop, and how she knew you would help. 'Emmy is magic,' she would say."

He paced as he spoke, coming to a halt in front of her and for a second, it was almost as if Maggie was standing before him again. He inhaled and allowed her lavender perfume to permeate his memories. Maggie Adams; the one true friend he'd ever had, with her bright robin's eye and ability to sniff out bullshit from a thousand yards. How she'd knocked some much-needed sense into him when it came to matters of equality and sexual politics.

"Yer a dinosaur, Jonathan," she'd once said, a dangerous smile on the gentle features of her face—a juxtaposition he'd never been able to square. *"A dinosaur, lumbering along the great pathway of life and love, and one of these days a woman is going to come along like a meteor and extinct the Cad-osaurus out of you."*

He'd changed since she'd spoken those words, of course. One couldn't spend centuries repenting for their crimes and not change. Plus, passing any reasonable expanse of time in Maggie Adams company would make even the devil himself want to become a better person. How she'd laugh if she could see him now: uncertain and floundering in Lady Emmeline's presence. He swallowed, banishing the memories, focusing instead on the impatient young woman before him. Maggie was gone. She couldn't help him now.

"But, I can't! I'm not a witch. I don't know magic." She shook her head. "And why didn't she tell me about this? About you?"

Jonathan offered his most winning smile, but Emmeline glared at him. She was not to be charmed then. A surprise for sure, but a tiny traitorous part of him found it a welcome one for reasons he couldn't quite pin down. He gathered his thoughts again and tried a different tack. "Would you have believed her?"

"Yes. Maybe. If you knew her like you say you did, you'd know she could be very persuasive, so don't you dare look at me like that."

Her eyes glistened, colour rising in her cheeks, and it took all Jonathan's strength not to reach for her. He had not bargained for this. *Focus, man! You cannot afford this distraction, as undeniably diverting as she is.*

"Lady Emmeline, it was never my, nor Maggie's intention to upset you. I will leave and never return if that be your wish. You need never read The Book again. Throw it in the fire and this will all be over." He made to tug The Book from her hands, but she was quicker, and surprisingly strong.

"I didn't say I wanted you to leave, and I'm not upset. Now, if you want my help, I'd appreciate it if you could arrive properly dressed next time."

Jonathan bowed again, "I don't have much control over the how and when, but I'll do my utmost to please you, my Lady."

"And stop calling me that! I am *not* your lady!" She stamped one heeled boot hard on the flagstones.

Oh, but you should be. An image of her, passionate and willing in his arms appeared completely unbidden in Jonathan's psyche, taking him by surprise again. What on earth was wrong with him? Stamping down hard on the seeds of his desire, he crushed the fantasy to nothing before it could take root and blossom. Let it wither and die. The alternative would be too precarious to contemplate. As much as he hated to change back, to wrench himself from *almost living*, it was time to take his leave. It would not do to linger on the young woman's bountiful curves or the way her dark eyes blazed.

EMMY STOMPED HER FOOT, but the anger was a cover. It was a stupid thing to be jealous of. But Maggie was *her* friend. Yes, she'd mentioned Jonathan in her letter, but why not before? Did Maggie not trust her? Maybe she'd been right not to. She grimaced at how deeply Jonathan's smile had affected her just moments before. She couldn't even trust herself.

"I apologise again," Jonathan was saying, his voice so smooth it could temper chocolate, "I must leave soon. The spell only last for minutes at a time. But I believe the more The Book is read, the longer each time can be. That is what Maggie surmised at least."

"But...wait!" Emmy held up a hand, stalling. "You must have some idea of how to break the curse."

He grinned again, and it struck Emmy how youthful he looked. Gone was the furrowed brow and mournful expression of a much older man, replaced with a beaming smile to make Hollywood's young guns weep. It was her turn to frown, however, as a horrific thought occurred to her.

"How old are you anyway?" She asked, studying her nails.

"Ahh, that is very much dependent on one's perspective," he began, "I had eight and twenty years the day of the curse. I am however preserved–forever to remain young for as long as I am caged within The Book. I have not aged a day since the year of 1568. How many years would you give me?"

Emmy's teeth chewed on her gum, her mind overflowing with impossible thoughts. *On the one hand, if he really is trapped in The Book, unable to age then he must be young. But that means he's been on this earth in some shape or form for over five centuries. Is he twenty-eight or five hundred and twenty-eight? And, is he even real? Things like this just don't–just can't–happen!*

"It doesn't matter what I think. The main thing is finding the answer." Emmy surprised even herself, but now that her mind was made up she immediately began wracking her brain for any clue, anything Maggie might have said or done which might help. Maggie had trusted him and that was good enough for Emmy. It was always like that. She'd weigh up the alternatives, trying to apply logic, analysing the best course of action, but once she'd decided to do something, once her mind was set in motion, nothing could deter her. A small voice–totally unlike the unwelcome kind she sometimes heard–piped up, attempting to whisper doubts into her resolve; a mischievous Shakespearean imp. But she shook her head, mentally shooing the mischief voice away. *Get to fuck, Puck.*

Jonathan was fading. The outline of him beginning to blur, and Emmy reached out in a futile attempt to pin him down. Her hand brushed against his forearm and it was like touching a bare wire.

"Goodbye Emmeline. Maggie insisted the answer was here, within the books. The answer has always been here."

Then he was gone, the letters dissolving into nothing again, and a whisper of static ran through Emmy's body, electrifying her blood.

EMMY'S HANDS shook as she resisted the urge to read The Book again. She had to stop and think. She placed it almost out of reach on top of the nearest bookcase, and with deliberate care, began putting misplaced books back on the correct shelves; a loving mother tucking her children in at night. Then she went to shut the still open door. She performed each action without fuss, but her mind in overdrive:

Think! Things like this don't happen in real life.

But he was just here.

Ahh, but was he?

Are you sure you're not imagining the whole thing?

Jonathan is real. And I can prove it by reading that bloody book again.

But why do you want to prove it? What is it you find so fascinating?

He's trapped in a book by a centuries' old curse. Of course, I'm fascinated. Anyone would be.

So, it's nothing to do with how his thighs looked in those tights then? Or how your chest tingles with delight every time he says your name?

Don't be ridiculous, I just want to help.

She'd put the same book on the wrong shelf and removed it again three times. Sighing, she rubbed the middle of her chest, the epicentre from where her grief radiated; a hurricane's eye of emotion. It was too difficult to make sense of the maelstrom whirling inside her. Too much had happened recently and over the past year for her to assimilate.

Old Emmy would have turned to her writing as an outlet. Expressing her emotions in prose or verse had been easy once. Second nature. The blank page was *the* best listener, never judging, always ready to be scrawled upon with half-baked truths, easy fictions and the lies we tell ourselves in the dead of night. And every now and then, something wonderful and shining with truth, something so precious it demanded to be preserved forever in ink and paper (or text on a screen) before it could take flight and disintegrate on the wind, was written on one of those blank pages. Maggie had taught her that. Words had power.

Just like a crackle of electricity between two near strangers.

But after everything that had happened with Dan, just the thought of writing again made Emmy's stomach writhe like a basket of snakes. Would she ever trust a man again? Would she ever want to write again? She hardly dared admit it, to allow herself to hope. But something about Jonathan, his curse, his need for her help, and the energy that had charged between them when she'd brushed his bare arm, told her that she would. But her sense of self was so inextricably interwoven with her ability to write and Dan had ripped that from her. Now she didn't feel like she knew herself at all. To open herself up again, to trust again, took more than words, especially when she could already sense herself falling.

If only Maggie was here to talk to.

Deeds not words, a voice whispered, and Emmy spun, certain she'd find Maggie's gentle countenance smiling at her. But there was only the empty shop; dust motes swirling silver and gold, and ghosts of the past slumbering in books, waiting to be resurrected.

Swallowing the sudden bitterness that had crept into her throat, Emmy set her mouth and picked up her phone, the very tips of her fingers still thrumming with that same strange static. She hoped Lizzie would have some answers, because, for the first time in her twenty-six years, Emmy Walker was scared stiff of following her heart.

"I KNOW what you're going to say, but it's true." Emmy said, sure her face was the exact deep red of Jonathan's hose. The magic, so easy to believe in back at the shop, seemed far away, the stuff of fairytales in the cold light of day in Lizzie's bright and airy lounge. Lizzie and Thom smiled down at her from their wedding photos on the wall opposite. The rest of the space was taken up with blow-up artworks of Lizzie's books and the odd framed newspaper article about her achievements as a celebrated historian. The contrast between the two friends' professional and personal lives had never been more obvious.

Emmy shuffled in her seat. She'd just spent a breathless fifteen minutes recounting everything that had happened with Jonathan and The Book, fidgeting with her phone, her hair and her water glass the whole way through. Lizzie had watched and listened without interrupting. If she was concerned, she masked it well with occasional nods of encouragement. The nods were almost extraneous, however, because Emmy was doing her utmost to avoid looking Lizzie in the eye since she'd started talking.

"Ems," Lizzie's voice was gentle as she pushed up the sleeves of her cream cardigan, "you've taken so much on. Maybe...you're overdoing it?"

"I know what I saw!" Emmy sprang out of her seat and paced between the sofa and the fire, hugging herself like a hypothermia victim.

"I know you wouldn't make this up," Lizzie said. "I believe you that *something* happened, but you've got to admit, it's pretty far out there. Even for you."

Emmy crumpled into the chair again. Her earlier frisson of hope twinkling out. The shooting star of excitement, long-since dead, eclipsed by the veracity of Lizzie's words. She reached for the glass and downed the remainder of her water in one large gulp. Then she closed her eyes for a beat before meeting her friend's waiting gaze with a heat-seeking stare.

"I know what you're thinking, because I'm thinking it too. Poor cheated on hopeless romantic Emmy and her schizophrenic hallucinations. If anyone's book boyfriend was going to magically come to life it would be *mine*, wouldn't it? How can I trust it–trust *him*? How can I trust anyone or anything when I can't even trust my own mind? But…I *know* he's real. I can't explain how or why, I just know." She paused, rubbing her temples. "Come back with me and I'll show you. Please Liz."

Lizzie threw an arm around Emmy's waist and pulled her close.

"Course I'll go with you. If I'm right, which I will be, I get to say I told you so. If I'm wrong, which I won't be, and your mystery man *is* real, I get to ogle a hottie from history. It's a win-win as far as I'm concerned."

THE LITTLE SHOP was in stupor. The ticking of the grandfather clock cut loud through the silence. Nothing moved, bar a cloud of dust waltzing in and out of the narrow shaft of sunlight. Breone appeared from behind the tallest bookcase and padded across the floor where he stood, ears twitching, the right one permanently bent at a jaunty angle. A sudden scraping followed by two loud clicks echoed through the room, sending the cat bolting as fast as he could for cover–which wasn't very fast at all. The door swung inwards, and the shop flooded with light, the old bell tinkling like a magical melody from long ago.

"I know you don't believe me, but he's real." Emmy shut the door behind Lizzie and retrieved The Book from the shelf she'd stashed it on earlier. "Read it and he'll appear."

Lizzie arched her brows as she took the tome from Emmy. "Okay, so what are the magic words?"

"Lizzie! Just read it, will you?" Emmy jammed her fists in her pockets, pacing.

"Okay, okay. I'm sorry." Lizzie held up her hands in mock surrender, "Which bit do you want me to read?"

"It doesn't matter. At least, I don't think it does. He just appears after I've read it. Sometimes it takes a while, but the last time it was almost immediate."

Emmy flipped through the pages with frenzy and stopped, pointing at the passage from earlier. "There! Read that bit there."

Lizzie's face was a mixture of doubt and foolishness as she read the sentence aloud:

"*I remove my doublet and shirt, affording me small, sweet relief from the stifling heat.* Really?"

Emmy snatched The Book in frustration. "It's *doublet.* You're saying it wrong."

"All right, all right! Keep your hair on! I remove my *doublet,*" Lizzie poked her tongue out, "and shirt, affording me small, sweet relief from the stifling heat. What the hell's a *doublet* anyway?"

"A tunic or jacket. Very fashionable in the Middle Ages. Surely you of all people should know? You're the bloody historian."

Lizzie laughed. "My specialty is local history circa 1800s to the early twentieth century. Not the sartorial choices afforded to scoundrels in the 1600s."

Emmy's eyes darted around the room, paying scant attention to what her friend was saying. Any second now Jonathan would appear, and Lizzie's big mouth would be stuffed with the biggest portion of humble pie ever. Any second now...

"Earth calling Emmy. Come in, Emmy," Lizzie shifted

a section of Emmy's hair and spoke into her friend's right ear in monotone. "I know you're not going to like this much, but I'm worried. Seriously, you've taken so much on and Maggie's not long gone. It's only natural for you to be stressed. I meant it when I said I believed you, but even you've got to admit how–and I'm sorry for using this word–how crazy this all sounds. I'm not going to mother you, because you're a grown woman, but I need to know...have you been taking your medication?"

Shoulders slumping with all the grace of an empty potato sack, Emmy sighed. Maybe Lizzie was right. *Maybe I am overtired and stressed. Maybe I am relapsing.* Hot, spiky tears itched at her eyes and throat, and she swallowed them back.

"I'm sorry. I don't know what's wrong with me," she said, sighing again before collapsing against Lizzie for support. It was a lie. She was aware of *exactly* what was bothering her, and it wasn't related to her health. She didn't know whether she wanted to cry or puke, or both.

"Hey! Come on. You'll be ok. You're Bulletproof Emmy, remember?" Lizzie loudly recited the lyrics to a popular David Guetta song, her tuneless voice echoing throughout the shop, sending small and claw-footed things inside the walls scurrying for cover

"And you're definitely no Sia," Emmy said, distracted by new worries about mice. Mice and old books? Not good. Was there such a thing as humane pest control? And how in the chuffing hell was she going to afford it? It wasn't as if she could rely on Breone to help. She cast an exasperated glance at the sleeping cat stretched out on a shelf. She really needed to do something about his weight.

Exhaling again, she chuckled inwardly. Her ability to

focus on the problem was something she'd always prided in herself. Now here she was, jumping out of her skin at the slightest noise, her thoughts and emotions scattered like confetti. Lizzie was the scatterbrain, Emmy the sensible one, while Dawn had always been the brainbox of the group. But as she thought about Lizzie's remarks, she conceded her friend might a point. Emmy had lost track of the number of times she'd stood strong in a crisis.

At sixteen, she'd taken charge when she and a group of school friends had got lost on Dartmoor, leading them all to shelter. Or there was the time when Emmy had stepped up as a last-minute replacement for a sick goalkeeper at a charity netball match Lizzie had organised, despite not having played since secondary school. And just last year, after her parents were involved in a light aircraft crash, she'd dropped everything, and dashed to New Zealand to take care of them.

Old Emmy always found a way of coming out the other side. What was the point in being any other way? You couldn't fix the past, only learn from it. But then, all those signs she'd ignored, all the little imaginings she thought she'd been having, turned out to not be imaginings at all, and the next thing she knew she was coming out the other side of a cheating fiancé with a serious mental health diagnosis to boot. None of which was easy, no matter how sensible or stoic she normally was.

The loose threads of Emmy's fragile mind had been yanked so hard by Dan's betrayal, her once cheerful, can-do nature had been dragged into a hole so dark she couldn't ever imagine seeing the light again. Her psychiatrist told her that her symptoms had mostly likely presented earlier, but because Emmy was such a positive person it had taken both her parents' near-death experience and Dan's duplicity to trigger such a strong and frightening reaction. It was only then that she, and everyone around her, realised something was terribly wrong.

High-Functioning Schizoaffective Disorder was what the doctors diagnosed. Emmy called it a high-functioning pain in the arse.

Thankfully, both Mum and Dad were fine now, and Dan the Dickhead had done her a favour with his philandering.

Dodged a massive bullet there, Em.

Throughout it all, Maggie was the one whom Emmy had confided in—even more so than Dawn and Lizzie. Knowing she was only a phone call or letter away (Maggie never did adopt modern technology, so emailing or texting were out of the question) was Emmy's safety net. Who was going to catch her now? Her blurring eyes fell upon the old red telephone box and she half laughed, half sobbed. No way would she ever replace the telephone inside it with a modern version, even if a clumsy electrician had cut the line last month and she hadn't gotten around to reconnecting it yet.

"I know. I've got to shape up and stop feeling sorry for myself." Emmy said, hugging herself. "But he seemed so real."

"Shit like that always does. Grief messes with your head," Lizzie said in a sage tone. "I hate to do this to you, sweet cheeks, but I've got to split. Thom's parents are coming for dinner, and I need at least half an hour to prepare for Sheila's inevitable advice about my dismal homemaking skills. Will you be ok?"

"Go! I'll be fine. I am fine. Thank you."

They embraced and Lizzie left, glancing back twice to make sure Emmy really was okay. The bell trilled again as she closed the door behind her, and Emmy squared her shoulders against the creeping loneliness.

Then the bell rang again, even though the door remained closed. Then again and again, the little hammer hitting the outside of the bell over and over. Emmy shrank back, fear crawling all over her skin like biting ants. Her shoulders banged into the wall and she sank to her knees, cradling her head in her hands.

Stop! Please just stop!

No sooner had she thought it, there was silence. But then a harsh trilling from the old phone inside the booth opposite made her jump, and she stared through the glass panes in disbelief at the receiver vibrating in its cradle. Emmy jumped to her feet, shaking her head again. But the ringing didn't stop. It pealed repeatedly, a clarion that echoed through the shop and Emmy's brain with a kind of urgency.

Unaware she'd been creeping forward until she was standing in front of the booth, Emmy took a deep breath and swung the heavy door open. The ringing intensified until it became unbearable. With trembling fingers, she lifted the telephone handset, both ventricles now threatening to burst out of her mouth.

"Hello?" Her voice trembled in the abrupt deafening silence.

A gust with the force of a February gale rushed her, pulling books off shelves; pages flapping like birds' wings before a storm. Powerless to resist, Emmy shrieked as she was dragged out of the box into the middle of the store, dark blonde hair whipping across her face as dozens of books fluttered around her. She couldn't see more than a foot ahead and held out her arms to steady herself, no longer able to tell if the loud thumping was her heartbeat in her ears or the sounds the books were making. Flap. Flap. FLAP. Something heavy and solid landed in her open hands and she nearly leapt out of her skin.

"Stop!" The hoarseness in her voice surprised her, the only human sound amongst a thousand fluttering pages.

The books crashed to the floor. She didn't need to look down to know what she was holding. Déjà vu washed over her as her fingers raced to open The Book again. But her hands were shaking with such irrepressible force she almost dropped it twice.

When she spoke again, however, her voice was clear, loud and deliberate:

"I remove my shirt and doublet, affording me small, sweet relief from the stifling heat."

She squeezed her eyelids shut, counting the beats of silence in between noisy, desperate, life-affirming breaths.

"Lady Emmeline."

CHAPTER 5

*T*he suddenness of being summoned was always disorientating, no matter how prepared Jonathan was for it. He didn't have much experience with the laws of physics, bar what he'd read during his brief excursions into Maggie's life, but the feeling of time stopping and compressing just before his body reanimated–the letters, ink and paper of his cursed self once more becoming living, breathing tissue and blood rushing through his veins–was something he'd never grow accustomed to.

Old eyes seeing the world anew, as if they belonged to a newborn's. Colours and shapes slowly coming into sharper relief. Flavours and aromas, both familiar and unusual, thick in his nostrils and on his tongue. The very ground beneath his feet; his own solidity, and the way air flowed around him in charged waves. The river of his senses bursting its banks and flooding the tributaries of his nervous system with life.

It all felt real enough, yet it was always obscured by a

maddening veil that hung between him and true reality. A membrane so fine it was barely there, tiny words and letters glistening like gossamer text in the wan light, a spell woven upon the air. The story of his cursed life. It looked so fragile, as if he could break it with a single finger. But Jonathan knew better.

The magick that had cast him into his captivity was too powerful to be undone by mere wishful thinking. Freedom always seemed so close, but as the seconds passed and realisation grew, he breathed in a deep sigh, cloaking himself in disappointment. The bitter smell of damp and old books hit his nostrils, and he exhaled, comforted by its familiarity.

But here was another scent. One he now recognised as only being noticeable of late. Yes, there was dampness, acrid but faint, but spiked with something more, something *intense*. He inhaled deeply again, allowing this new perfume to hit the back of his throat with such force he could almost taste it. Floral and powdery, yet spiky, like the roses that had grown in the walled garden of his family seat.

He'd pricked his finger on one once. He must have had barely more than six years on him at the time; hiding from his governess in the rose garden, the hot sun burning the back of his neck, a bee buzzing nearby. Mother always loved to decorate Powderham's draughty halls with fresh flowers. He would take her some to bring her cheer, for she had been most unwell lately. He reached out to grasp one particularly leggy bloom. Its proud red petals were soft to touch, their sweet perfume tickled his nose. But too late did he spot the sharp thorns dotted along the stem, and as his forefinger closed around one, he let out a yelp that sent a flurry of finches hiding in a nearby bush fluttering into the air. He'd yanked his hand away and inspected the drop of ruby coloured blood blooming on the tip of his finger. Eyes watering, he'd swallowed the tears back down. Father wouldn't approve.

Now, as Jonathan waited for Emmeline to respond, to acknowledge his whispered salutation, he fought to marshal his thoughts back to the present. He couldn't afford to allow the melancholy of his past to interfere with his goal in the here and now. But even as the blood returned to his extremities, even as an echo of that sharp pain resounded in the forefinger of his right hand, he couldn't deny that those precious moments in the garden, planning to gift his mother a posy of her favorite blooms, was perhaps his only happy memory in a childhood blighted by fear and misogyny. Even as a child, he hadn't regretted his decision to pluck the rose and he still could not bring himself to regret it now.

He searched for something–anything–for distraction before the memories overwhelmed him. Emmeline then. Her eyes were closed, her chest rising and falling with laboured breaths. When she finally looked at him, he almost staggered. Would she always affect him so? He had never reacted like this with any other witch he'd encountered. However, he could not deny this new sense of wholeness–of *almost* being–that occurred in Emmeline's presence. She was obviously a much more powerful enchantress than either of them knew. She stood so close now heat radiated off her in waves, daring him to reach out for her. However, her expression filled his heart with icy dread. What if she had read the whole book? She would want nothing more to do with him.

"I don't understand." Emmeline said at last, as she rubbed the bridge of her nose. "Why didn't you come before, when Lizzie was here?" She sounded weary, and Jonathan's heart sank further. He rebelled at how readily he had permitted her to affect his emotions. How weak his mind to have allowed her perfume to affect him so. He must be stronger than this. Maybe if he didn't look into her eyes? Yes, surely that would release her hold over him.

"Countless are the times I have asked your forgiveness, but I request that you accept my apologies once more. I wanted to come, but something prevented me." He inclined his head, careful to look at the floor.

"None of this makes sense," Emmeline said, turning away from him, "how can you be trapped in a book and appear and disappear at will? Things like this don't happen in real life."

He didn't know what made him do it. Maybe it was the way she'd so easily given her back to him, but for all his promises to avoid her gaze, to resist her charms, Jonathan found himself grabbing Emmeline's wrist, twisting her back to face him and tugging her hand to his chest.

She snatched it away.

"You should ask before you do that." Her eyes and mouth dripped with reproach and Jonathan's cheeks flamed as he experienced an unexpected stab of guilt.

"I apologise unreservedly. I shall not touch you without your consent again, my lady."

Emmeline nodded. "Good," she said, her lips set in an unforgiving line.

Jonathan opened his own mouth to say more but before he could speak, Emmeline was continuing. "I want to believe you. But, how can I? Why didn't you come?"

Her brown eyes were the colour of dark oak; warm, comforting and made of the same kind of solidity as supporting beams.

Get a hold of yourself man! It's an illusion, a ruse. She's doing everything in her power to put you at ease. You were just hoodwinked into reliving a painful memory from your childhood because of her perfume and now you can't even honour your own seconds-old promises about not looking into her eyes.

Maggie trusts her.

Yes, but Maggie has been wrong before. If Emmeline truly is the key, she may be more powerful than perhaps even she knows. Just...take more heed. Don't allow yourself to be foolishly guided by that part of you which leaps from slumber at the sight of a mere handsome face. Goodness knows it led you into enough trouble before.

"I could see and hear you and your lady friend, but no matter how hard I tried, some unseen force prevented me." Jonathan said, shaking his head as he tore his eyes from hers again. "Maybe it's because she is a non-believer. I heard how she scoffed at your tale. Or perhaps it is because she does not possess any magic. *You* however are a witch, and thus I am compelled to appear before you."

"Oh, don't start that nonsense again. I am *not* a witch! And don't talk like that about my friend."

"I have provoked your disapproval yet again. Are you always this pugnacious? No, don't answer that," Jonathan added before she could respond. He wrung his hands together, surprised by the clamminess of his palms before holding them up in front of him in a what he hoped was a gesture of peace. "Might I propose a truce?"

His smile was genuine. He could not risk incurring Emmeline's ire. He needed her. He paused, cautious as he considered how his need for her might be interpreted, but then gave himself a slight shake. Debating the definition and shape of his desire was an argument he knew he would lose with himself. There was certainly nothing cautious about the way her eyes made him burn.

He had to get control of himself, fast. "Contrary to what you probably think, I do not take pleasure in displeasing you, Emmeline."

"Okay, I'm on edge, that's all. It's a lot to take in." She exhaled, seemingly letting her anger out with the breath and the tightening around Jonathan's chest lifted. Indeed, she was powerful.

"You scared the living daylights out of me with the phone stunt though." Emmeline continued, nodding her head towards a strange scarlet and glass structure.

"Phone stunt? I do not follow. What is this 'phone' of which you speak?"

Emmeline's musical laughter caught him off-guard. "The telephone," she said, still laughing, "you made it ring even though it's not connected. I don't know how you did that, but you get top marks for effort, even though it did make me jump."

"Forgive me, Lady Emmeline, but you have me at a loss." It was Jonathan's turn to laugh but his quiet chuckle sounded uncertain and alien in his ears. "What is a telephone?"

"It wasn't you calling?" Emmeline asked, her dark eyes drawing together.

"*What* was not me?" Jonathan threw up his hands in complete confusion.

Emmeline yanked on his forearm, presumably to get him to follow her to the telephone, but Jonathan didn't budge. When she rounded on him, he gave her what he hoped was his best look of mock disapproval, waggling one finger in her direction. "Ah-ah, no touching without consent, remember?"

Her eyes shot a warning. "I'm glad you find it such amusing subject matter." But then her blazing expression softened. "You're right though, so I apologise. Follow me." She marched over to the imposing red box near the far wall.

Grinning inside, Jonathan bowed and replied, "As you wish, my lady."

But she whirled to face him again, hands on her hips, one foot tapping against the flagstones. "How many times do I have to ask you not to call me that? This isn't *The Princess Bride*, you know."

"The *what?*" Jonathan smiled again despite everything he'd settled with himself about being cautious. Infuriating Emmeline wasn't part of the plan, but he was enjoying her reactions too much to stop. Besides, if he had to use every ounce of his roguish wile to resist her, then so be it. His competitive side immediately awoke, sniffing the air with interest at the wager he'd just made with himself. It was a game he wasn't prepared to lose.

Emmeline shook her head, "Never mind. Do you want me to show you this or not? I've got plenty of better things I can be doing."

Jonathan dipped again and gestured for her to continue. With some reluctance, he forced himself to listen as Emmeline proceeded to open the door of the case and demonstrate how the odd contraption worked, though his reluctance was not born out of a lack of interest in what she had to say. Quite the opposite. She was delightful company–knowledgeable, spirited, funny. It was because he couldn't get the feeling of her touch upon his arm out of his mind. The strange charge which had sent delicious, nervy flutterings throughout his skin. Or the way she moved with innate grace for such a tall, large woman, and the fire in her eyes when she spoke of things she was passionate about.

Not again, you ridiculous fool. You utter boblyne. How many times do you need to hear it before it penetrates that thick skull or yours? She's a witch, and if you don't pull yourself together and start resisting her charms fast, you shall have lost this wager before the day is through!

"*This* is a telephone. A nineteenth century invention. It's a method of communication," Emmeline was saying. "You lift the receiver, like so." She placed the handset in his palm and held it up to his left ear. "Then you put this part to your mouth..." Her voice trailed off and he steeled himself to brave a glance down at her lips. "...With your free hand, you dial the number of the person you want to speak to, like this."

She placed her finger in a small hole cut into an odd metallic disc and twisted it all the way around, only for the disc to rattle back to its starting position. The whirring dial was loud in the cramped space and Jonathan was still none the wiser about the modern invention. His instincts of mistrust and suspicion warned him to keep his guard up. For all he knew, this was yet more evidence of Emmeline's powers of witchcraft, but when she asked if she could take his hand again, all his wary inhibition flew out of the window.

"You try," she said, as she placed his forefinger in one of the holes on the dial. She was so close her warm breath tickled his ear. One thing he hadn't expected was for this thing, what was it she called it–telephone–to be so sensuous. Could she feel it too?

"Then when you've finished dialling the number, you wait for the person on the other end to hear *their* telephone ring and pick up *their* receiver. At least, that's how you used to do it. This is an old phone. Before my time." She was speaking again, faster this time and he sensed the moment was coming to an end. "Now we have cordless phones and mobile phones... but that's perhaps best left for another day."

Jonathan shook his head, "Are you saying that you can hear people *talking* on this? You can converse with them without having to wait for a letter to be delivered? But why do I not hear anything right now?"

To his surprise, Emmeline squeezed herself into the glass box with him, and his heart rate quickened from a cantor to a gallop in seconds. She took the handset from him and placed it to her ear. "Yeah, it's dead. There's no connection. The line was cut by accident, by an electrician...But you won't have a clue what an electrician is either." Heaving a sigh again, she slipped the receiver back into the cradle and turned to face him, incomparable eyes searching his face. "You really *are* from the past, aren't you?"

Jonathan nodded. How could he make her understand? Pressed up against her in this suffocating space, it became the most important thing ever. Yes, he needed her to believe in him because that would be the only way of getting back to his time, but it was more than that. He wanted–no, needed–her to trust him.

"So... if it wasn't you who made an unconnected phone

ring," she said as she replaced the odd-looking handset, "Who was it?"

"I cannot help you, I'm afraid, which seems unjust when I consider how you have agreed to assist me." Still somewhat disquieted about the telephone business, Jonathan was cheered to find his earlier and usual mischievous charm hadn't completely deserted him. "I must confess I very much enjoyed the lesson. The twenty-first century surely is a wondrous place." He charged his words and gaze with as much indecency as he could muster. They were still squeezed together in the confined space of the telephone box, the back of his knees against the small, cushioned bench built in to the side, her face upturned to his, her chest inches from his own. But before he could say or do anything else, Emmeline ducked out from under his arms and pushed her way out of the door.

"Didn't Maggie introduce you to the wonders of the future?" she asked, putting space between them, and beginning to tidy up various books. Then she paused with a large tome in her hand. "Yeah, that's a silly question. Maggie was more of an antique than these things."

Jonathan moved out of the baffling telephone box. He should be relieved the atmosphere was broken but the flames of his libido were not so easily extinguished. He wandered over to the seating area and perched on the edge of the sofa, steepling his fingers under his chin. "Maggie and I talked. She had a wonderful knowledge of my time. I can forgive her for not explaining her world–*your* world–to me. I doubt that I would have believed her. I can barely believe it now. In fact, I am tempted to call it another kind of sorcery."

"*Sorcery?* You're standing there, magicked out of a

book and you think a telephone is sorcery?" Emmeline rolled her eyes, "You're welcome for the history lesson. If you plan to hang around, I have a feeling we'll be doing another soon." She laughed. At first just a quiet giggle, but then another and soon she was doubled over in a fit of mirth, tears streaming down her cheeks.

"And what, may I ask, has caused such hilarity?" He raised an eyebrow, but this only served to make her laugh harder and she snorted a reply.

"You. This. *Everything!* It wasn't a history lesson for you, was it? This is the–*your*–future! Oh, this is all far too confusing. Maybe Lizzie's right and I am losing it, but if I'm going to help you, I might as well have some fun doing it." She placed the pile of books she was cradling on to the counter and came to sit on the sofa next to him, still wiping the tears from her eyes.

Jonathan beamed, and Emmeline's laughter ceased. "Yet again, you bewilder me, but I am grateful for once to be the root of your happiness. If we are to fail and I should be imprisoned within this curse for the rest of eternity, I will remember you in this moment."

This was the requisite amount of charm he needed to remain in her favour, surely? But a moment later, when he dropped to one knee before her, gesturing to her hand, Jonathan surprised even himself.

"May I?"

She nodded, wide eyes twin pools of blackest night.

"Thank you for consenting," he whispered, before taking Emmeline's palm in his, and grazing her knuckles with a soft, chaste kiss.

～

THEY SPENT the rest of the evening searching the store. Maggie had said the answer was here somewhere, but where to begin? Emmy scoured the old shelves for likely stories, pulling anything that alluded to witchcraft, magic and fairytales, but considering Maggie's love of romance and mystery, this amounted to over half the contents of the shop.

She was now curled up on the sofa, a wall of books towering high on the table between her and Jonathan, a notebook open on her lap. The only sounds were the scratching of her pen on paper, the clock ticking, and a whisper promised in every turned page. Every now and then he would glance over the top of the pages he was perusing, catch her eye and quickly look away again. As strange as it was to observe him sitting bolt upright on Maggie's chair, his presence was also oddly comforting. He belonged here and yet, didn't.

Emmy closed *The Lord of The Rings* and placed it on the table next to a copy of Olivia Butler's *Kindred*. She stood and stretched, scraping her fingertips on the low beams before glancing at her phone. Two-thirty? They'd been at this for hours! Her brow furrowed as something occurred to her.

"How is it you've stayed so long this time? Usually you're in and out of here faster than the Flash." She waited for him to ask who the Flash was, but there was a far-off look in his eyes.

"If I tell you, do you give me your word that you won't be displeased?"

Emmy pursed her lips. How could she answer this honestly? "I'll give you the benefit of the doubt, just this once." She smiled, knowing he wouldn't have heard the now-common expression before.

The old chair squeaked as he got out of it. "If I had to wager, I would say it has something to do with you, but I know you will not like that. So let's just call it *your willingness to believe* in magic."

"But...but, what about Maggie? Are you trying to tell me she was a witch too?" Emmy regarded him with interest. "Not that *I* am, remember," She added before he could get any ideas.

"There are many different forms of magic. For some, it presents as witchcraft." He gave her a pointed look, which she pretended not to notice. "Maggie was not one of them. She did, however, *believe* in me. We would talk for hours. Mostly about you."

Emmy closed her eyes, a vortex of emotions twisting in her stomach. "Please, can we not talk about Maggie? It's hard enough wrapping my head around all this as it is."

"Well, you were the one who brought her up." He folded his arms across his chest. "Maybe if you'd known her as well as you think you did, this wouldn't be so confusing for you. She assured me you would have the answer to my predicament. I'm starting to wonder if she was mistaken."

He hadn't raised his voice, but Emmy was on her feet and away from him as if he'd lashed out at her. Stinging from his attack, she couldn't speak. They stared at each other, the moment stretching on into the near silence. Each tick from Maggie's clock echoed inside Emmy's head like tiny clicking beetles. The clicking morphed into whispers and chattering, threatening to become an accusatory voice from the past.

No! She wasn't going to give it anymore headspace, and she wasn't about to back down either. Panting, she fixed Jonathan with her eyes and gave him the full benefit of her judgement. Her shoulders and chest ached from the effort, but she was determined to win this battle of wills.

Across the room, Jonathan's face and posture were similarly set. His jaw solid, brows bunched. A muscle in his cheek pulsed. He swallowed and Emmy had the sense he was warring with something inside himself. The moment stretched on and Emmy's shoulders sagged an inch before she squared them again. Jonathan relinquished his stare first. Exhaling, he raked through his hair with a double-handed swipe and made to close the space between them.

Coming up short, he hesitated just before reaching her, his eyes filled with an emotion Emmy recognised too well. Grief.

"I am sorry, Emmeline. That was uncalled for, but she was my friend too. I should go."

"Maybe you should." Her voice was quiet but firm. She couldn't look at him, wrestling inside between needing to be alone and wanting him to stay.

"May I return tomorrow?"

"I said I'd help you, didn't I?" The words left her mouth before she could think. Pushing him away wasn't going to bring Maggie back, but she wasn't ready to share her sorrow. She tried to ignore the voice which inquired why she wasn't being honest about her feelings over Maggie and Jonathan. Unlike the hallucinations, this voice was completely real but just as difficult to silence.

"I do not recall requesting more from you. Thank you

for your kindness, my lady," Jonathan said bowing low, the merest hint of sarcasm detectable in his voice.

"Jonathan, wait!"

It was too late. He was already gone, leaving Emmy alone with nothing but the books, her final plea echoing in her ears like a ghost from the past.

CHAPTER 6

*E*mmy's dreams were an unnerving tableau. A bare-chested Dan the Dickhead was professing his undying love for Maggie. Except it wasn't a Maggie Emmy recognised. This was a young, beautiful and slightly terrifying Maggie, a Witch Queen of the forest Maggie, all haughty looks and elven features. Distressed, Emmy tore her eyes away, catching her alarming reflection in a mirror. Her features and body were morphing into a disturbing familiarity. She glanced down at her feet, now large, bulbous and hairy, whipping her head back up in time to see Hobbit Emmy shout, "Wait!", before the scene switched.

A bleak chamber this time, the walls dripping black slime, air thick with despair. As Emmy approached the open casket at the far end of the cavern, her every movement was replicated in the grotesque, deformed shadows cast on the low vaulted ceiling by a single torch that flickered in a cold draught.

A voice chanted in Latin, but it was only when they

intoned the word "Magicae" did she understand that *she* was the one speaking a language she didn't know. But how could that be? How could she speak in a tongue she'd never studied? Emmy didn't know, but something inside her stirred and grew as she approached the casket. She clutched The Book in her hands, unable to ignore the power radiating not only from it, but also from deep within herself. She should be afraid, but her heart was filled with a strange sense of resolution and duty. A sense of awakening magic as old as the world itself. The Book pulsed in Emmy's hands and as she glanced down, it began to glow. She gasped as it fell open in her hands, the words and letters within it springing to life in golden threads which swirled in the air around her, casting even deeper shadows on to the cavern walls.

Witch Emmy drew nearer to the coffin, dragged toward it by the uncontrollable urge to see the man who'd rained misery and murder on her sisters brought low at last. She was connected to them by those same golden words, a shimmering thread that wove throughout history in old tales and folklore; stories of wronged women, unfairly accused, mistreated and punished for crimes they hadn't committed.

A frigid wind whistled through the chamber, a vengeful banshee in the night. The sound of Emmy's bare feet on the chilled stone floor was the scuffling of rats, which turned to silence as she reached the casket. But then there was another noise: the scratching of a pen nib on parchment. Realisation rose like vomit inside her throat as Emmy looked down to find a quill in her hand, now scrawling indecipherable words on to the pages of The Book. She tried to yank her arm away, to release it from her grasp, but still the words came, spilling from the quill's savage tip in ink the colour of blood. Each word inscribed upon her soul. Then Jonathan's corpse sat bolt upright, and the shriek became a scream ripped from Emmy's throat, as his decomposing body begged for her forgiveness, over and over, in a voice that echoed like an open tomb.

Emmy woke in a web of tangled sheets, sweat-slicked and breathing hard. She got out of bed fast, as if the nightmare had impregnated the bedding. Then she stripped the bed and stuck everything on a hot wash before going anywhere near the coffee machine, as per as her usual routine. The diary app on her phone told her she had three weeks before her prescription was due for assessment, but maybe she ought to give Doctor Harrison a call, just in case.

It was just a dream. A crazy, messed-up dream. The Book, Jonathan, the magic–all of it!

Emmy shook the tension out of her shoulders and let the fragments of the nightmare fall away like discarded clothes. She swallowed her morning cocktail of pills without preamble, before humming along to the radio around mouthfuls of cornflakes, where a gravelly-voiced Jack Savoretti was crooning a *'Whiskey Tango'*. When Breone leapt on to the kitchen counter a few moments later–quite a feat given his bulk–she didn't even flinch. She was fine.

"We're going to have to do something about this, B," she said, stroking his back. "You and I are going to the vet. Don't look at me like that. Now, where did I put your carrier?"

Still singing, she skipped down the stairs an hour later,

swinging a protesting Breone squashed inside a woven cat carrier in one hand. Emmy felt lighter than she had in days, but also strangely hollow. The nightmare had seemed so real. Was it so surprising given her love of romantic heroes and everything that had happened with Dan and then Maggie that her subconscious had dreamt up Jonathan? Her mobile jumped in her palm and she yelped as she banged her head on a beam. A withheld number, but she swiped the screen with her thumb to accept the call on speaker, setting the carrier down as she massaged her bruised scalp with the fingertips of her other hand.

"Hello?"

No one answered, but the faintest whisper of static told her the line was open. "Hello?" she repeated, emphasising the 'o'. Nothing. She was about to end the call when a soft voice chuckled. Emmy narrowed her eyes, observing the phone with bewildered impatience.

"I think you've got the wrong number." A beat of silence followed by the same snigger. Emmy scowled, tapping the 'End Call' option with undisguised annoyance. Rattled, she skirted the coffee table to turn off the alarm and unbolt the door, her breathing loud in the empty space. It was probably bored teenagers dicking around. She exhaled, letting go of her anger. She had much more important things to deal with. An overweight moggy being the top of her list.

Stepping out of the shop she took a moment to enjoy the sunshine warming her face, before placing Breone down on the doorstep below the eaves. Turning back, she placed one hand over the door handle and tugged it towards her. That's when she saw it. The Book. It lay open on the table where she'd left it last night. Emmy's throat constricted. Her hand slipped from the knob, her stomach suddenly flipping. A roaring in her ears drowned out the noisy city.

Gone was the overhead symphony of blackbirds, tits and gulls fighting for birdsong supremacy. The steady hum of the traffic from surrounding streets and the inner bypass was also silenced, as if someone had turned a tuning fork. The only sound in Emmy's head now was an unwelcome and familiar whisper, one of the voices she knew all too well.

Emmy's lungs suddenly felt too small. Her head swayed dizzily as if her brain was being starved of oxygen. Leaning against the outside wall, she tried to remember her grounding techniques. Five things to see, four things to touch, three things to hear, two things to smell, and one she could taste. A gull swooping overhead. The blast of car horn in the distance. The roughness of the wall behind her back. The salty sweetness of her own blood from where she'd bit her tongue. But here was another sound: a plaintive mewing that cut a direct route to Emmy's need to be loved. Breone! She dropped to her knees and sprung the cat from the carrier, who leapt into her lap with a meowed thanks.

"Oh, Breone. What would I do without you? It's not far, I'll carry you if you promise not to run off." She nuzzled the cat's face, hoping to transfer some of the warmth from his furry body into her own shaking, cold fingers, as her senses grounded again. She scrambled to her feet, letting the remains of the panic attack fall away. She was fine.

Wisdom is caring yet remaining immovable with our words."

Then, when she'd reasserted control over her breathing, she back heeled the carrier inside the shop. She wouldn't risk glancing in the direction of the table again. She couldn't think about Jonathan now. It was too stressful.

THE VISIT to the vet took longer than Emmy expected. The veterinarian had insisted on weighing Breone and to no one's surprise, the cat was diagnosed as clinically obese. Then they'd asked questions about Breone's age and Emmy had to admit she didn't know it. She cast her mind back to that very first day when she'd visited Adams' Antique Books as a little girl, meeting Maggie and Breone for the first time. Even then, both she and her cat seemed too old to be real. But Emmy didn't dare tell the vet this, so mumbled something about Breone being around nineteen, crossing her fingers that they would let the matter drop.

On the way back, she and Breone took a detour to the pet shop, Emmy's mind weighed down with problems real and possibly imaginary. But she'd dealt with the imaginary before and it hadn't broken her. Put a huge dent in her armour, maybe, but she was still here, still on this strange and unusual journey called life, writing her own story. Telling her own tale. And whatever lay in wait for her back at the shop, she knew she had the tools to cope. She hardly dared to allow herself to imagine that The Book and Jonathan could be real.

But as she neared Adams' Antique Books, Emmy's mind became more vociferous and her knuckles gripped white around the handle of Breone's roomier new carrier. The morning's sunshine had given way to a sky the colour of dirty water, with great globules of soap scum clouds floating across the grey. Setting her jaw, she turned into West Street allowing the familiar cobbles and Tudor buildings to strengthen the new-found resolve blooming in her chest. She hushed the voices before they could derail her. She could do this. She *would* do this.

She unlocked the door, pleased to see her hands did not shake. First things first. Emmy busied herself with freeing Breone, who turned his nose up at the special diet food packet she now waved at him.

"I know you don't like it, but it's vet's orders," she called as his bushy orange tail flickered once before disappearing with the rest of him behind his favourite bookcase. Rolling her eyes, Emmy dug into her bag and pulled out the veterinarian's instructions, plus the other items she'd purchased at the pet shop: a green retractable lead, yet more diet food and a wind-up mouse, designed to encourage fat cats like Breone to play. She eyed the leash for a moment, testing the retraction button beneath her finger, yanking on the length with her other hand. Pull. Click. Pull. Click. Her eyes narrowed as she took in the fastening system to fix the lead to a collar. *That was going to be interesting.* Pull. Click. Pull. Click. Pull...

If only reining in her wayward emotions was as easy.

She clicked the button one last time, pressing down on it with grim determination. She'd avoided things for too long. If The Book was real, maybe that meant Jonathan was real too. She paused to consider why it had been such a shock to see it earlier, worrying at a random thread on her blouse. Was it so difficult to believe? Would a part of her always refuse to accept what she'd seen with her own eyes? Touched with her own fingers? In books and movies, the characters were always quick to believe in the fantastical—once they'd got over their hot minute of shock. But this wasn't a story, this was real life. *Her* life. Maybe it had been easier to accept it had all been a dream because of her illness? Maybe.

For the first time since returning to the shop, Emmy turned to face The Book in a slow, deliberate pirouette. Using her upper limbs to shield her chest, like crossed swords on a coat of arms, she approached the table with scavenger care, eyes fixed on the old volume. Nerve-endings on high alert.

With each beat her heart felt like it was growing, engorging her throat. She tried to swallow it back down into her chest, but her sandpaper tongue scraped the roof of her mouth. She gulped in several deep, steadying breaths. A shiver crawled through her scalp, tiptoeing down her spine, and she belatedly acknowledged that she was afraid. Afraid to feel, afraid to summon him, afraid of letting go, afraid of facing what had happened last night, and how all her feelings for Jonathan were wrapped up in grief about Maggie and her fear of relapsing.

Her earlier pretence of armour was gone.

Now cast aside and battle-damaged, it hadn't protected her where she'd needed it most. Her arms reached for The Book almost as if they belonged to someone else.

If he comes back, if he's real, I'll never doubt myself again.

She closed her eyes, unable to deny it any longer.

Maybe he *was* little more than a ghost, but he haunted her now, in more ways than just in her dreams.

She waited for the air to change, for the stillness to fill, for her breathing to regulate, before opening her lids again. Even then, it was like staring into the sun. Jonathan's hopeful expression instantly morphed into one of concern as he reached out with hesitant fingers, brushing at her cheek with his thumb.

JONATHAN'S MIND RACED. The last thing he expected was for Emmeline to summon him again, not after his behaviour last time. If Maggie was right–and he could only assume she was–Emmeline was his only hope and he'd lashed out, wounding her first before she could inflict a similar low blow on him. But it was folly of him to risk hurting her so. He needed her much more than she needed him, and the realisation hit him with sudden and unexpected melancholy, a poisoned blade twisting in his guts. How could he get her back onside?

"I can only hope," he began in a voice he did not recognise as his own, "that I am not yet again the cause of your sadness, but I fear my hope is in vain. I apologise for upsetting you. It was thoughtless and insensitive of me to talk of Maggie in that manner. I pray you can forgive me. For too long, I have been trapped between worlds, with Maggie my only source of companionship. I am unrehearsed in social discourse and unprepared for your friendship. Too long have I wished for liberation. Now, at last, my wish may come true. But...I am afraid, Lady

Emmeline. I'm afraid of where I will go should we find the answer. Or rather, I should say, *when* I will go."

"I don't think I'm following you. This is what you want. Your freedom."

Jonathan ushered her to the sofa and took her hands in his. "How do I explain this confliction?" His eyes scanned the shop, as if searching for the answer within the books, "It is you. You are both the answer and the question. No, hear me out, please. According to Maggie, you are the only person who can help me. I have no reason to doubt her. I understand that this is unjust, and I fully expect your rebuttal, but since I met you...I have been in awe of you."

There. That should do it. He didn't enjoy toying with her, but if he had to use every ounce of charm to win her trust again, so be it. A pretty blush crept into her cheeks and the blade twisted again, this time stabbing at the space where his heart should be. What was this hold she had over him? No matter, as long as he remained true to his goal and took every precaution to guard himself against her powers, he would be safe. But her generous mouth had fallen open with a slight gasp at his words, making his fingers itch with sudden longing. She was so close. Close enough to kiss.

EMMY'S BREATH caught in her throat as Jonathan spoke. He was gazing at her with such guile, such warmth that she fancied the icicles in his clear blue eyes were melting. A swift blurring at the end of his arms distracted her and she glanced down to catch his long fingers flexing, as if he was about to reach for her. But the movement happened so fast, Emmy couldn't be sure she hadn't imagined it and she quickly looked up at his face again. He was closer now. Her brain struggled to keep up with not only his words and movements but also how her own body was responding, as if drawn to him by an unknown magnetism. Closer. His eyes held hers. Closer. Inches between his lips and her own…

The bell jingled, Jonathan vanished, and Emmy whipped her head to the opening door with reluctance. Shame scorched her cheeks, pouring water upon the now smoking embers of her lust. Irritated that she'd allowed infatuation to distract from the more important task of running the shop, she sprang up, a smile for the customer on her face.

"Good morning! It's a hot one out there," she said, but her eyes glazed as the woman launched into the uninspiring tale of her bus journey into the city that day. Nodding and laughing in all the right places was easy, yet her thoughts rarely strayed from Jonathan. He was still there. Her body responded to his presence now in ways she didn't understand and was afraid to explore. The atmosphere was super-charged, humming with electricity, and moments later, when a book flew off a shelf and appeared to float in midair, she nearly jumped out of her skin.

"I'm sorry, which Beverly Jenkins did you say?"

Emmy nodded, certain that the very book the woman had asked for was now dancing an aerial waltz behind the old dear's back. Her mind danced with a heady brew of delight, and she beckoned to the customer to follow her to the back of the store, in completely the wrong direction.

"*Forbidden*," the customer replied, unaware of the magic occurring in her wake.

Emmy pressed her lips together to keep from dissolving into giggles and made a charade of searching for the novel on a random shelf. Manoeuvring so that the lady couldn't see back into the main part of the shop, she glared in the direction of the dancing book, her eyes expressing a silent plea. The book drifted with agonising sluggishness back to its shelf, and Emmy's shoulders slumped with relief.

"Oh, *Forbidden!* Of *course*. I'm so sorry, I've been looking in the wrong place. I–err–changed this around recently. Please follow me."

At last the woman was gone, happy with both her purchase and the service she'd (eventually) received. Emmy closed the door behind her and spun round to give Jonathan a tongue-lashing, but before she could, the door opened again.

It was gone four when the shop was next empty. Fourteen customers. *Fourteen!* Not nearly enough, but Emmy grasped the inkling of hope with her whole being. It didn't escape her attention either that the majority of those purchases, like Beverly Jenkins' *Forbidden*, were from Maggie's selection of paperback romances. Jonathan's exploits had increased in inventiveness and daring, disappearing and reappearing behind oblivious customers at will, and by the time Emmy was serving the last customer, he was juggling three books at once, putting Emmy in mind of *The Sorcerer's Apprentice*. Then he took form again, a battered copy of *Tom Jones* wrapped around one finger, and an expression of mock outrage etched on his handsome features. Emmy didn't know how she managed to hold her composure, especially when he began mouthing Fielding's raunchy prose at her over the customer's shoulder.

"I can't believe you just did that!" Emmy lunged for the book in Jonathan's hands once they were alone. "Books cost money, you arse! You could have damaged them."

"Ahh, but I did not." Jonathan's eyes blazed full of playful danger and Emmy gave in to the giggles she'd been trying to quell. "I am *scandalised*, however, by what I have read." He glanced down at Henry Fielding's novel again and intoned: "'Now the agonies which affected the mind of Sophia, rather augmented than impaired her beauty; for her tears added brightness to her eyes, and her breasts rose higher with her sighs.' Is this impropriety indicative of the literature of your time?"

Emmy laughed again, sweeping her hair off her forehead. "Impropriety? *The History of Tom Jones* is actually more *your* time, I'll have you know. But if it's improper you're after, you need to read D.H. Lawrence." She turned on her heel, beckoning him with a crooked finger, hyper aware she was flirting, but unable to restrain herself. She led him to the nook of shelves at the back of the store, the same place where he'd appeared yesterday, and ran her fingers along the spine of the books with deliberate leisure. When she found the volume she was looking for, she took it down from the shelf and, with a salacious grin, flicked through the pages for a few moments, before stopping approximately halfway through. Without a word, she handed it to Jonathan and leaned back against the bookcase, waiting for his reaction.

"'That thrust of the buttocks,'" he began, one eyebrow raised in interest, "'surely it was a little ridiculous. If you were a woman, and a part in all the business, surely that thrusting of the man's buttocks was supremely ridiculous. Surely the man was intensely ridiculous in this posture and this act!' What is this filth?"

"Filth? Don't act so pious. This is one of the most important works of literature of the twentieth century—*and* one of the most controversial. It caused a scandal when published and is still the source of much titillation today, but it's tame compared to everything else out there. And to be honest, I'd much rather read this than Tom Jones. Am I supposed to overlook that he's a complete and utter misogynistic dickhead because he's an interesting character?"

Jonathan's head snapped up from the Lawrence novel.

"A *dickhead*?" he almost choked. "Pray, do explain the meaning of this term and what debauchery our good Mister Jones is accused of which makes him one."

"He's a cad, a scoundrel. He sleeps with virtually every woman he meets, just because he can, and tries to defend his cheating by claiming that his heart wasn't in it—only his lustful body." Emmy crossed her arms in front of her chest. This wasn't turning out as she'd expected; Dan the Dickhead had a lot to answer for. She huffed and looked down at D.H Lawrence's famous work again, hoping to rekindle the mood, but Jonathan's expression was unreadable.

"It grows late. I must take my leave of you." He deposited the old volume on the shelf with an odd sense of finality.

"You're leaving? *Now?*" Emmy pressed her lips

together to soften the edge to her voice, but even to her own ears, it was unmistakable. "Will you come back tomorrow?"

He was already fading but hovered long enough to take her hand in his and bring it to his lips again. "Of course, sweet Emmeline."

He was gone again, and Emmy was left wondering what she had said to make him leave so fast while hating herself for how desperate she'd sounded for him to stay. She busied herself tidying the store, reliving her earlier elation at the number of customers that day. Maybe she could make this work after all. If Maggie could keep the bailiffs from the door for all those years, then so could she.

Her phone vibrated in her pocket and she drew in a sharp breath. She shook her head as she answered it. She'd never been this skittish in London. Or anywhere, for that matter.

"Hello? Adam's Antique Books?"

Silence.

"Hell-*o*?" she repeated about to terminate the call, but then a voice spoke:

"Go back to London if you know what's good for you."

Click. The line went dead, but Emmy wasn't dissuaded from shouting into her mobile, her heart thundering like a runaway train. "You can't scare me, you sick fuck! I'm not going anywhere."

She covered the space between the counter and the door in three strides, locking it fast. Her hands hardly shook as she continued picking up misplaced books and returning them to their rightful homes, but her eyes darted to the street each time a shadow darkened the window. Maybe she should call someone? She tried Lizzie but got her voicemail. Dawn was in the middle of studying and as it was the middle of the night in Auckland, she ruled out her parents. They'd only worry. She considered Leticia, her old boss and London bestie, but the Frankfurt Book Fair was coming up. No, Leticia wouldn't appreciate the interruption.

Anyway, it was probably nothing, right? Just a coincidence that the harsh voice had mentioned London. Easier to pretend it was a wrong number and not another in a long line of strange and unexplained occurrences that had happened to her lately. Maggie, The Book, Jonathan. Her unsettling dream from the night before flickered across her mind and she brushed it away as if flicking a page in a novel which had taken an upsetting turn.

Not every story has a happily ever after and what if this is one of them?

She clenched her teeth against the unwelcome notion. It was a prank caller and her over-stimulated mind had jolted her thoughts into trepidation and melodrama. There was no need to call anyone. She *wasn't* in danger and she *didn't* need rescuing, thank you very much.

The one thing she absolutely, positively, one hundred percent was not going do, was read The Book and summon Jonathan.

CHAPTER 7

*L*izzie swept into the shop a week later, flinging the door open with such gusto that the bell's usual mellow tinkling echoed though the store with the tenor of a fire alarm. Emmy–elbow-deep in a large cardboard box–straightened up, massaging the small of her back, relieved for a break from unpacking the delivery she'd taken possession of that morning.

"Thanks," she grinned as Lizzie handed over a steaming takeout coffee and choc au pain from their favourite bakery.

The smaller woman bounced from foot to foot, a mischievous sprite in black Louboutins. It was clear she had something on her mind, but Emmy was too engrossed in the caffeine and sugar fix to pay much heed. Besides, she hoped that keeping Lizzie from whatever it was she'd come to say would distract her friend from the contents of the box at Emmy's feet. She could all too easily imagine what Lizzie's reaction would be if she knew Emmy was ordering yet more romance novels.

Never mind that they were some of the books Emmy was proud to have worked on before she'd left Happily Ever After. It wouldn't even register that the box also included some of the biggest selling titles in romance of the last two years, plus perennial bestsellers in the genre. Lizzie just wouldn't–*couldn't*–understand the appeal, either as a reader or from a business sense, even though she'd worked in the old shop for a spell too.

But Emmy was no fool. She'd crunched the numbers (Maggie's atrocious bookkeeping skills notwithstanding) and romance made up thirty-five percent of the shop's entire turnover for the last five years. Maggie Adams knew what her customers wanted, and for every rare and ridiculously expensive old tome she'd traded, she'd sold another ten vintage romances by Kathleen Woodiwiss or Johanna Lindsey. Plus–as Emmy had recently discovered during a long and frustrating search on a popular auction website–many Woodiwiss and Lindsey books, along with their contemporaries, could be just as highly sought after as any old Austen. It was simply a matter of finding the right buyer.

Emmy popped the last delicious morsel of buttery pastry and chocolate into her mouth, chewed for a moment and washed it down with a big gulp of coffee. Then she backheeled the box out of sight behind the counter and grabbed Lizzie's hand, leading her to the seating area.

"What's up?" She asked as they slumped into the cushions together.

Lizzie straightened up almost immediately, an expression of pure exhilaration on her pretty features. She rummaged in her massive handbag–designer, of course–

before extracting an A4 folder from its depths. With her diminutive stature and bobbing curls, she resembled an over-excited child going through their stocking on Christmas morning and Emmy smiled to herself at the notion.

"Remember this?" Lizzie slid a faded newspaper cutting from the folder, laying it out on the coffee table with care.

Emmy's heart quickened in her chest. The cutting was from the local paper, the Express & Echo. Yellowing at the edges, it gave off a slightly foxed with age odour, even though Emmy knew it couldn't be all that old. A glance to the top right-hand corner confirmed this: Thursday 17th May 2009. Her mouth went dry as she quickly scanned the headline and article below it.

EXETER TEEN CASTS SPELL OVER PRESTIGIOUS POETRY COMPETITION

An Exeter teenager has won first place in a nationally acclaimed writing award. Emmeline Walker, 15, from Ide on the outskirts of Exeter, was announced as the winner of the Spellcasters Poetry Prize 2009, an award which recognises the writer of the best verse based on a theme of magic, the supernatural and witchcraft, for her poem Say The Magic Words at a prestigious ceremony recently held in London's Old Vic Tunnels. About Emmeline's winning entry, Spellcasters founder and co-judge, Gwendoline Alwood, had this to say, "We were impressed by the standard of entries for this year's competition. There were so many wonderful poems submitted to us, but Emmeline's breathtaking metaphor about the magical healing power of words and books simply blew us away, and to think that she wrote it at only fifteen. We can't wait to see where her writing goes next!"

Emmeline, who goes by the name of Emmy, is a student at Exeter's Maynard School. She also works part-time at Adams' Antique Books, the popular rare and secondhand bookshop in Exeter's West Quarter, owned by local literary luminary, Maggie Adams. Adams is a well-known figure on the Devon book scene, fellow of Exeter University and Exeter library, and co-chair of the Exeter and Devon Institution, the private members library in Cathedral Close, which houses a collection of manuscripts, artworks and local topography, some of which are believed to be over five hundred years old.

Of her win, Emmeline said, "I was amazed that my poem was picked as the winner. Writing is something I've always loved, and I hope to make a career out of it one day."

You can read Emmeline's winning poem in full at www. spellcasterslit.co.uk

Emmy reached out with one hesitant hand to brush her fingertips across the black and white dot matrix photo which accompanied the story, almost unaware that with her other hand she was rubbing at the sore spot in her chest. The pain au chocolat and coffee sat stodgy in her sternum, threatening to reappear in a soggy caffeine and pastry mess. An uncomfortable prickling crept across her shoulders, up her neck and goosebumped into her scalp.

She closed her eyes, trying to shut out the memory that was forcing its way through the doors of her psyche. Maggie, proud as a parent, bustling around the old shop, instructing the photographer on where the best possible setting for the photo would be. Shifting her chair into the light by the big picture window, grabbing young Emmy by hand and plonking her unceremoniously into it so that the old leather let out an audible creak and a whiff of old tobacco and vanilla. Emmy, red cheeked from the all attention, simultaneously trying to hide her size by slouching her shoulders and juggle the photographer's demands: clutch her trophy–a sculpted glass quill–in one hand, tap a pencil against her teeth as if in the middle of the creative process with the other and "Smile, love. It's not the end of the world". But Maggie's repositioning of the chair sent the sunlight blasting through the window into Emmy's eyes like golden arrows, and for a brief moment, a tiny voice inside her head whispered that it was a blip, that she'd gotten lucky, or they'd taken pity on her.

That she wasn't good enough.

Of course, the photographer had chosen that very moment to start clicking and so the image accompanying the article was less than flattering. Emmy opened her eyes again, letting out a held breath as she did so. The large young girl in the photograph scowled back, eyes stormy below her fringe and Emmy choked back the same flicker of resentment she'd experienced at the time, not only for the photographer and her ridiculous "local press" demands, but also for Maggie and the hateful voice, full of spite.

"Maggie kept it all these years. She wanted you to have it." Lizzie said and Emmy jumped, having forgotten her friend was there.

Emmy's heart charged in her chest, making the pain from the undigested food even more uncomfortable. Her fingers rubbed faster. Maybe she could erase it all away. It was easy enough to do with words on paper, why not hurt and grief on a person's soul? Where was the eraser for that?

Lizzie didn't appear to notice and pressed on, enthused, "There's more where that came from too!"

She opened the file again, and for one horrifying moment Emmy saw herself snatching it out of her friend's hands and tearing it to pieces. Her head thumped, creating a champion tag-team partnership with the aching of her heart. She had to get a hold on herself. It wasn't Lizzie's fault. She drew in another deep breath, disguising it by stretching her arms up high above her head as a yawn. What was there to be afraid of? They were just memories.

She should be grateful to Maggie for having kept them safe for her. And Lizzie didn't deserve this either. It was good of her to have taken them from Maggie, especially as she had her own grief to deal with. Lizzie had been there when Emmy wasn't, taking care of their friend, right up until the last. An entirely separate stab of guilt caught Emmy unawares, right between the ribs, but this one she didn't attempt to rub away. No, she had to deal with this. Or at least give a reasonable facsimile of appearing to. She could cry all her hurt out later when Lizzie was gone.

Fixing a smile on her face, Emmy gave Lizzie her full attention as the other woman took what Emmy recognised as one of her old university notebooks from the folder and laid it on the coffee table. The cover was blue. *The same shade of frozen sky blue as Jonathan's eyes.* Emmy shivered as the unbidden image popped into her head. She forced it away and picked up the notebook, losing herself in old memories. Writing her name in her best cursive in the top right-hand corner of the first page came rushing back to her now, as clear as the sunshine that poured through the high windows in Professor Doherty's draughty English rooms. That electric buzz of sheer *possibility*, which had vibrated through her body making her hand shake. The way she'd had to concentrate so her trembling wouldn't transfer to the tip of the pen gripped between her fingers and ruin her otherwise perfectly blank page. The stories she could tell in this book.

She flipped through the pages, pausing every now and then as a story or poem she'd written while studying at Durham leapt out at her. Most of her notes were incomplete, the scribbled meanderings of a creative mind attempting to make something beautiful out of a blank page. Struggling to find the exact words in the right order with just the right amount of honesty that would perfectly encapsulate the emotion she was hoping to express without sounding trite or earnest. God, she'd had a lot to say. She'd forgotten how she used to add a mountain of notes in the margins, an editor even then.

One story caught her eye; a piece entitled *Modern Witchcraft: Feminism and The Magical Power of Romance Novels*. It was the story that had formed the basis of her dissertation. She scanned the story, smiling at some of her more laboured metaphors. But right at the bottom there was another note, written in a fragile, spidery handwriting Emmy knew not to be her own. Maggie.

Words ARE Deeds

What could it mean? It didn't make sense. Maggie was fond of reciting the oft-quoted motto of the Women's Suffrage Movement, "Deeds Not Words". The message in their bold statement clear: it was a cry for action, for radicalism. A call to arms so loud, it was heralded the length and breadth of the country and beyond. Of course, staunch feminist Maggie Adams had always identified with such a battle cry. She was known for getting things done, for challenging the status quo. But one thing had always troubled Emmy about Maggie's apparent attachment for the slogan.

It had never sat right with her that someone such as Maggie, someone whose love of literature, who's fondness for the magical power of words rivalled even her own, could dismiss them so handily. There was a duplicity about it that Emmy didn't understand. What was she saying in this note? Was she admitting that her insistence of prioritising action over expression might not have been the correct mantra all along?

She couldn't shake the uncomfortable feeling that Maggie was trying to tell her something. Something about her writing, something along the lines of "Why are you wasting your talent, Emmeline?" and the lump which had been forming in Emmy's chest became engorged and herniated, and suddenly she couldn't think about words and their meanings anymore.

Emmy gathered the newspaper clipping and tucked it and the notepad into the offending folder before tossing the whole thing back on to the table. She sighed again and rubbed her temples where the headache was threatening to take root. Lizzie noticed this time and lifted her head to regard her friend.

"You okay, Ems?" Her voice was hesitant, quite unlike her usual breathless tone. "I didn't mean to upset you."

Emmy smiled, but it was forced. There was too much going on in her head for her try to decipher Maggie's mysterious word games, none of which was Lizzie's fault. "I'm-I'm fine. I'm just tired." She flung one arm around Lizzie's shoulders and pulled her close, hoping to convey every iota of gratitude she felt for her best friend's unfaltering support. "Thanks for bringing this round." She smiled again and this time she meant it, but she couldn't shake the feeling that she was missing something important.

That Maggie was trying to tell her something, which would solve the mystery of The Book and Jonathan's curse, once and for all.

CHAPTER 8

*T*he problem with searching for elusive secret magic to break a centuries-old curse, was that neither Jonathan nor Emmeline had the faintest idea where to look, nor even what it would be if they found it. It could be anywhere within the shop. Maybe they walked past it every day without realising. The odds of it being in a book were, of course, sky high, so this is where they continued to search.

Fifty books later, they were no closer to achieving their goal. After one particularly long session browsing the shelves, Jonathan looked up from the novel he was perusing to catch Emmeline as she stretched, brushing the ceiling with her fingertips, and cricking her neck from side to side. The hem of her modern tunic inched up to expose a tantalising flash of bare stomach. Ivory smooth and deliciously rounded, just as he liked. Not washboard flat as seemed to be the fashion with the young women who appeared on Emmeline's magic screens. A stirring in his belly needed quashing before it could unman him, and he tore his gaze away, less she capture him staring.

"I need some fresh air," she said. "Do you fancy a walk?"

Jonathan glanced up again, eyebrows raised. "A walk? With you?"

"Yeah, I have to take Breone out anyway, but if you'd rather not..." Emmeline turned her head this way and that, presumably scanning the nooks and crannies for Maggie's funny ginger cat. She gave up and shrugged, facing him again with those soul-searching mahogany eyes. "It was just an idea."

Jonathan got up off the stool behind the counter. "I would be honoured to partake in a walk with you, but alas, I think it would be quite impossible. I am bound to this place. I cannot leave." He gestured around at the shelves.

"What? But the first day I met you, you walked in through the door—and I watched you leave and walk past the window." Emmeline mimed the actions as she spoke.

"I cannot leave the vicinity of the shop. I lose form if I cross the boundary. As long as I remain within the immediate purlieu, I am able to return. I do not know what would happen should I attempt to go further. I fear I may not return again."

"But...how do you know all this?" Emmeline's left eyebrow raised, awakening his sleeping libido again. "Have you ever *tried* to leave?"

Jonathan shook his head. "Well...no. But it was part of the witch's curse. Let me tell you:

"Bound by word
Bound by paper
A life captive
Bound forever
Bound in flesh
Bound in blood
Gaol eternal
Bound to book"

EMMELINE WANDERED over to perch on the stool he'd just vacated, an indecipherable expression on her face.

"There's something I don't understand. Why here?"

Jonathan came to lean on the counter in front of her. What was she asking? "I do not follow. What do you mean, why here?"

Emmeline pushed up the sleeves of her tunic and grabbed a notebook and pencil from the shelf below the counter. "I mean...why can't you leave here? Is *this* where you were cursed?"

His ability to think on his feet was something Jonathan had always prided himself on, but Emmeline's line of questioning was perilous. How to explain without alerting her?

"Maggie interpreted the curse in this way so long ago now that I never thought to question it. I hazard a guess that it has more to do with the location of The Book, than any specific connection to a place. I confess, I have been too fearful to try." His pulse roared in his ears as he finished speaking, but he could not afford to allow her to see how troubled he was.

Noticing her studying him, Jonathan rearranged his face into a nonchalant smile before heading back to the seating area and pretending to immerse himself again in the books he'd been scanning. But it was hopeless. His mind raced with impossibly warring thoughts. On the one hand, there were his growing feelings for Emmeline; a shining seed of truth that he was afraid to expose to the cold light of day, lest it expose him once and for all. On the other, a sixth sense told him the deception was necessary, not only to keep Emmy on side but also to protect her from matters she didn't need to know. Matters which would alter her opinion of him and Maggie in an instant. Preserve her memories of Maggie, for both their sakes.

Yes, that was his best course of action. He had to keep Emmeline from knowing the full truth, even if it meant lying, even if it meant despising himself for such treachery. He could not lose her now. A muscle which had been twitching in his cheek came to a sudden stop as this last thought flashed across his consciousness. It was true, in more ways than he cared to admit.

He willed himself to focus on the text he was pretending to read. The book he'd picked up was unfamiliar. It wasn't a printed manuscript, like the majority of the tomes in Maggie's—no, *Emmeline's*—shop. Instead, it appeared to be a journal of some kind, the fine paper had a series of equally spaced horizontal lines printed across each page, and someone had scrawled a mountain of notes upon them. The hand was untidy and harried, words and entire phrases had been crossed out, rewritten, tumbling over themselves, as if the author had been exorcising something from deep within their soul in a frenzied rush. Jonathan flipped through the pages to the beginning and had to stifle a gasp when he read Emmeline's name. The date, September 2013, intrigued him almost as much as learning the identity of the author. As accustomed to modernity as he was becoming, the very notion of the twenty-first century nevertheless had the power to take his breath away. There were times when the past was still real to him, but it felt distant, a long-lost brother he hadn't known existed. Other times he felt the hand of time pressing down on him with menace, the slow suffocation of history; drowning in days.

Yanking himself out of this sudden melancholy, his fingers worked fast to relocate the page he'd been reading. Here was an essay penned by Emmeline in 2014. She had struggled with it, he could tell. The crossings out were numerous, deep indentations left behind by the pressure of a frustrated pen upon paper evident beneath his searching thumb. He pressed down harder, almost unthinking, the only thoughts in his mind now the words Emmeline had printed. The spell she'd woven. Maggie was right. Emmeline *was* a sorceress, for only a mind and soul touched by magic could have penned such beautiful prose, such truth.

There was the smoothness of the paper beneath his thumb. The imperfections in its surface where she'd bore down. His forefinger joined his thumb in tracing the text and a strange warmth began to vibrate in their tips, as if the message of hope within Emmeline's stunning prose could have somehow impregnated into his skin. Her scruffy penmanship belied a magic truly wonderful to behold, although he had to smile at that. Pen*woman*ship Emmeline would insist on rechristening it, glowering at him in that peculiar way of hers which made his pulse race. He read on, becoming increasingly aware of the blood singing in his veins, of the glow that seemed to emanate from the very page into his own being. He'd never felt more alive.

EMMY COULD HAVE SWORN a fleeting veil of fear crossed his face at her questioning. But before even a ghost of doubt could materialise in her mind, the look was gone, and Jonathan's expression reverted to that serene and unattainable movie star handsome look she'd come to recognise. Satisfied she'd imagined it, she allowed herself a moment to study his impossible beauty. Even now she had to pinch herself that he was real and not another figment of her imagination. She had to laugh at that. She certainly couldn't have pictured Jonathan, not even in her wildest dreams, and she doubted there was a romance writer on earth who could have created such an archetypically perfect book boyfriend.

Damn it, Emmy! You need to get over this infatuation, this ridiculous fantasy. Perfect book boyfriend indeed! There's no such thing as perfection.

Even if there was, Jonathan was far from perfect boyfriend material–book or otherwise. There was the small matter of him being cursed for starters. Still, he *was* extraordinarily pretty, even with that strange blurring at his outline, which gave him the appearance of being behind an Instagram soft-focus filter. Emmy couldn't help but steel another glance as he wandered back to Maggie's armchair. Nothing wrong with looking *respectfully*, right?

Jonathan now selected a random book from the pile on the table, flipping through pages in a distracted fashion. Then he gazed into some unknown far-off distance, lost with his thoughts. As beautiful and untouchable as a Hollywood actor gracing a magazine cover. Then he turned the book to the first page and his expression changed. His posture went rigid, his mouth dropped open in an expression of surprise and wonder. She couldn't see which novel it was because his body was angled away from her, shielding the cover from view. He rifled through the pages again and for a moment Emmy was transfixed by the way his long fingers seemed to caress their surface, even in his haste.

Emmy's stomach did a slow loop-the-loop as Jonathan continued to stare at the mysterious book. His face took on a look of undisguised longing and Emmy's own excitement increased. What *was* he reading and why was watching him like this so erotic? Part of her was desperate to stride over and join him, but another part felt like she was intruding on something private. He began stroking one page with the ball of his thumb and the forefinger of his left hand, and Emmy's mouth widened as a wonderful glow began emanating from the book. All the air was sucked out of the room and Emmy felt a curious tightness in her chest totally unconnected to the usual ache in her sternum. Before she knew what she was doing, she'd left the stool and taken five steps toward him, compelled by some unknown magic.

This is too much like your dream.

She shook her head to rid herself of the unwelcome memory. No, this was good, she was sure of it. Jonathan looked happy, delighted even. Nothing bad could come of this. Not something as pure and magical as this. She took another step closer, electricity charging the air around her in a crackle of static. She was so close, she could almost see what book it was that had triggered the spell. For it was definitely magic, there was no denying it.

She smiled, one arm outstretched to brush Jonathan's hand with her fingers. Excitement and fear tiptoed across her skin. She didn't want to shock him. But as she peered over his shoulder, as the unknown book came into view, Emmy's heart shattered into a billion pieces. The electricity which had hummed around her in a nimbus of light exploded and blind rage washed over her in its place. *How dare he?* How dare he read her private words? Tears spiked at the corners of her eyes, but she mentally bottled them instead, allowing them to mutate and course through her veins like venom. A feeling of indescribable power pulsed inside her and the parallel with Witch Emmy of her dream struck her anew.

"What the hell do you think you're doing?"

Jonathan whipped his head up to face her, astonished bewilderment written all over his face. "I-I...I meant no harm, Emmeline." He placed the offending book on the table and held up his hands like a cornered criminal. "I did not realise my reading it would upset you so."

Emmy wasn't having it. She folded her arms across her chest and continued to give him the full benefit of her thermonuclear stare. "It's mine, damn it! You had no right. Where did you get it from anyway? Have you been snooping in my things?" It was an unfair accusation, she knew, but lashing out was her best form of defence right now. She was *sure* she'd hidden the folder upstairs in her wardrobe, so why was her old university notebook down here where anyone could read it?

Does it matter if someone reads it, though?

Oh, shut up! Of course it matters. Those are my

private thoughts, my stories. If I wanted to expose myself for all to see, I'd run through the streets of Exeter naked.

But it's not for all to see. It's just...Jonathan.

Thought I told you to shut it.

Fine. Enjoy you pity party for one.

Pity party?! I am not throwing a pity party!

Emmy almost screamed this last at her subconscious. Wasn't she allowed to feel a bit sorry for herself after everything that had happened over the last year with Dan, Maggie, her writing, her illness? Surely losing your fiancé, livelihood, longest friend *and* having your mind break all within the same twelve months qualified you for a smidgen of self-preservation? It's not like she went around attention seeking, trying to get sympathy from everyone. No, she'd done quite the opposite. She'd just gotten on with it like she always did. Strong, dependable Emmy.

The tears which she'd bottled moments earlier threatened to make a reappearance then and it took every ounce of self-worth she had not to give in to them.

Wouldn't want a good old cry to gatecrash your party, would you, Em? Why can't you let go? What are you so afraid of?

What? What's that supposed to mean? Actually, don't answer that. *I'm* not the one in the wrong here.

This whole discourse swept through Emmy's mind in a matter of seconds, but it wasn't the same as the hallucinations she associated with her mental health, which could be both terrifying and terrifyingly real. This conversation was concise and mostly logical, even if she had found herself arguing with her inner voice or subconscious, or whatever it was called. Usually, she had to admit, her inner voice got it spot on, but on this she could get in the sea. Jonathan should never have taken and read her private writing, and she raised one eyebrow as she waited for his explanation.

But Jonathan's confounded expression only deepened. His own brow furrowing in dismay. "Emmeline, I apologise again, but I implore you, I found the book here on top of the pile with all the others." He swept one hand towards the stack of books on the table. "Believe me, I would not lie about this.

Emmy's ice-old resolve thawed a little under the boiling heat of his gaze. And that strange and frightening oneness with the vengeful Emmy of her dream dissipated, melting into nothing like the Wicked Witch of The West. "Okay," she pursed her lips, "but why did you continue reading it when you realised it was mine?"

At this, Jonathan threw his head back and bellowed a laugh so loud, Emmy's heart stuttered. He clapped his hands together and stood up so that their eyes were at almost the same level.

"I continued to read it, Emmeline, because it was magical, breathtaking writing, and your words had me entranced. I know you will only scoff at this, but I was captivated, as if you'd cast a spell over me. I have only ever experienced such a powerful feeling once before. I am sure you can guess what that was."

A glow appeared in the depths of Jonathan's eyes as he spoke, and Emmy was mesmerised by their growing radiance. A crackle of supercharged air hummed between them and she took an involuntary step closer, her heart pounding in her ears, fingers itching to touch him. There was another urge in them too. A dormant need which she barely recognised within herself, a part she'd long ago locked away and buried. It was the itch to feel the weight of a pen between her fingers. To hold that power of the unknown in her hand and let it and the blank page see where they would take her. But opening that particular sarcophagus would only allow all her writing ghosts to escape and haunt her as Dan once had, so she had to fight it. As wonderful as Jonathan's words were, as warm as his eyes made her feel, she couldn't afford to expose her heart like that again. Plus, he was just trying to distract her with magic and all that bull about her being a witch and she was still mad as hell at him, goddamnit! Besides, what did he know about "breathtaking" writing? What did he know about writing at all?

She broke eye contact and moved around him to pick up the notebook from the table, before brandishing it in his face. "Fine. I believe you. But please don't read it again."

"Of course, Emmeline. I am sorry." Jonathan inclined his head, the hurt in his eyes evident. He looked as if he wanted to say more.

Emmy turned on her heel and headed back to the counter. She didn't enjoy being rude to him, but it was better this way. So why were her eyes threatening tears again? There had to be a scientific answer to explain how easily her emotions ran to crying these days. It was fast becoming her default setting. A natural phenomenon, like forecasting weather. Cloudy with a chance of waterworks.

But that wasn't quite true. The words of her inner voice rang out again, loud and clear:

Why can't you let go? What are you so afraid of?

Nothing.

Everything.

Almost every instance lately when she'd been on the verge of tears, something inside had compelled her to hold them back, to not give in, and trying to understand why made her head hurt.

Casting the net of her mind wide, she fished in her thoughts for distractions. What had they been talking about before all this? Yes, Jonathan's curse. She tried to remember the words, but random phrases leapt out at her. Despite everything she'd just promised to herself, she tugged the pencil and notepad she'd dug out earlier closer to her. Jonathan had retreated to Maggie's armchair, the stack of books now a wall between them. A literary no man's land. Maybe she'd overreacted a little? She ought at least try a peacekeeping mission.

Clearing her throat, she called his name, her voice low and hesitant. "Jonathan?"

He looked up. His face was a closed book.

"Can you repeat it for me–your curse, I mean?". The pencil twirled between her fingers until she made herself stop, resting it on the counter. Why was she so jittery?

He still didn't reply, only studied her, as if he was battling with himself to acquiesce or tell her where to go. She wouldn't completely blame him if he chose the latter.

"Please," she added.

As Emmy watched, Jonathan closed his eyes, rubbing both hands over his face before opening them again. The battle was won, it seemed, but it didn't feel like victory.

"Of course," he breathed, smiling widely, as if she was his favourite person in the world and Emmy's breath caught in her throat. An urgency she didn't understand swept through her. The only thing that mattered was breaking his curse and a tiny alarm inside her head warned her that she'd already lost the war. There really was no point trying to resist him. But even as she acknowledged the warning signs she pushed them away again. She wasn't quite ready to capitulate just yet.

For a few moments, the only sounds within the little shop were Jonathan's baritone, the scratching of Emmy's pencil against paper as he dictated the curse, the ubiquitous ticking from the clock, and the rhythmic patterns of their breathing. Even the mice seemed to have stopped their incessant scurrying inside the walls to listen. When he was finished, Emmy began reciting the curse to herself in a whisper.

> *"Bound by word*
> *Bound by paper*
> *A life captive*
> *Bound forever*
> *Bound in flesh*
> *Bound in blood*
> *Gaol eternal*
> *Bound to book"*

As she spoke, the air deepened and flipped. A breeze drifted through the small space, filling it with magic, and Emmy's skin prickled. A strange electricity thrummed in her veins. Colours bloomed in her vision and she blinked rapidly, her mouth falling open with a small gasp. Jonathan became clearer, an old television picture coming into sharper focus, and Emmy almost jumped as she saw him completely real for the first time, no longer unattainable and trapped behind a filter or shimmering like a mirage as he had during their first meeting.

"I feel it also," Jonathan's eyes were wide, glistening with wonder, "I haven't felt this alive in centuries."

He reached out to touch her cheek, fingertips brushing her skin and this time she did jump.

"I'm sorry," he drew his hand away, but she stopped him, taking his palm in her own, before returning it to her cheek. The power pumping through her was like nothing she had ever experienced before. Even more potent than the Witch Emmy dream feeling. Her fingers tingled as if they were glowing. Her chest constricted. The usual stab in her sternum usurped by something magical and portentous. But that regular pain–the Maggie and Dan pain–could not be quelled and a sudden flash of doubt unleashed all her insecurities, bringing her other hand up to rub at her chest once more. Maggie, Jonathan, Dan. Emmy. Would she ever trust anything or anyone again?

Will you ever trust yourself again?

She wrestled her gaze from his, the moment broke, and Jonathan returned to that same mirage-like state; heat haze edges and perpetually out of reach.

JONATHAN WAS PERPLEXED. Emmeline was gone, walking Breone, and rather than disappear as was his usual wont, he remained in the shop listening to the clock ticking in the corner, hoping it would drown out the warring factions of his mind. Intuition told him that Maggie had been correct in her assessment about Emmeline's latent powers. Perhaps it was woven in her magical writing or the way her words had charged the air around them when she recited his curse, flooding his veins with life? Or maybe it was just Emmeline herself? Something about the way she spoke, the cadences and patterns in her voice sang to him like no melody ever had, and the thrill of hearing her laugh, knowing he was the cause of her mirth comforted him in a way he didn't completely understand.

His freedom was so close, it was almost tangible. That brief moment when he'd come fully alive assured him that they were on the right path. The membrane had dissolved, and he'd found himself staring into Emmeline's eyes, lost and found all at once. But then the veil reformed and shifted back across his vision and the bitter taste of freedom disappeared on his tongue, only to be replaced with that intense spiky perfume again.

He flung the book in his hands across the room, regretting his moment of pique as quickly as it had come as he pictured Emmeline chastising him, eyes blazing. But then again, something about the way Emmeline's expression flashed ignited a desire in him too dangerous to mention. By gods, she was exciting! He exhaled and laughed at himself, the noise too loud in the silent space and the tremor in his voice sent another wave of desire swooping low into his gut. Rising out of the chair, he strode with purpose to where the book had landed, retrieving it with a sigh of relief that it wasn't damaged. He cradled it in his large hands as he moved into the shadows at the back of the shop.

In his former life, his trade as a cloth merchant had taken him far from England's shores. He'd learnt from his father and grandfather before him. It was his family's *other* ventures which today would call their status as upstanding pillars of the community into question, and which had set his moral compass adrift at a tender age. Even so, he'd undertaken many a perilous journey across land and sea, either as a legitimate merchant, or in his more clandestine, nefarious role. So why should he be fearful of the unknown now? His destination, so clear to him for centuries, appeared unmapped and fraught with danger. Yes, this path was still the right one, but he was suddenly unsure about where he was headed and why. And the only illumination his mind offered was that Emmy and her magic was the difference. But she deserved better. She was light and life and he was a man without a true north, no matter how many years he'd served of his sentence.

Even within his curse, he'd always understood his place in the world. It was his penance. He'd tried to make amends. But not even eternity would be enough to absolve him of his crimes. The brightness of Emmeline only served to illuminate the darkness surrounding him. Everything he thought he'd learned about himself felt wrong, as if whatever it was that anchored him to reality had shifted, as if the words and letters that told his story were now written in a language he didn't understand. He struggled to translate it, to make sense of it, but its cryptography was woven so intricately, so irrevocably, it was a riddle that confounded his mind and tied his soul in knots.

~

EMMY'S MIND was a battlefield as she walked Breone. *This can't go anywhere. He's over five hundred years old and he comes from a time when the world was very different. He probably doesn't even think women should work. Help him, that's all. Help him be free and you'll never have to see him again... But he said he's in awe of me. He's probably said a lot of things he didn't mean. You survived the damage Dan caused, don't let anyone break you again. Help him, and then he can go where he needs to go, and you can get on with living your life...*

...But... what if I want my life to be with him?

Breone yanked on the leash, it was time to go back. Shame replaced the warm glow inside Emmy's chest. Too often lately, she'd neglected him, never mind the business. Jonathan and his curse were proving too big a distraction.

CHAPTER 9

*E*mmy's heart dropped like a stone into the pit of her belly. Alarms trilled in her head and her hands shook as she took in the bank statement total. How could it be so low? Eyes scanning the statement breakdown, she zeroed in the anomaly: a missing ten thousand pounds. What? Why? She and Dan The Dickhead had been in the process of buying a flat in Bethnal Green when Emmy had finally left him, and she'd been counting on getting her half of the deposit back this week. Why on earth had she ever trusted him, dammit? With gritted teeth, she picked up her phone and swiped until she found the number she needed. While it rang, she mentally sieved through everything she wanted to say, breathing hard through her nose.

Twenty minutes later, she slammed down the mobile, before snatching it back up again to inspect the screen for damage, and a tide of relief swept over her. The last thing she needed right now was the expense of replacing a broken phone. She sank her head to the counter and let out a groan, aware she was being dramatic but not caring. From the change in the weight of the air, she sensed Jonathan had left the sofa and was now hovering over her. She lifted her head and glanced up. Sure enough, his expression was one of puzzled concern.

"Something vexes you, and for once it is not me. At least, I believe it is not." His eyes searched hers with the forensic detail of a microscope, making Emmy shrink inside a little. She made a show of straightening up.

"Course it's not you. My arsehole of an ex has only gone and fucking stolen my fucking deposit! So, it's definitely not you." She threw hers arms about in violent, jerky motions as she spoke. Anger speckled her chest and neck like a virus. Jonathan's mouth hung open, and Emmy let out an exclamation halfway between a laugh and a sob. "Don't tell me I've offended your delicate Tudor sensibilities because I won't believe you. Surely people curse where–*when* you're from?"

Jonathan shrugged, "Well yes, it is not uncommon to hear profanity. I confess myself to having used it on occasion, but never have I heard such language fall from a lady's lips."

"Jonathan, this may be a surprise to you, but I'm no lady. I may be female but I'm not here to adorn your arm or make house or babies, or whatever other expectations your time might have put upon women."

A beat.

"Why are you here, then?" Jonathan's eyes shone with such wonderful sincerity that Emmy had to collect herself before answering.

Emmy stood up, gesticulating again, a combination of white-hot anger and Jonathan's intensity driving her muscles to react and before she knew it, she was in the middle of the floor.

"I don't know. Why is anyone here? I'm a person with hopes and dreams just like everyone else. I want to make a go of *this*," she gestured around at the books, "for Maggie's sake and because I want to prove to myself that I can do it." She took a deep breath, steeling herself for what she was about to say next. "I want to...write...

"I want to explore and travel and create. I want to love and *be* loved in return, and not treated like a doormat. And help people and be a good person and recycle more and reduce my carbon footprint because I'm scared stiff of climate change and how we're slowly killing the planet. I never want to stop wandering, wondering, questioning, and dreaming. I want to be hopeful because hope is a tiny act of defiance against what sometimes feels like a cruel and cynical world.

"I want to be free of the stigma that surrounds people like me." She snatched her eyes from his at this, hurrying on before he could interject.

"I want to be paid the same as the next man for a job I can do just as well. And to be able to walk down the street without a constantly suppressed fear of attack. I want to eat what I want, drink what I want, wear what I want and do what I want without guilt or shame, and if that means saying 'fuck', I'll fucking well do it, and I don't care who it offends. I want the same as you. Freedom. Thankfully, times have changed a lot since the dark ages. And yeah, I'm aware that being a cis white woman affords me certain privileges not everyone my gender is lucky enough to have, but it's still not enough. Time's up. Time is so *definitely* up."

She exhaled and almost laughed again at the astonished look on Jonathan's face. "I'm sorry. You didn't deserve that–well, not all of it anyway. Things are different nowadays. Women are taking the lead roles more now. No longer just the bit parts, hidden in the shadows–or only illuminated to exploit or use by a patriarchal society that values our worth in looks, youth and fertility. If you think I'm shocking, wait until you see the rest of us."

"If they are anything like you, I should imagine they are quite something to behold," he smiled. His eyes glowed again, making Emmy's belly do a loop-the-loop. Her phone buzzed on the counter between them and, with some reluctance, she dragged her eyes from his to answer it.

"Hey, you two!" Emmy smiled as her parents' faces filled the screen. "What time is it over there? Must be getting late."

"It's nearly eleven," Emmy's mum said, "but we wanted to catch you before you got too busy."

"Good idea," Emmy echoed her mother's cheery, hopeful tone, praying neither of them would mention Dan the Dickhead. They couldn't see Jonathan, who was now peering with undisguised fear at the mobile over her shoulder, but she twisted away from him to be sure.

"How's it going then, Emmeline?" Dad was the only person other than Maggie–and now Jonathan–who insisted on addressing Emmy by her full name.

"Great! I haven't stopped. What have you two been up to? I hear there's a heatwave."

"Yeah, freaky weather for late September but it's not too bad here. The South Island is super-hot. They put out warnings about forest fires and there's a hosepipe ban again... Anyway, your dad and I just wanted to check that you're okay. With the memorial and everything... We're really sorry we can't be there, Hun."

Emmy swallowed. She'd known this was coming. "It's fine. *I'm* fine. I don't expect you two to drop everything and fly halfway around the world for one day, and even if I wanted you to, you can't. How's the leg, Dad?"

"As good as can be expected, least that's what Doctor Grimm says, anyway–

"Don't call her that!" Emmy's mum interjected.

"She gives me the creeps, you know, with the way she stares at you without blinking. I feel like a fly being eyed up by a praying mantis. Still, she's a bloody good doctor and that's what matters." Her dad turned his attention back to the screen, "I'm doing good, Emmeline. With a bit of luck, I'll be up on my feet in no time."

Emmy laughed as her mum rolled her eyes. Jonathan was still watching them, his face full of incredulous trepidation.

"That's great, Dad. Maybe I can come and see you once things have settled down here." She twisted her hair, hoping they'd say their goodbyes soon. The day they'd returned to New Zealand two years ago had made the first chink in Emmy's carefully forged armour and she still missed them terribly. But the longer they kept her talking, the harder it would be to keep lying to them. The tinkling of the door opening came to her rescue. *Saved by the bell*, she thought looking around for the customer, but there was no customer. It was Jonathan. He grinned as he closed the door again, looking at her in a shy, hopeful way that made her mouth go dry.

"Good morning!" she directed in his direction before whipping her head back to her parents, who'd no doubt heard the door opening and closing too. "I gotta go. I love you both. Byeee!"

"Bye love. Take care and call us if you need anything. Anything at all."

"Bye Emmeline. Love you!"

They waggled their fingers at her, and mum blew several kisses before the screen went blank. She stole a moment just staring at it, trying to assimilate everything that was threatening to tear her apart inside. Her heart overflowed with emotion as she thought about her parents. Mum, forever anxious but not organised enough to make sense of her worrying. And Dad the complete opposite, always larking about and cracking jokes. It was a wonder how they managed to get through each day. But at least they had each other, especially now that Emmy wasn't around to tell them to buy milk or remind Dad when his hospital appointments were. What on earth would they think if they knew just how topsy-turvy Emmy's own life had become? She turned to Jonathan, grateful for his intervention.

"Thank you, but you didn't have to do that."

Jonathan didn't look convinced, "Why were you avoiding their questions? Why did not you tell them the truth? You are in trouble. They are your parents. Or do parents not aid their children in their time of need in this strange new world of yours?"

Emmy lifted her chin a fraction, "There's no law against wanting to be independent."

"No, but in my day, there were many against witch-craft. I am torn between fear and my natural inclination to help. I respect your desire for independence, but I must offer to settle this score against the man who stole from you, even though I am certain you will decline. Maybe you can *conjure* the means you require to keep your shop open, because it appears to me that you are indeed a great sorceress. The witch who cursed me must have been a mere amateur, for my prison is nothing but a humble book. You, on the other hand, have your parents incarcerated within this strange device," he left the door and strode to her side, pointing at her mobile, "I do not understand the sorcery here, but I must admit to being both in awe and terrified of it."

"Witchcraft? Sorcery? Get a grip." She rolled her eyes. "Remember I told you about the telephone?"

He arched one eyebrow, morphing from ruggedly handsome to suggestive sex god in a nano-second. "It is forever imprinted upon my memory."

"Well…err," Emmy's psyche involuntarily reminded her of the moment in the phone booth and how close his lips had been to her own, their bodies squeezed together tight in the cramped space. Her mind shouted 'Phone Sex!' and it took all her resolve to shove her libido back down before she could humiliate herself. Certain her fiery cheeks gave her away, she gulped and continued, "This is also a telephone, except this one is mobile. No leads or wires. I'm not even going to try to explain it to you because it would take forever, and we probably don't have that long. Now, for the last time, I am *not* a witch and I can't do magic or sorcery or whatever you want to call it. My Mum and Dad live in New Zealand—that's an island in the Pacific Ocean thousands of miles away—we use our mobiles to keep in touch. I know this must be overwhelming for you, but just go with it, okay?" She closed her mouth with a snap.

All the talk in the world wasn't going to conceal her rekindled desire. It was only making it worse. The memory of pressing up against Jonathan's hard torso inside the phone box was too much to take on top of everything else right now and she moved behind the counter again for protection. She couldn't allow herself to be distracted by him, no matter how her body responded to his smile. And she *definitely* wasn't going to let him play the knight in shining armour riding to her rescue. A role he seemed determined to carve out for himself.

"And as for your kind offer, you're right. Thank you, but no thank you. I can fight my own battles."

Jonathan face was nonplussed. "I do not doubt it," he said with a small shake of his head before looking at the phone in her hand the way a man might eye a snake he'd just realised was venomous. When Emmy offered it to him, he backed away.

"Oh, come on! Don't try to tell me a tough guy like you is frightened of this little thing!" Emmy laughed, "It's just a phone. Here."

Despite everything she'd just promised herself, she darted around the island counter again to his side and made to grasp his hand in her own.

"You're going to have to trust me on this," she said when he only looked at her.

Jonathan was quick to react. "It is not you I do not trust, Emmeline. It is that thing. That apparatus. I have been taught to fear dark magic. In my time, rumours spread like disease. It was not uncommon for one's neighbours or even family to be accused. Suspicion and superstition prospered. At first, it was mere whispers that the evil from Europe had spread into Britain, infecting all it touched. This was before the witch trials of the following century, I believe. Darkness had begun to descend upon us long before the history books began to record it, but I guess this much is true for all history. It is only after that fact that people truly take notice. I have had much time to ponder this, but I still fear the unknown, for it was forbidden to dabble in these darkest of arts, by both My Queen and my God."

"Your god? You're religious then?" Emmy couldn't hide her surprise.

"I used to think I was a religious man." He gazed out of the window. "A man of faith, yes, but after the curse, I began to question that faith. Five hundred years is a long time to be abandoned by one's deity… And now you cause me to question it further. I am both humbled and awed by knowledge, but I must confess to being fearful to learn more."

Emmy looked him squarely in the eye. "I am not a witch. I have told you this so many times. If my world scares you so much, I won't show you anymore, but if you truly want my help you must accept that you're going to see and hear and touch stuff that is alien and possibly even blasphemous to you. It's just a phone. A form of communication. Let me show you."

She took his hand again, leading him to the sofa and he allowed her to nudge him into a sitting position. She sat opposite him in Maggie's chair without thinking. It hit her like a wrecking ball and her stomach flipped with an unexpected wave of nausea. Gripping the armrests, she brushed the feeling away.

"With my mobile I can call anywhere in the world, just like on the telephone over there. But this does so much more. I can use it to read the news or books. I can check the weather. It has apps that allow me to type and schedule my day. I can create an online presence that allows me to interact with anyone, anywhere in the world. You're right. It *is* a bit magical and scary, but that's thanks to technology and science, not witchcraft."

Her fingers worked fast as she spoke, swiping and clicking across the screen as she demonstrated the phone's capabilities. Jonathan watched with wide eyes, occasional utterances of surprise leaving his lips. When Emmy clicked on YouTube, he leaned forward and tried to touch the person on the screen with a hesitant finger.

"She's not really there. That's a recording," Emmy said nodding at the video now playing. "This is Beyonce. She's a singer, actor, businesswoman, activist, one of the most famous people on the planet, and a goddamn queen...But, not a queen in perhaps the sense you're used to. Oh, never mind. It's just an expression. I don't imagine you've seen many Black people."

Jonathan tilted his head, "On the contrary. Once again, your history books are inaccurate. There are–*were*–Africans living amongst us. In fact, one came to court in the entourage of Catherine of Aragon. This lady–this Beyonce–is most impressive. I take it she must be a witch, also? I jest," he added as Emmy opened her mouth to protest. "What does this do?" He pointed to the camera icon.

"It's a camera. It takes photos–or videos. Like a painting but more realistic and it captures the image instantly. Like this." Emmy flipped the mobile over and snapped a photo of him before he could reply. When she showed him the image, his expression mirrored the one in the picture: complete and utter bewilderment.

"Are you saying," Jonathan began, eyebrows shooting up, "that this tiny little thing just painted that portrait of me, and you expect me to believe that it is not sorcery?"

"I know, but honestly, humanity made some pretty phenomenal advancements in technology in the last five hundred years. We even landed on the moon."

Jonathan stood up too fast, banging his head on a beam. "Now it is you jesting with me. I refuse to believe that a man has stepped foot on the moon."

"You're not alone." Emmy said rolling her eyes. "Now sit back down so I can make a video of you."

"A video?" His incomparable face was a mixture of pain and incredulity as he sank into the seat again, rubbing at the back of his skull with one hand.

"A *moving* portrait. Like Beyonce." An image of Jonathan in a black leotard strutting his stuff to *Single Ladies* popped into Emmy's head and she pressed her lips together to stifle her giggles.

"Surely you cannot expect that I gyrate and twirl like that? The only dancing that I know is much more refined."

Emmy permitted herself the briefest of daydreams to imagine what Jonathan's refined kind of dancing might be like. "Don't worry. I just want to try something, that's all. I didn't expect you to show up on the photo. I thought you'd be invisible like you are to everyone else. What do you think would happen if I sent it to someone? Would they be able to see you?"

Jonathan's furrowed brow made two deep trenches in

the otherwise perfect landscape of his face. "I do not know. It depends on whether they believe in magic. Do you want people to know about me?"

Emmy nodded. "Yes, why wouldn't I? Of course, no one would believe me if I told them the truth. Lizzie didn't believe me did she, but no matter. They don't need to know who you really are. Will you let me video you?"

"If it makes you happy, I acquiesce," he bowed theatrically, and Emmy laughed again before leaping up and disappearing into the warren of shelves at the rear of the store. When she returned a few moments later, her lips couldn't contain a bubble of delight as she held out a copy of *The Complete Poems of Sir Thomas Wyatt* to Jonathan, who took it from her with a question etched on his handsome face.

"Will you read it?" She hesitated before adding, "Please? For me?"

"Ahh, young Sir Thomas. A more wonderful turner of phrase I have yet to meet. Now *this* truly *is* a spell book."

He flipped through the aged pages with an excited smile. When he found the poem he was looking for, he paused for a moment before speaking. Wordlessly, Emmy raised her phone in front of her face and pressed record.

"The lively sparks that issue from those eyes
Against the which ne vaileth no defence
Have pressed mine heart and done it none offence
With quaking pleasure more than once or twice.
Was never man could anything devise
The sunbeams to turn with so great vehemence
To daze man's sight, as by their bright presence
Dazed am I, much like unto the guise
Of one ystricken with dint of lightning,
Blinded with the stroke, erring here and there.
So, call I for help, I not when ne where,
The pain of my fall patiently bearing.
For after the blaze, as is no wonder,
Of deadly ' Nay' hear I the fearful thunder."

At first, his eyes were fixed on the book, his rich voice bringing Wyatt's words to life as a sculptor moulds clay. Then he lowered the tome and stared at the phone, reciting the sonnet by heart, and Emmy shivered. It was as if he was dedicating the verse to her; each word sending sweet bolts of nervous energy catapulting around her system. She shook herself. How many women had he tumbled into bed by reading sonnets to them? *Distracted again, Emmy? Focus goddammit!* His on-camera presence was undeniable. He had a certain magnetic quality that filled the space around him, yet also made the room seem intimate, as if there was no one else on earth but the two of them. Others would feel it too, so before she could talk herself out of it, she crafted a Tweet on the store account and sent the video out into the ether.

"Done," she said, avoiding his eyes, "You're on Twitter." She perched on the arm of the sofa next to him, too aware of his closeness as they watched the recording back together, him mouthing the words. When he reached the part about the sunbeams, he shifted to face her, his eyes blazing. He leaned towards her and the magnetic pull was there again, dragging her body to his, as both he and the on-screen Jonathan intoned in unison: "Of one ystricken with dint of lightning."

A flash enveloped the room. Emmy leapt from the couch and sprinted across the floorboards, shocked at how gloomy the sky had turned outside. A steady pat, pat, pat of fat, heavy raindrops hit the window with a sound that meant business.

"Quick! Help me with this," Emmy called from inside the small cupboard into which she had half crawled. She emerged carrying five plastic buckets, which she instructed Jonathan to place in various spots on the floor and shelves. "The jettied roof leaks rain through the ceiling. At least it always used to, and I can't imagine Maggie ever got around to having it fixed."

When they'd finished plugging gaps in the beamed ceiling, the steady drip of water into the slowly filling buckets was only punctuated by the pattering of the rain on the roof and windows outside. A new roof would cost a fortune and the sudden downpour wasn't going to help with business today. Emmy pushed up the sleeves of her blouse and drifted back to the counter. Keeping busy was always the answer. Instead of turning to the computer, however, she found herself drawn to her notebook. Picking it up, she began whispering the curse again.

Propping the notebook against the till, she bunched her hands inside her pockets and her fingers brushed against Maggie's letter once more. *Deeds Not Words* and

Words ARE Deeds flashed across her mind like a bizarre radio commercial jingle. Then Jonathan's deep voice reading Wyatt's sonnet came back to her and soon everything was intermingling in her thoughts, until she was dizzy. Drunk on a lyrical, literary cocktail.

Something half-formed tugged at the edge of her psyche. A mere wisp of an idea like a small child demanding attention by tugging at their mother's skirt. Emmy scrambled to drown everything else out, willing the idea to take shape before it could get away, but it was like trying to hold smoke. She snatched up a pencil and started scribbling. It was moments before she remembered that she was writing again and heart banging in panic and confusion, she knocked over the stationary pot, sending pens and highlighters flying, and Breone–who'd been dozing on the countertop–gave a startled yowl before fleeing to his favourite bookcase with a rather disgruntled look.

Her hand shook as she wrote, and her fingers quickly cramped from gripping the pencil too tight. Faster and faster she scribbled, her breath held and heart galloping. The lights in the chandelier flickered on-off-on-off, as the storm outside intensified, until finally, the little shop was plunged into near darkness. A huge crack of thunder erupted overhead, and Emmy's pencil snapped in two, driving a sharp splinter into her left forefinger. She threw the broken half still in her grasp on to the desk with a small yelp.

Jonathan was by her side in an instant. "What is it?"

Emmy shook her head, eyes wide. Her temples throbbed and her chest ached. She removed the finger she was nursing from her mouth and gave it a few quick shakes before picking up the notebook.

"Free from paper
Free from words
A life released
Time re-turned
Freed in flesh
Freed in blood
Life eternal
Rewrite the book"

The ornate hands on the grandfather clock began turning in reverse as the air decompressed. Emmy's stomach performed a series of dizzying somersaults as she looked up at Jonathan with unfettered animation.

"I think... I think I've got it."

CHAPTER 10

*J*onathan was becoming more real every day. Emmy's spell, as he insisted on calling it, was like the breath of life. Emmy remained unconvinced, but even she couldn't deny the changes in him. He was able to stay with her for increasing periods at a time now, and Emmy only had to read The Book briefly for him to appear. Fascinated by the account of his life, she had to keep stopping herself from devouring the whole story. Just one more page, she'd tell herself. When was it ever just one more page? Besides, what would happen if she read it all? Emmy had never divulged her guilty secret to anyone—not even Maggie.

She always read the last page of a new book first.

She'd been burned too many times to count by books that promised a Happily Ever After in the blurb, only to discover the plucky heroine tragically dying by the final page. Who could blame her for wanting to sneak a peek at the ending of this one? But she was good and resisted.

One thing she couldn't deny, however, was that she

found The Book fascinating. In one excerpt Jonathan surprised her by sacrificing his claim over a land dispute that had raged since his great grandfather's time, giving a young Catholic family a reprieve from almost inevitable eviction.

"Irrespective of my great grandfather's will, I was not in need of it," he told Emmy when she questioned him later, "Thirty acres already within my possession, what benefit would half an acre more afford me? Besides, it was rotten land, liable to flooding. Better to let them stay than adopt the pitfalls and problems that accompanied it."

Emmy suspected he was downplaying his role as the family's benefactor but said nothing. Who was Lord Jonathan Dalgliesh? At first glance he appeared to be the stereotypical scoundrel hero of every historical romance Emmy had ever read. But peel back the layers of his rakish exterior and Emmy found a man conflicted by his faith, lineage, duty to his queen, and sense of nobility. A good man at his core, perhaps? But this would be ignoring his penchant for misogyny and she found herself challenging some of his more archaic viewpoints on women on more than one occasion. Each time she did this, he merely shrugged and told her he no longer held the same opinions.

"What about here, where you describe one of your many conquests–the wife of a prominent local business-man, no less–as 'an entertaining plaything, a charming, yet utterly unrewarding diversion.'?"

Jonathan removed The Book from her hands, taking them in his. "I am not proud of it. I have had many life-times to understand that my behaviour was unpleasant and ill thought. What would you have me do? I cannot alter my past, as much as I would wish to. But on this, I give you my word: I was no infidel. As many women as there were, it was only ever one at any given time. Perhaps this does not mean so much to you, but for me it is an important distinction. I may have been a rogue, but I was, at least, a faithful one."

His expression was so sincere Emmy almost found herself believing him. She pulled away from his grasp and pretended not to notice the crestfallen way his eyes dropped.

"How many were there?" Even as the words left her mouth, Emmy wanted the ground to open up and swallow her. It was a wholly unreasonable question. What business was it of hers anyway?

"I'm sorry?" Jonathan said, looking at her with a baffled expression.

"How many women did you seduce?" *Shut up, just shut up!*

Jonathan began pacing the floor again.

"I cannot say," he held up his hand when Emmy made to interrupt. "You are asking me to give you details about my life from over five hundred years ago. I do not recall the numbers. I am twenty-eight. I lost my virginity at fifteen–*she* seduced *me*, if that makes any difference. I was promiscuous. Can we agree on that?"

Alarm bells about centuries-vanquished STDs clanged in Emmy's head, but she let it drop. It wasn't as if she was planning on jumping into bed with him. However she made a mental note to ask Alexa to add condoms to that week's shopping list–just in case. Then she blushed at her presumption. Why couldn't he have been a boorish oaf, or at least not a sixteenth century philanderer? But that was crossing dangerously into slut-shaming territory. Who was she to tell him how to live?

How long would she be haunted by Dan the Dickhead's betrayal? Would she ever trust anyone again? It was ridiculous to connect Jonathan's five-hundred-year-old philandering with Dan's recent duplicities, but her wounded heart couldn't help but join impossible dots. Maybe one day she'd be confident enough to think about dipping a wary toe into the dating pool again. Maybe it wouldn't bother her so much if Jonathan wasn't such a sex god. And considering buying protection was, at least, a start. So, if she had to start somewhere, why not with Jonathan? A quick roll in the hay with him might be just what her trust issues needed.

Her cheeks burned. Perhaps it was reading about his exploits, or maybe it was her own fertile imagination, but this was the effect Lord Jonathan Dalgliesh had on her whether she liked it or not. But Emmy wasn't about to let her runaway imagination ruin everything she'd worked so hard to build. Not when she knew, deep down, that there was no way she ready for any kind of relationship.

Brushing Jonathan's Tudor sex life aside, she decided to check Twitter, but something wasn't right. The little red numbers were off the charts. She *never* got this amount of notifications. Her heart leapt to her mouth when she clicked on the icon bringing up like after like after like for Jonathan's video. And there were comments too!

Hot damn! Now there's a tall drink of Tudor water.
Where can I find me one of these?
Marry me!

"Jonathan, look!"

Jonathan ceased wearing a track in the old stone, as had become his custom, and came to look over her shoulder. "You will have to explain what it is you are so delighted about, because I am, yet again, perplexed."

"It's your video! People love you! I don't know how or why but you've gone viral!" Emmy spoke fast, giddy with excitement, as another ten likes totted up on her notifications. "Read what they're saying! They want to marry you! This woman wants to marry you and have lots of sex and babies. Ugh, this one is cringeworthy: *'Shall I compare thee to a summer's BAE?'* Ouch! That's just blasphemy."

Jonathan was inspecting his hands and arms with forensic scrutiny. "But I am not sickening. What is this virus of which you speak? Pray it is not the Dreade Sweat returned to bring doom upon these lands again."

Emmy let out a party popper of a laugh. Jonathan's bemused expression only made it worse and she doubled over, unable to stop giggling, clutching at her sides. When she finally got herself under control, a huge hiccup escaped her lips which started her off again. It was only when Jonathan spoke, did the giggling fit cease.

"It pleases me to see you liberated from the woes that normally shackle you, Emmeline, even if this is naught but a temporary state. You should have reason to laugh often and I am gladdened to be the cause of your mirth and not your distress for once."

"I'm sorry," Emmy said wiping her eyes, "It was your face. Going viral is an internet term for when something is virtually passed from one user to another. It doesn't mean you are sick. It's a metaphor for how quickly things spread on the internet. I never expected that video to go viral. I thought a couple of my friends and maybe some of our more tech savvy customers might like it. I've honestly no idea how it happened, but I'm over the moon it did because–look!"

She swivelled the computer screen so that he could see and pointed out the messages. "All these people want to order books from us! This is the best thing that could have happened, so thank you."

Standing on tiptoes, she surprised them both by lifting her head to his and depositing a light kiss on his cheek, noting how his stubble scratched against her lips. A fast blush heated her face and neck, and she sat back down again, busying herself with the messages. Then she immediately turned back to him, tapping a pencil on her teeth.

"You know, it's *you* they want. You should be answering these messages, not me–if you don't mind, of course." She tried to keep voice level but inside she cringed at asking for his help again.

"Me?" Jonathan laughed, "In case you have failed to observe, your modern inventions leave me utterly flummoxed. I am floundering here. I do not think I would be of any use to you."

Emmy got to her feet. "You already have been." She grew in confidence. "And I'll show you how. You don't have to reply to them all–there's thousands! You'd be here another five hundred years! *Please?*" Ugh. Begging would be a direct arrow to his sense of chivalry, and she resented resorting to it, but if it helped the shop? Well, she could afford to swallow her pride just this once, couldn't she?

The far-off look in Jonathan's eyes told her he was considering it, then his solid jaw broke out in a wide, dazzling grin that left Emmy breathless. Yesterday's storm had made way for glorious wall-to-wall sunshine, but it was nothing compared to Jonathan when he smiled. Her suppressed libido awoke again, stretched in an exaggerated fashion and did a slow tango in her stomach, sending delicious thrills of delight around her body. Okay, she had a crush on him. Surely, she could admit to that without compromising herself? And to be fair, anyone would have to remind themselves how to breath if they were on the receiving end of one of Jonathan's smiles.

"Emmeline," Jonathan said, still smiling his million-dollar smile, still giving Emmy respiratory problems, "it would be amiss of me not to help you, especially as you are assisting me. But even without a reciprocal exchange, I would acquiesce. Nothing would give me greater pleasure."

1568

A cold breeze creeps at my neck as I slip into St Martin's Lane. I yank the cords of my cape tighter around my throat, but a trickle of fear sweeps down my spine as I try to rid myself of the unsolicited feeling the action conjures. Would I be for the Hangman's noose or beheaded if caught? Peering through the soft settling fog, my eyes tighten. Are the shadows around the base of the cathedral moving? I should have brought a torch, but the flames would attract attention.

Looking skyward, I can just make out the silhouette of the incomplete South Tower; black against the inky sky like the heart of a witch. Horses hooves on cobbles clip-clop into the distance and the thick stench of ale and piss assault my senses. I take one last glance back down the alley and duck through the door of The Ship Inn, hopeful Lady Catherine has undertaken as much heed getting here as myself. To say her summons surprised me is an understatement, and I remain unconvinced she will attend and that this is not a hoax–or worse, a trap.

I shuffle through sawdust and goodness knows what other debris littering the floor to make the bar, stooping as is my custom. The beamed ceiling is low, and I have been caught out before. Most buildings are not built for giants of six feet. It is perhaps why I am happiest outdoors, where I can be free to stand up straight and tall without fear of concussion, or my own home, Powderham Manor, with its high ceilings and airy, capacious rooms.

Laughter now fills this *room. A circle of men is grouped around a large wooden table in the centre of the inn. Cards are strewn across the table, and sovereigns and medallions glint like gold teeth inside a decayed mouth in the candle-light. The faces of Exeter's rich and powerful in varied states of intoxication leap out at me. They are accompanied by several young ladies who are not their wives. My eyes widen a fraction in greeting. It is out of a mutual, unspoken treaty that we do not disclose each others' nighttime procliv-ities. There is danger, yes, but the tales that could slip from my mouth are as equally–if not more–dangerous for these men should they ever think to unmask me.*

I order a flagon and signal to Tom, the innkeeper. He nods, and I make my way to the back of the room, careful no one pays me heed. The shouts and guffaws from the crowd grow ever bawdier as the game progresses, and a fiddler in one gloomy corner struggles to make his melody heard above the din. I sip at my beer, watching the foamy scum on top dance and wobble as I place the tankard down on the rough table. The taste of hops is strong on my tongue, recalling the last time I was here, six months ago, when Lady Catherine, wife of the Marquess of Somerset, told me our affair was over. I gulp the rest of my ale and wipe my mouth with the back of my hand, hungry to taste hops on her lips once more.

It is almost midnight when Tom nods again and I smile, standing too fast, banging my head on a beam. Thankfully, the bar is all but empty now. Exeter's great and not-so good have dispersed like wraiths in the night with their entertainment for the evening, many a good deal poorer than when they first arrived. No-one but Tom notices as I wince and rub at my forehead.

"Every time, without fail. I shall have to put up a sign for you." His voice dances with amusement but his eyes are deadly serious. He is no fool. He understands the gravity of our actions. "She's 'ere, but I don't know how long for. She seems troubled."

He sets down the tankard he is drying with an old rag onto the bar top, and kicks over a heavy looking wooden barrel with ease. The stone steps beneath it are revealed, curving in a downward spiral out of sight. With a smile of thanks, I hurry to them. My footsteps echo into the encroaching silence as I descend.

Lady Catherine is waiting for me in the cellar below. Her beautiful countenance is flushed, eyes fevered, but whether from fear or desire I cannot discern. Shadows wax and wane across her face and bosom in the candlelight. The room is simply furnished with a small wooden table and two chairs. She has already poured the wine that Tom has left for us. I take it as a good omen.

"I did not think you would come," she says with a

whisper quite unlike her usual direct manner. "I thought I was strong enough to do this alone. The plan has changed."

My fingers ache to touch her. I hesitate, shocked by my own reaction. To think that after all this time she could still...

The candles gutter and die as a gentle breeze sweeps in from under the closed door behind her. The same door she would have crossed through to arrive at this clandestine chamber. The same door she slammed in my face the last time. I know the risks she has taken to get here, for only I and few others are aware of that door and where it leads: the rabbit warren of secret tunnels that snake beneath my great city. Follow the right path, and within minutes, one could reach the quay, stowaway aboard one of the many ships on the Exe–perhaps even one of my own–and abscond from the city undetected. For her to yet again make the dangerous journey in the opposite direction tells me everything.

"I imagine you have much to tell and little time, but I demand you kiss me first."

I unlace the ribbons gathered at the side of her pale blue satin gown as I speak, waiting for a rebuttal, but it doesn't come. A tiny muscle in her cheek pulses, her eyes spit fire, but she does not resist. Whatever strange power that is holding her back– self-control or some other higher influence I cannot comprehend–suddenly breaks and her fingers work faster than my own until she is stripped from the waist up, her glorious pale breasts almost glowing in the dim light. My groin strains uncomfortably against my codpiece in response. The look on her face as she fixes me with the full strength of her brilliant green eyes almost unmans me.

It is I who is not strong enough. Yet, even as I acknowledge that this woman will be my eventual downfall, my mouth closes around first one perfect ruby nipple and then the other. I trail slow, agonising kisses down her now naked body, marvelling as ever at the smoothness of her skin. Then my ego growls in triumph at Lady Catherine's soft sigh of resigned lust, as I claim her most precious jewel with my tongue and lips.

CHAPTER 11

2018

*E*mmy and Jonathan worked on crafting tweets together for the rest of the day, giggling like children at some of Jonathan's racier replies. Each time their fingers brushed as they hovered over the keyboard they'd start, and with furtive flushed glances, try to ignore the Van De Graaf charge rising between them. At six o'clock, when Jonathan suggested making another video, Emmy couldn't hide her surprise.

"You'd be up for that again?" She looked up, fingers frozen in place above the laptop.

"Why not? What worked once should work again. Maybe we could make it a regular feature for your Titterings."

Emmy had to duck her pride back down out of sight again. "Okay, let's do it. What do you want to read this time?" She browsed the shelves for something suitable, running a fingernail along the spines.

"Oh, I do not need a book this time. If it pleases you, I would like to recite some poetry of mine own." His soft smile was like a thousand hopeful puppies, wide-eyed and begging to told 'Yes'.

Powerless to resist Emmy nodded, but before either of them could say or do anything further the bell rang. They turned to the door in unison, and Jonathan's mouth fell open as a young Black woman with bright blue hair burst through it. The bracelets at her wrists jangled in an echo of the bell. She bustled up to the counter, a steady stream of words gushing from her lips, as if she and Emmy had been chatting all along.

"Saw your Tweet went viral, so had to come and see what the fuss was for myself," she planted air kisses next to Emmy's cheeks before regarding Jonathan. "Are you going to introduce me or stand there gawping?"

Emmy's mouth went dry. Dawn and Jonathan stared at each other as if they were both explorers who'd just discovered a new country. It was difficult to say who was the more outlandish of the two. Dawn, with her electric blue crop and Instagram-worthy sense of style, was perhaps the antithesis of anyone's preconceived notion of what a lawyer or trainee lawyer should look like. Today, she wore a grey marl sweater with the word "feminista" emblazoned across the front like a brand, a pair of red tartan flares the Bay City Rollers would be proud of, high-heeled black ankle boots, silver hoop earrings the size of saucers, and a chunky necklace in every colour of the rainbow. As ever, she carried off the look with the kind of panache Emmy knew *she* would never possess.

If I wore that, I'd look like a bloody clown.

Bubbling with a mixture of awe and quiet resentment,

Emmy swept her hair back and turned her attention to Jonathan. Resplendent in today's ensemble of black leather breeches and a silvery grey blouson trimmed with gold embroidery and piping and mother of pearl buttons, her mind went blank when she looked at him. He had such an aura, such presence, it was as if nothing existed but him and everything else–Dawn, the shop, the outside world even–fell away. As her senses returned, Emmy was irresistibly reminded of something.

"Hold on!" She called back over her shoulder as she disappeared into the part of the shop that Lizzie had once dubbed the 'Ripped Bodice & Shredded Abs' section thanks to Maggie's obsession with historical romance. Her breath quickened as she scoured the shelves. *There*! Snatching the paperback from the ledge, she hurried back to Jonathan and Dawn, who waited for her with bemused patience.

Emmy settled on the stool again, dropping the book down harder than she meant to in her excitement, and they both flinched.

"Sorry. Erm... Dawn, meet Jonathan."

There was a moment of polite greeting between them where Jonathan bowed, and Dawn responded with a quick nod before she resumed staring at Emmy with question marks written in her eyes. Emmy pressed her lips together. What could she say? For all her fun appearance and flirty conversation, Dawn was as pragmatic as the day was long and even less of a believer in the supernatural than Emmy. If *anyone* should believe in this stuff, it would be Lizzie. She was the one obsessed with those ghost hunting shows and checked her horoscope daily. But Lizzie had scoffed. Better to say nothing to Dawn about Jonathan's past, perhaps. It wasn't as if Emmy didn't trust Dawn, but a girl shouldn't have too many confidants.

And one of yours is dead, remember...?

Emmy pushed the unhappy voice away, took a deep, ragged breath and opened her mouth again. "Jonathan is a friend of Maggie's. He very kindly offered to help with the video and even brought his own costumes with him." She was never any good lying. Time seemed to slow the blood in her veins to treacle while she waited for Dawn's reaction, but to her intense relief, the other woman's face broke into a radiant smile.

"How thoughtful!" She whirled to face Jonathan. "So, you're an actor, or what–a model?"

Emmy shot Jonathan a look. She crossed her fingers behind her back and prayed he would go along with the subterfuge.

"Yes," Jonathan said, "And it has been both an honour and pleasure to offer Emmeline my assistance. In fact, we were just about to make another one of her virus videos when you appeared. However, I am curious about her choice of literature this time." He cast his eyes down at the book Emmy had flung on the counter moments before.

A bubble of gratitude rose in Emmy's throat and she looked at Jonathan, hoping to convey her thanks for his changing the subject. Grabbing the novel again, she studied the cover. Juliet Landon's *The Mistress and The Merchant,* the stylized white lettering proclaimed across a close-up image of a couple in a romantic clinch. The woman wore a bright vermillion gown, heavily embroidered with shimmering threads. The male had one arm on the small of the woman's back, his other hand resting near her elbow. Their foreheads were touching, the woman's face upturned to the stubble-jawed Adonis as if they were about to kiss. The man's silver and gold quilted doublet caught Emmy's eye again and she shivered as she glanced back up to Jonathan, who was standing there looking as if he'd just stepped from its pages. Which wasn't a million miles away from the truth.

"What you're wearing today," Emmy nodded at Jonathan's clothing, "it reminded me of this. I thought you could read some of it. Maybe? As well as your own poetry, of course." Her gut twisted as she waited for him to respond. She didn't know if Dawn's presence was making it better or worse.

Dawn snatched the book from Emmy's hand, causing Emmy to cry out.

"Hey!"

Dawn's dark eyes scanned the cover with delight. "Oh, it's a Mills and Boon. Remember how we used to devour these, Emmy?" *Temptation in the Italian's arms!*" she quoted, her voice rising with glee as she performed another of her infamous exaggerated swooning motions.

Worse. Definitely, much worse. Heat bloomed in Emmy's chest. Flames of embarrassment licked at her ears and swept across her cheeks as she remembered how Juliet Landon's steamy tale about betrayed woman Aphra Betterton and her scandalous relationship with Venetian merchant, Santo Datini, belied the genteel restraint of its cover. But Dawn hadn't finished. She whipped her head between Emmy and Jonathan and the book in her hands, like a spectator at Wimbledon during a prolonged and fascinating rally.

"You know, you look a bit like her, Emmy. I mean, apart from the hair, of course, but you have similar bone structure and features. How would you guys feel about a photoshoot?" Her eyes sparkled as she brought her head up to face Emmy and Jonathan again. "I dabble in photography," she explained to a bewildered Jonathan, who shuffled on the spot but said nothing, clearly not enamoured with the idea.

Emmy had only ever once been more mortified. She wished she could say the flames of her desire were extinguished, but instead they mutated and raged into a fiery humiliation that seeped into her pores, turning her usually pale complexion into what she now imagined must resemble sunburn. Angry, red-hot and painful. But then a tiny voice pointed out a possibility she hadn't yet considered, and she clung to it, as docile as the model on the cover of *The Mistress and The Merchant*. It was a voice she knew well and for once one not to be feared, for it was her own true voice; always questioning. Always asking: *what if?* It was the reason why she became lost in books, where her passion for storytelling had spawned, nurtured over the years by first her parents and then Maggie, who taught her to seek yet more tales, stay curious and never settle. It was a voice which only came to her when she needed it most and she remembered the older woman's letter now:

It is a truth universally acknowledged that a single woman in possession of neither good nor bad fortune, must be in need of nothing more than belief in herself.

Of course, it was entirely plausible that Jonathan didn't have the first clue what Dawn had suggested, but what if he, in that ever-so-courteous way of his, was waiting for Emmy to accept Dawn's offer? What if he *did* want to do it? Emmy shivered, her belly clenching with fear and delight at the possibility. Couldn't she get over herself for once and open herself up to something new?

"Oh, I don't think that would work," she replied to Dawn, who wasn't listening but instead was rummaging through her capacious yellow shoulder bag. "You don't have to do that, Jonathan. You've done more than enough already."

Dawn removed an intimidating and professional looking digital camera from her bag with a flourish. "Nonsense. You two would look scorching together. You don't mind if I take a few photos do you, Jonathan?"

Jonathan shrugged, still nonplussed. "If Emmeline is amiable, then I have no objection. I imagine she has much to tell on this matter, so far be it of me to make any demand of her."

"You're good at this," Dawn punched Jonathan lightly on the upper arm, catching him off guard. He stumbled back a step. It was clear from his dumbfounded expression that he found this tiny, Black powerhouse of a woman fascinating. He rubbed at his shoulder where she'd hit him and smiled his most winning smile. Dawn responded with a shriek of delight and began snapping his picture, bracelets jingling again as she raised the camera in both hands. Out of the side of her mouth, she addressed Emmy.

"Girl, imma be serious with you. What you have here is an opportunity. Now, I'm quite happy to take this gorgeous man's photo all day long but the real magic would be you and him together looking like *that*." She inclined her head to the book now propped up by the till. "I'm sure I can source a costume for you from my theatre group, and we could do a whole series of romance covers and videos. Of course, if you could hire a model that would be great, but fact is, you can't afford it. And to be honest, I don't think we could find a model who'd look as good as you next to Jonathan anyway. Please say yes, Emmy."

Words formed and died on Emmy's lips. Nothing coherent seemed to want to leave her mouth. Excitement swirled in her stomach like a butterfly dancing in a breeze. Part of her was mortified by the idea. She hated having her photo taken and was happy to let others hog the spotlight. Another part doubted Dawn's insistence that she'd be able to source a period-appropriate costume that would fit her, and a very small voice from somewhere in the deepest recesses of her mind where shy, body-conscious sixteen year-old Emmy still hid, had to questioned Dawn's judgement. She couldn't see what Dawn was seeing as far as a resemblance between herself and the slim pale blonde model on the cover went. Emmy was twice that woman's size for starters. Maybe if she screwed her eyes up a little there was a slight similarity. But an image of herself in Jonathan's strong arms had already bloomed in her mind's eye and wouldn't quit. Their bodies pressed together closer than they'd ever been, her breasts heaving against his torso, faces turned to one another, lips on her cheek, millimetres from her own...

She tore herself away from the fantasy with reluc-tance, suddenly aware of how hard she was breathing. *Get a hold of yourself, woman.* Maybe it was because of the scene she'd read in The Book earlier, featuring that hot as hellfire secret tryst between Lord Jonathan and Lady Catherine that Emmy was finding it hard to focus on Dawn's plan. Models and actors all over the world did this kind of thing every day without going all gooey-eyed over their co-star. But she was neither and if Hollywood was anything to go by, on-screen intimacy had a regular habit of spilling over into real life. *Focus, Emmy! This isn't some blockbuster romance. It's just a few photos.* She could do that if it meant even the slightest chance of helping her business.

She stole a glance at Jonathan who was now lounging in Maggie's chair, long, muscular legs swung across one armrest like a louche as Dawn snapped away happily. He lifted his dark to head to lock Emmy's eyes with his in a come-hither stare so suggestive Emmy's cheeks flushed again.

"Okay," she found herself saying as if from far away. Jonathan's eyes tightened a fraction of an inch and sudden low swooping desire gripped Emmy's lower belly with another unmistakable and delicious clench. Yes, he was (and probably still is) a womanising bastard. But he was also unbelievably, impossibly sexy. Lady Catherine knew it and she didn't let that knowledge stop her. Lucky Lady Catherine, Emmy thought, squeezing her thighs together in quiet desperation.

Dawn did a fast pirouette. "Fabulous!" She grinned at Emmy whose legitimate insides felt as if they'd been scooped out and replaced with jelly. "Don't worry," she said, "we can't do it now. I need all my equipment and we don't have a costume for you yet. Besides, I've got a paper to finish first. How does next Saturday evening work for you both, assuming I can borrow a dress or two from my drama club? I'll call Lizzie too. She can be my assistant."

Emmy's heart rate, which had been hovering some-where in the upper atmosphere before plunging down to earth when Dawn had said they couldn't do it immediately, soared right off into outer space again. So soon? She expected Dawn to say it would take weeks. She gulped and nodded, unable to speak.

Jonathan however was nowhere near as reticent. "Excellent," he said in a voice that rang with jubilation, making every nerve ending in Emmy's body stand to attention.

Breone, who'd been asleep as usual in the window, shook his furry head and stretched from nose to tail, before jumping down and entwining himself first around Dawn's tartan clad legs and then Emmy's. Emmy bent down to stroke him, smoothing his coat with the palm of her hand. She had to avoid Jonathan's eyes. The hold he had over her was becoming unbearable. She picked up the cat and cuddled him close as she wandered over to the counter again and began rummaging in the cupboard for the cat's lead.

"Great. Sorry to change the subject but I need to take Breone for a walk. Do you want to come with me?" She yelled over her shoulder to Dawn, who was stuffing her camera back into her bag.

"I'm good, thanks. I better get this paper started, plus I've got a date with Mark tonight. Did I tell you he texted me?"

Emmy's eyes widened at the news that Dawn was seeing Mark, her on-again, off-again boyfriend, but before she could say anything in acknowledgement, Dawn had hurried on. "Anyway, I best be off. Lots to do. If I don't call, I'll be round about ten on Saturday. I don't have your number, Jonathan."

"He doesn't have one," Emmy said too fast, heat rocketing up her neck once more.

Dawn gave her a knowing smirk which Emmy could interpret all too easily. Dawn obviously thought Emmy was staking a claim on Jonathan, but it wasn't like that. She was only trying to avoid any unnecessary questions about Jonathan's lack of phone ownership, that's all. Nothing more. She busied herself with locating the lead and almost cheered when her hand fell upon its rough length. Jonathan had left the chair and was saying goodbye to Dawn, who giggled like a schoolgirl as he took her hand and kissed it.

With one last look at them both, and an especially exaggerated and quizzical glance at Emmy, Dawn exited the shop in the same attention-grabbing manner with which she'd entered. "Okay, my lovelies, I'll see you both soon. Don't do anything I wouldn't do. Ciao for now." She blew a theatrical kiss over her shoulder, swept a pair of oversized, acid-green sunglasses onto her pretty face, and was gone.

Emmy kept her head down as she wrestled with a fidgety Breone to fix the lead to his collar. The cat twisted his fat body away from her and dashed out of reach. Huffing, Emmy trailed him across the shop, still avoiding Jonathan's waiting gaze. The silence between them pulsed as if it were alive, punctuated by Emmy as she cooed to an unresponsive Breone, who was now curled up on Maggie's chair.

"I know you're not asleep. Come on, it's just a little walk," Emmy's fingers worked fast, twisting the collar on Breone's neck before he could escape again, but something caught her eye. A metallic gleam inside the bell that hung on his collar reflected in the light from the chandelier and she peered closer. The hairs on the back of her neck bristled as she deftly unfastened the clasp, removing the collar from around the cat's throat. The bell was large and shiny but also slightly transparent, and Emmy's heart skipped as the thing she'd spotted a moment ago came into clearer focus. She worked fast to slide the bell from the collar and opened it up like an oyster, eager now to get to the mysterious object inside. Turning to Jonathan, she spoke with a mixture of awe and nervous energy in her voice.

"Look!" she said, holding a small, ornate key between two fingers.

Jonathan sprinted to join her, peering at the object in her hand with a curious expression. Then he gripped her around the waist, scooping her up into the air before spinning on the spot. He laughed as she shrieked, and his voice rang with jubilation.

"This could be it, Emmeline. My freedom!"

WHILE EMMELINE and Breone were gone, Jonathan remained in the store. For what seemed like an age, he didn't move. The key Emmeline had found lay on the table in front of him. They had spent the last half an hour checking every door and window for the lock it would fit, but to no avail.

He should be excited. Ecstatic. The discovery of the key could be significant in their search, so why was his mind now gripped with a confliction so strong, powered by emotions he couldn't name? The more he forced himself to take heart from the find, the more the tug of war inside him grew, pulsing inside his gut, until it was eating him alive, tearing him in two. But even then, he knew he wasn't being completely honest. He was sickened by his performative enthusiasm for Emmeline's discovery, but he couldn't afford for her to think he was anything but overjoyed. For a while now, one part of him had been dominating the fight. He'd just been too stubborn to admit it, of course, preferring to whisper comforting lies to himself about bewitchment and sorcery. He might be able to hide his true feelings from Emmeline, but he no longer had anywhere to hide from himself.

Yes, Emmeline was magical, and it was true in every sense of the word. All this time he'd resisted, afraid that by allowing himself to covet her, to fall for her, he might lose himself, but what truly scared him was the possibility of her rejection. Because surely there was no hope of any kind of relationship with her, not if she found out about his past. So why torment himself like this? Why continue with this merry-go-round of despair? Why not rejoice in the discovery that was the probable key to his freedom? Why was he not, at this very second, tearing down every wall in this place to locate the door that key fitted?

Because finding it would mean leaving her.

He would lose her either way, and the dawning realisation of this gripped his heart in an iron vice.

The trouble with coveting a thing you can never have, is that it only serves to highlight the distance between you and it. Sea and sky are destined to never meet. The horizon, an unattainable whisper of air between. And the more one coveted, the further Fate tugged the prize from one's grasp until only Distance itself remains. Distance growing closer and closer, engorging everything in its path, until the very weight of It suffocates all other want or desire.

For centuries he'd coveted one thing and one thing alone. His blood still yearned for freedom, so close now he could almost taste the grime of the sixteenth century on his tongue. But that very blood was also intoxicated by Emmeline. If only he wasn't so enthralled by her, if only *she* wasn't the Distance suffocating him, he could pick up that key and eventually unearth the correct door. Yet, he feared if he did, he would risk incarcerating not only his mind, body and soul for all eternity, but also his heart.

EMMY PUSHED OPEN THE DOOR, unclipping a tugging Breone from the leash, who sprinted away in case she made him go outside again. Night was setting in and the shop was shadowy and quiet. Too quiet. The hairs on Emmy's arms stood up. Something was wrong.

"Jonathan?"

He'd been right there a few moments ago, lounging on the sofa in that gloriously disheveled way of his. It wasn't as if they'd been gone long. But her mind returned to how excited he'd been when she'd shown him the key, only to be replaced by a kind of melancholic indifference when none of the doors and windows had fit. It shouldn't matter so much but the realisation that he still wanted to return to his time was crushing and she brought a hand up to her chest.

Her earlier fantasy of being in his arms smashed into smithereens. Was she really allowing herself to fall for him? After everything she'd done to protect herself? Feeling absurd, she slumped on to the sofa, determined not to think about where he might be now, and failing miserably.

Emmy was about to watch the video of Jonathan again when a clattering on the cobbles outside snapped her head up. A hooded figure darted away from the window. She gave a cry of dismay and sprinted to the door. Crossing to the opposite side of the street, she scoured the shadows for any sign of the hooded stranger, adrenaline kicking through her system. When she turned back to the shop, the overheated blood in her veins froze. Spray painted four-foot letters screamed at her from the white-washed wall:

LEAVE BITCH!

"Emmeline!" Jonathan appeared by her side as if he'd been there all along, eyes loaded with concern.

Emmy pointed, her mouth half forming the word, 'That', but when she spoke, it was something different that fell from her lips.

"You're *outside*. Outside *the shop!*"

∽

1548

EACH BUMP and divot in the dirt road vibrates through the carriage, jostling me into the men towering at my sides. Father picks at something in his teeth, eyes narrowed. I follow the heat of his gaze to the barred window in the door of the wagon in front. The woman beyond the bars doesn't speak, but she doesn't have to. We all know what she is.

Sweat slides down the back of my neck and between the ruffles of my silk tunic. Maybe I should remove the doublet? But then I think better of it. Grandfather would not approve. I glance at him from the corner of my eye. He sits on my left side, Father on my right, their broad shoulders almost touching above my head. Two great men, bookends for my body and mind.

Grandfather arches his back, as if recoiling from something.

"Smell that, son? That's the stench of a dead witch."

Father laughs, a cruel braying sound and is on his feet before the carriage comes to a halt. Grandfather wasn't wrong about the smell. The air is ripe with high, sweet horseshit and I stuff a neckerchief to my nose and mouth as cover for my gagging. Fortune favours me because both men are too concerned with the removal of the woman from the other carriage to notice. Once the choking fit has passed, I dash away my wetting eyes on the back of my hands and jump smartly from the wagon. My eleven-year-old muscles make light work of it despite the three-day journey from Exeter to Blackabrook River. The same it seems, can't be said for Grandfather, who's legs bow as if he'd made the trek astride his horse.

The other men with us are a mixed lot. Some are representatives of the local judiciary, but most are here for the spectacle only. One, however, a bulbous nosed fellow of sallow skin and sunken eyes looks around lost, as if unable to comprehend how he comes to find himself on the edge of a river in deepest Dartmoor.

A crow caws loudly, causing a flock of smaller dozing birds in an overhanging tree to explode into flight.

Father calls to one of the other men for aide. The woman,

though shackled at wrist and ankle, puts up a good fight, all gnashing teeth and feet that kick like a mule. Father dances out of the way of one viscous hoof and my gut clenches and unclenches with an odd mixture of cheer and fright. One of grandfather's horses once dealt me a swift, sharp blow in the privates and I can still remember how it made my eyes water. Grandfather said it would put hair on my chest. Father laughed.

It takes five men to drag the kicking, screaming woman to the water. She stills as the cold liquid first touches her bare feet, soon creeping up her once fine dress. One man ties a length of rope to her ankles before taking the other end and fastening it to a blacksmith's anvil. Another fills the pockets of her skirts with stones and black tar from the bank of the stinking bog. Her lips move swiftly, but no sound can I discern. Maybe she is praying. Or perhaps she means to curse us. One of the men from the judiciary steps forward and unrolls a length of parchment. His voice as he reads the condemnation is reedy and thin.

"Lady Sarah Dalgliesh, you have been tried and found guilty of the charge of witchcraft; specifically of cursing your lover, a Mister William Johnson Esquire, a blacksmith of Magdelene Road, Exeter."

The sallow faced man shuffles uncomfortably under the hot sun and nods once, almost imperceptibly. The judiciary clears his throat and continues.

"You will be executed by dragging in Blackabrook River until you are drowned. Do you have anything you wish to say?"

A murmur rustles through the crowd like disease and suddenly I want to be somewhere, anywhere but here. My head splits from a combination of the glaring sun and sickly stench. Father and grandfather are at the woman's side now, bookending her like they did me earlier. She stares at Father, her face all eyes, but remains silent. I don't know whether it's for my benefit or hers, but grandfather produces a small, roughly hewn sack from inside his tunic and tugs it over her head like a hood. At the sound of the first splash I turn away, a slick fist of vomit ascending in my throat, before splattering my shoes.

CHAPTER 12

To Emmy's surprise and delight, business boomed that week. Her original Twitter video had been shared over thirty thousand times and there was even a Buzzfeed article waxing lyrical about Jonathan–or as they'd dubbed him, 'The Literary Lothario'. A series of excited texts from Dawn confirmed the photoshoot was on for that evening:

Lizzie can't make it, but I got you the most amazing dresses. You're gonna look ravishing! the first one said, followed by three heart-eye emojis and two photos, each depicting a stunning Tudor style gown. Where Dawn had found them was anyone's guess. Emmy's stomach flipped with the sudden urge to regurgitate her tuna salad lunch. Tonight! Her eyes fell upon the passionate cover of *The Mistress and The Merchant* and she gave an involuntary shiver. One mystery *was* solved however, when Leticia from HEA called.

"I can't believe that video you posted. I retweeted it

from the HEA account just before I went to bed the other night and now look at it!" she squealed down the phone in a most un-Leticia like way, adding before Emmy could respond, "*Who on earth is he? Does he have a brother?*"

"Err, he's just a friend. His name's Jonathan. I'm pretty sure there aren't any brothers on the scene but thank you for the retweet. My phone's gone into meltdown. Seriously though, the response is incredible. I don't know how I'll ever repay you."

Anxious to avoid further grilling, Emmy made an excuse about having a customer waiting. It wasn't a total lie–there were lots of lovely online orders to fulfill and the steady stream through the door sent her spirits soaring. By closing time, she'd almost forgotten about Jonathan's new-found ability to leave the shop, the eerie message on the wall outside (which looked even worse in the daylight) and her impending humiliation. She'd been too exhausted to discuss yesterday's events last night and there hadn't been time in between customers today to have a proper conversation. Now she rolled up her sleeves and whirled to find Jonathan waiting for her, a frown upon his gorgeous face.

"You can leave the shop now? How? Why?" Emmy asked before he could give voice to his worries.

Jonathan scratched the stubble on his chin. "I honestly do not know. If I had to guess, I would suggest it is something to do with your spell–but I know you will not appreciate that."

Skirting the whole 'Yer a witch, Emmy' conversation, Emmy's spirits brightened at the prospect of being able to go out with him. She'd spent too much time cooped up inside this shabby old building lately and it wasn't doing her health any good. She needed to get out and take a walk, or go for a meal, or see a movie. She needed normality. Or whatever normality was these days. But they had to get this nonsense with Dawn over with first, not to mention sort out the mess outside. She dug into the cupboard under the stairs again, this time emerging with a tin of white paint and a brush that she'd taken delivery of earlier.

"Right," she said, "*I* am going to paint over that rubbish out there and then once Dawn has gone, *we* are going out." She looked Jonathan up and down. "First stop, if you're amiable, is to buy you some new clothes. Literary Lothario or not, you can't go everywhere dressed like that."

Jonathan nodded, the haunted look his eyes eclipsed by a gleam of excitement. At least one of them was looking forward to Dawn's plan.

"Good," Emmy said, heading out of the door into fresh air. There was still time to call it off. Her earlier nervousness had been superceded by the fluttering of a million migrating butterflies in her stomach.

What was there to be worried about? They were just two people who hardly knew each other, who were going to recreate some of Romancelandia's sexiest book covers. Okay, so one of whom happened to be a sixteenth century Tudor sex god, who'd appeared out of a book by magic. What of it? And when they'd finished, she was taking her sex-on-legs historical 'book boyfriend' shopping for new clothes. (*It's not a date. It's not a date. It's not a date. It is* not *a date.*) Nope. Nothing unusual about any of that.

Emmy puffed out her cheeks as she regarded the graffiti, and the swooping in her belly intensified. If a butterfly shot up her gullet and flew out of her mouth right now, she wouldn't have been surprised. She dipped the brush in the tin and began spreading it on the wall in long, sweeping strokes. If only covering up her emotions was as easy.

DAWN INSISTED on doing Emmy's hair and make-up. A treasure trove of opaline eyeshadows and ruby lipsticks lay glittering on Emmy's bed. Every now and then, Dawn would rummage around in the pile and with an exclamation of triumph, her hand would emerge clutching a new wonder product guaranteed to give Emmy glowing skin, pillow lips or "eyebrows on fleek", whatever that meant. Emmy tried not to grimace as Dawn worked her magic. After what seemed like an eternity, in which Emmy had been poked, prodded, buffed and teased, Dawn took a step back.

"And voila! I'm good at this, even if I do say it myself." She spun the chair around, so Emmy could see the results in the mirror.

It took Emmy's eyes a moment to adjust. In the soft glow of the dressing table lamp her skin really was radiant. Her normally too-close-together eyes were now defined, wider spaced and framed by a heavy fringe of black lashes. And her lips! She brought a finger up to touch them to be sure they were hers. How on earth did they look fuller? Emmy stared at her reflection. Okay, she might never be a supermodel, but lately she'd been happy enough with her appearance. *This* Emmy, though? Wow! Her eyes found Dawn's.

"You *are* good at all this. How on earth did you do that?" She leaned in closer to the mirror to get a better look at Dawn's expertly applied eye make-up. "I mean, I look like me, but better, and I don't actually look like I'm wearing ten layers of warpaint, which is what happens when I do it."

Dawn beamed, gathering up the cosmetics and hair-brushes from the bed before stuffing them into a professional looking case. "Just call me your fairy godmother. Now, dress."

She held up a sumptuous scarlet gown, similar to the one on the cover of The Mistress and The Merchant. It's heavy satin sheen and bright pop of colour made Emmy's retinas hurt. *Why does it have to be bright red?* She wriggled into it, the nervous tension in her chest spreading, but even she had to admit the shade complimented her pale skin. There was nothing she could do about the neckline though, a deep square cut which revealed far too much cleavage for Emmy's liking. She tugged ineffectually at the heavy material, shoving her large breasts down, but it was no use. This dress was designed to show the puppies off.

"It's too small." She rounded on Dawn who giggled.

"Em, we can't all have boobs to die for and curves for days. Flaunt it, girl!"

Emmy stopped fidgeting and drew in a set of deep, fortifying breaths. Why had she agreed to this?

Dawn smiled reassuringly and cocked her head to one side. "You look lovely. Anything you're uncomfortable with, just say. We don't have to do this."

Emmy took a deep breath and shook her head. "No, it's okay. I want to. How did it go with Mark, by the way?"

It was wrong of her to use Dawn's love life as a

distraction technique, but she nodded and made all the right noises as her friend regaled her with the tale of her recent date. Following the other woman to the door she promptly tripped on the hem of the gown. *Serves you right for being such a rubbish friend.* Her earlier butterflies were now enormous moths whose nightmarish wings flapped inside making her sick with every beat. She lifted the skirt and began tiptoeing down the stairs, trailing Dawn's back. Each step sent a dizzying wave of adrenaline to her head. Too soon she reached the bottom. She stood, waiting for Dawn's instructions, aware that Jonathan's eyes had been on her the whole way down the staircase, but unable to look at him yet.

Emmy took her eyes off the floor long enough to absorb the scene. Dawn had positioned a tall wrought iron candelabra in a dark corner of the shop next to two imposing bookcases, creating a kind of doorway between them. Oversized church candles gave the spot an intimate, clandestine feel. Music started playing and Emmy turned to spy Dawn's i-pod propped up in a portable speaker on the counter. Emmy grinned as the familiar strains of Jack Savoretti's *Candlelight* began to swell. Two years earlier she'd dragged Dawn and Lizzie to see the enigmatic singer in London. It was no secret he was one of Emmy's favourite recording artists. Emmy had to give her friend credit, she certainly knew how to push her buttons.

"Emmy, over here," Dawn said, with a little gesture of her head as she fiddled with the studio lights and camera that she'd set up earlier. Emmy dutifully complied and shuffled over to where Jonathan waited. Inside she trembled, but as she raised a hand to remove a stray strand of hair from her eyes, she was relieved to see it didn't shake. Jonathan was dressed in the same silver doublet with fine golden threads woven in intricate detail along the cuffs and neckline. Emmy's breath caught as he moved, revealing an off-white tunic with a half-frill collar and a very deep slashed v-neck beneath. This, along with leather breeches and over-the-knee boots, gave him the aura of a sexy, Tudor rock god. She busied herself adjusting the boobie neckline of her dress to avoid staring at the alluring triangle of dark hair on his chest. But that only drew more attention to both, so she dropped her hands to her sides. Her fingers itched for something to do. When she looked up again, he was leaning against one of the bookcases, his tall frame and broad shoulders filling the space and a seductive stare ready and waiting on his incomparable face.

Emmy allowed Dawn to take her by the arm and pose her like an oversized Barbie in front of Jonathan's Ken Doll. He didn't speak, only watched, that lazy, sexy fire still scorching in his eyes. Emmy had to look away. She'd never felt so detached from herself, as if she was nothing more than a mannequin in a shop window suddenly come to life.

"Okay, you two. Let's do this." Dawn barked orders from behind the camera, glancing down at The Mistress and The Merchant every few seconds. "Emmy, can you put your right arm around Jonathan's shoulder? That's it. Lift your chin… Jonathan, I need you to place your left hand on Emmy's back…

When Jonathan spoke, Emmy wasn't expecting it and she gave a little start.

"May I touch you, Emmeline?"

Emmy's heart skipped. "What? Oh, yes, of course. I should have asked you first too."

"Well, if it helps," Jonathan whispered into her ear, raising goosebumps across her shoulders, "I give you full and irrevocable permission to do so whenever you desire." He placed his hand on her ribcage sending her thoughts into orbit.

"A little to the right, a little more... perfect. Now bring your heads together so that they're touching" said Dawn.

They were almost the same height but as she was the taller, she dropped her forehead to Jonathan's so that he had to look up at her rather than the other way around, the way it was depicted on most romance covers. His hand crept along Emmy's torso, inching closer and closer to her breast, coming to a halt with his fingers cupping the soft flesh from beneath. The dress was so restrictive, Emmy gasped for breath, her bosom now swelling and receding inches from both their faces. From somewhere far away, Dawn started clicking.

Emmy was certain the cover they were creating was nowhere near as intimate as this. Gazing directly into his eyes for the first time since venturing downstairs all thoughts other than him were immediately banished from her brain. She was lost at sea, and found herself inching closer, tightening her grip around his muscular shoulders, his eyes promising a lifeline and so much more. His lips opened a fraction, his breath ragged and shallow. Emmy couldn't fight it any longer. Her breasts heaved. Her own lips parted. Closer still...

Something crashed to the ground behind Dawn, plunging them all into near darkness. A fluffy orange streak darted across the floor and bolted up the stairs away from the devastation he'd caused. Flustered, Emmy leaped out of Jonathan's arms and whirled to find the source of the commotion. Dawn's studio light lay on the flagstones like a drunk passed out at a party, the glass bulb inside now a billion smashed and gleaming diamonds, glinting at her wickedly like Jonathan's blazing eyes.

CHAPTER 13

*B*y the time they'd cleaned up the mess and Emmy had apologised at least twenty times to Dawn, it was too late for their shopping trip. So, first thing Sunday morning Emmy grabbed Jonathan by the hand and whisked him out of the store. Neither of them mentioned the photoshoot, but their almost kiss hung heavy between them. *Not just an elephant in the room but a whole blinking herd.* Emmy's foot tapped with nervous energy as she waited for Jonathan to emerge from the Marks and Spencer changing room.

When he did, in blue-jeans and a checked shirt looking like a hot cowboy from a Mills and Boon cover, Emmy had to stifle a giggle. It's wasn't as if the new garb didn't suit him, because of course they did. Jonathan could wear a sack and still be mister sex on legs. But it was the thought of the typical Hollywood makeover scene in all those frothy romantic comedies she loved that did it. She didn't like to dwell on how she might be trying to mold him into something he wasn't for her

own ideals, or how posting that video of him could be slightly exploitational. Of course, Jonathan had agreed to be filmed, but that didn't completely remove the sour taste from her mouth. When had she become such a cliché?

Jonathan's face was a picture of confused hurt and Emmy was quick to reassure.

"I'm sorry. It's not you. It's me." *Wow, Em. More cliches?* "You look great, honestly you do. It was a shock to see you looking so *normal*, that was all. If you don't like them, we won't get them."

"No, they are very good." He kept patting himself down, self-conscious, as if he'd lost something. "I confess, this is a rather liberating experience for me, but I'm not entirely convinced about this... polyester garb." He titled his head at a seventy-degree angle to read the label inside the bottom of his shirt, before eyeing the bundle of embroidered velvet and silk Emmy now clutched in her arms with undisguised longing.

"Put these back on if it makes you uncomfortable. You don't have to do this." She held his old attire out to him as a peace offering.

"It will take some growing accustomed to, that is all. I must admit, The Twenty-First Century surely bests the Sixteenth for haste. I don't think I've ever dressed so fast, although I must admit, the absence of a codpiece is some-what disconcerting."

Emmy pressed her lips together to stifle more laughter, distracted by daydreams imagining how quickly he could now undress too. She gulped and turned away, picking out extra pairs of identical jeans, a handful of shirts and several cable-knit jumpers. She held them up for Jonathan's approval, before heading for the tills. Jonathan trailed after her looking bemused.

"Allow me." He reached for the bundle of clothes and as their hands touched, Emmy jumped as static passed through them again. The expression on Jonathan's face confirmed he'd felt it too but as they were now standing in front of the expectant cashier, neither mentioned it.

"Can we pay for all these, please? And the stuff he's wearing too." Emmy gestured in Jonathan's direction as he placed the new items on to the counter and tried to ignore the sales' girl's eyes as they travelled over every inch of Jonathan's incredible face. Then he flashed an encouraging smile and Emmy was sure the assistant gave an audible sigh. Emmy's eyes made at least three revolutions in their sockets as the girl took an inordinate amount of time to scan the items Jonathan wore. He jumped at each beep from the point of sale device, as the girl wafted around him in a cloud of perfume.

"That's three hundred and thirty-two pounds and fifty pence, please." The girl's smile was so wide, lipstick marks were visible on her back teeth.

Jonathan was fiddling with the tassel of a small velvet pouch, which he opened and tipped the contents of onto the counter. Several large gold and silver coins spilled out and one spun for a few seconds before falling flat with a drunk's wobble. The coins caught the florescent lights from overhead and Emmy read sovereign on at least six, before she came to her senses. A quick glance at the cashier almost had her guffawing again and she whipped a card out of her purse before the girl could ask.

"I'll get this," she gave Jonathan a pointed look, paying

for the transaction over his protestations. She'd worry about the cost later.

"Thank you, but you must allow me to repay you. It is improper, and you cannot afford it." Jonathan's eyes were confused, then he smoothed his brow and turned to address the sale's girl. "And thank you too, my lady. Please pass my sincerest gratitude to Mister Marks and Mister Spencer for the fine threads."

The girl's jaw hung open like a cartoon character and Emmy locked her arm through Jonathan's, steering him from the counter with a hasty thanks and a self-satisfied smirk.

"YOU SHOULD HAVE SEEN the way she was throwing herself at you!" Emmy smiled again at Jonathan's confused expression. "I swear I've given myself an injury from rolling my eyes too far back in my skull. And then when you tipped those coins on to the counter, I thought the poor girl was going to faint. Can I see them? Your coins, I mean?"

Jonathan fished in the stiff pocket of his new denim, extracting the small burgundy velvet pouch with difficulty. He passed it over to Emmy with a grin. "Of course."

Emmy undid the gold tassel at the top of the pouch and removed a large, silver coin, squinting at it in the dim pub lights. They were tucked in a corner far from the only other patrons propping up the bar. The sixteenth century Ship Inn had seemed a great idea for lunch, but from the moment they'd arrived, Jonathan had watched the door, his eyes wary. Then the waitress appeared at their table with their food and Jonathan shot to his feet as if stung.

"What's wrong?" Emmy asked when the waitress had gone again.

Jonathan swept back his wavy hair and regarded his plate of steak and chips with interest. "It's nothing. The fare looks... good."

Putting down the coin, Emmy rested her elbows on the scratched wooden table and waited until Jonathan looked up again.

"It is not nothing. Please tell me what's bugging you. You've been like a fly trapped in a bottle since we sat down. I know you've been here before. I thought it might helpful to go somewhere recognisable, but if you want to leave..."

Jonathan opened his mouth and closed it again. He took another quick, furtive glance around. When he spoke, his voice was quiet, as if encumbered with the weight of history. "Yes, I frequented this house often, although now it appears changed. I do not even know whether to speak of it in the past tense, because to me, this *is* my present.

"I should take a sovereign and make my way to the bar—which incidentally was over there," he indicated with a nod towards the opposite wall, "and ask Mister Holmes, the innkeeper, for a flagon of his finest ale and a Daily Special. Tom Holmes would nod and admit me to the hidden chamber beyond the cellar. Did you know there used to be a secret network of tunnels beneath this city? They were initially built to house water pipes to carry the supply to the Great Conduit and Cathedral, but they soon became invaluable to those who wished to move about undetected."

Emmy nodded. "Yes, they're still open today but it's a tourist attraction now. Maybe we should go one day…"

Her voice trailed off, but Jonathan was leading forward across the table.

"Really?" His eyes shot up. "Remarkable they are still intact. We must visit. So many tales this wondrous old city can tell, so many voices past… Speaking of the Cathedral, did you know there was once a cat on the payroll? Yes, paid the handsome salary of thirteen shillings a week to catch rats and mice, its own hole cut into the base of a door so he could roam those tunnels as it pleased."

"You're pulling my leg," Emmy smirked, shaking her head.

Jonathan looked affronted. "I would not dare. I've seen your foul temper up close. But I digress. Down in the chamber, I would await my monthly meeting with the wife of the Earl of Somerset. He was a confidant of Queen Elizabeth but also a suspected conspirator, practised in dark arts. If we were caught without proof of his plan to overthrow the Queen, we would, all of us, have been beheaded for treason." He ran a finger across his throat. "And now, here I sit with you, trying to comprehend how everything can remain the same and yet be so different. It is almost alien to me to accept that what I consider to be fresh, merely days-old memories, are long since forgotten pockets of history, and that Holmes and Lord and Lady Somerset are nothing but the ghosts of dust….As I myself should be. I should not be here."

For the first time, Emmy could imagine him as the man he was, the man who had lived all those years before, and yet who still existed today. The conundrum made her head hurt. Maybe she'd read too much into things. Surely the poem and the way he'd looked at her while reciting it couldn't be solely her imagination? But the passion with which he spoke about his time brought all her nagging doubts to the surface again.

"I know this is hard for you to comprehend but do you realise how special you are? To historians I mean," she added in a stammer at his raised eyebrow. "I'm sure lots of people would be interested in your clandestine meetings with the mysterious Lady Somerset. What was she like?"

Jonathan smiled again, his eyes lighting up in recollection. "She was very astute, very unpredictable and very beautiful."

Emmy picked up her fork and began prodding at her spaghetti carbonara, her appetite gone. It was irrational to allow stories from his past to put her off food. She swallowed a large chunk of pasta along with the jealousy monster. It had been foolish to ask such questions. What was the point in torturing herself like this? Hearing him speak of another woman with such warmth made her green-eyed and she didn't like it one bit.

"Lady Catherine did not care for the Queen, nor her rule, but she cared for her husband even less. Her marriage was an unhappy, and I suspect, violent one. Yet throughout, she remained wicked of humour and delightful company. I do not doubt for one moment that she would have given me up in an instant and gone back to playing the part of the good lady wife if her pretty neck had depended on it."

Emmy nodded. "She sounds like an amazing woman. How's your steak?"

"If I did not know better," Jonathan began, his eyes dancing with scandal, "I would wager that you are jealous."

"Jealous? Don't be ridiculous." Emmy's fork clattered to the plate. She took a swig of water and snatched up her napkin, before taking a long time to wipe her lips. Then she balled up the tissue and placed it on her plate before meeting Jonathan's waiting gaze.

"Emmy, I apologise. I jest. Am I forgiven?" Jonathan held out a chip by way of a peace offering. "These triple-cooked chips–deep-fried potato wedges par-boiled, fried and roasted in goose fat–are incredible." He was reading off the menu verbatim.

His expression was so pathetic, Emmy couldn't help but laugh. She reached out for the chip, but Jonathan was too quick and snatched his hand away so that her fingers ended up grasping thin air. With deliberate slowness, Jonathan made a big deal of dunking the chip in the little ceramic pot of ketchup on the side of his plate before offering it to her again, one eyebrow raised with heavy suggestion. Emmy made to grab it but before she could, laughing. Jonathan stole it away and popped it into his own mouth.

"You!" Emmy spluttered. Two could play that game. She retrieved her lost fork and removed the napkin from her plate. Twisting the fork in slow, deliberate turns through the pasta, she loaded it with a good mouthful of spaghetti, careful to ensure there were several long, enticing strands dangling from the tines. Eyes narrowed, she held it out toward Jonathan, who's pupils dilated as his mirth rescinded. He stared at her and the fork as if hypnotised.

"Carbonara?" Emmy said, a playful laugh dying on her lips. She'd never said anything more ludicrous in her life, but the way Jonathan was now staring between the food and her mouth sent synapses of delicious fission exploding throughout her body. Suddenly she couldn't care less about how she sounded.

"How could I spurn such a tempting invitation?" Jonathan said before leaning towards the fork and taking it into his mouth. His blue eyes were now almost black thanks to the low-lit mock candle style bulbs, artificially flickering in the alcove where they sat. He chewed for a moment, then swallowed. "Delicious."

Emmy broke eye contact first. It would be all too easy to fall for him. But what good could come of it? How could they have a future when he was from the past? But why worry about the future? Couldn't they have some fun without expectation or hope that it could turn into something more? Would it be so wrong to jump into bed with him? There was no denying the obvious attraction they shared but maybe it was because he was *from* history that made him so enticing. *Or maybe you're so desperate to be loved, you're believing this half-baked fantasy and any minute now you're going to wake up in the hospital to find out you zoned out again.*

The voice Emmy hadn't heard in months was back and she dropped her glass, this time smashing the plate below into three pieces. Hot, itchy tears sprang to her eyes and her throat constricted, suddenly dry.

"Emmeline?"

Jonathan's worried voice seemed to come from far away and Emmy zeroed in on it, surprised that her hands were now tugging at hair.

Diazepam and get out of here. Now!

"In my bag. The little white packet... please find it," she said, throwing her handbag across the table to Jonathan, who blinked in surprise. Emmy nodded in encouragement but then the spiteful voice–the one she hated most of all–spoke again and she couldn't react quickly enough to block it out:

Stupid cow! Why would you think he'd want you when he could have any other woman? When he's had lots of other women? Beautiful, sane *women.*

Emmy closed her eyes and groaned. Why did the bitch voice have to come back now? Her only hope of silencing her was medication and a quiet room.

"I don't underst–"

Jonathan was peering into the bag, pulling out objects at random. Her mobile, purse, a hairbrush, tampons in their neon green packaging. Then a small, white cardboard box with words printed on the side in bright blue letters. *Meds!* Emmy lunged for the box, grabbing them from Jonathan's hand before he could speak. Her fingers shook, and she fumbled the packet before opening the flap. *The wrong end! Every fucking time!* Gritting her teeth, she dug past the information leaflet and extracted the blister pack from the box, popping three of the pills out on to the table. Then she shoved the tablets into her mouth and downed them with a large swig of water.

Jonathan was speaking again.

"Emmeline, what is it? What can I do?"

She couldn't look at him. She wanted to run and hide. She wanted to throw up. He must be repulsed, but she couldn't waste time on what he thought. She had twenty minutes– thirty tops–before she started slurring and desperately needed to get home and into bed before the meds kicked in. Without opening her eyes, her fingers crawled across the table to where Jonathan had placed her purse.

"Please...just...go and pay. There's money in here," she said in a weak voice, pressing the purse into Jonathan's hands. "I need to go home."

CHAPTER 14

*E*mmy's head pounded. The general malaise that always came after taking diazepam was like being buried alive in mud, but at least her mind was quiet. As a distraction from her thoughts about the previous day she grabbed her mobile. Dawn had sent the photos over as promised and Emmy's stomach tightened with an unexpected pang of desire as she scrolled through them. *Shit!* Dawn was right, they did look hot together. Especially the shots where they'd come a hair's breadth from kissing. Blushing, she uploaded a few to Twitter with a quote from *The Mistress and The Merchant*. Then a reminder she'd set weeks ago popped up on the screen and her shoulders slumped. Maggie's memorial service. How could she have forgotten it was today?

She hovered between tears and the urge to throw up. *Ugh. This isn't about you. Pull yourself together and get ready.* Nodding to herself, she turned to the kitchen to feed the now yelping cat and take her regular meds. Then stopped when she spotted The Book lying on her bedside table.

Where was Jonathan? He'd been a near-constant presence in her life in these last few weeks and she'd come to assume he'd automatically be around. Would she have to read again to bring him back? Or…was he so appalled by what happened yesterday he now chose to stay away?

The grandfather clock downstairs chimed ten and Emmy rushed into the shower, allowing the sting from the hot water to scold her for caring what he thought. She wouldn't be late. Not today. Not for anyone.

THE SKY WAS A PREGNANT OPALINE, a solid block of colour that no flash of blue was permitted to peek through. It looked to Emmy as if it was waiting for something to happen. The recent glorious September sun seemed far-away, and Emmy shivered, linking arms with Lizzie for warmth as they entered the gloom of the centuries old church. Maybe it was the open, cavernous space but churches always gave her the sensation of being naked, as if the minute she stepped inside one all her clothing disappeared–her secrets laid bare for all to see.

The group now huddled on the cold and rigid pews consisted of an eclectic mix of Exeter's finest. Local business owners, Bridge Club friends, young community leaders and their families, fellow Devon and Exeter Institution members, even the mayor. Maggie had known them all. The good turnout warmed Emmy's soul. It was clear that Maggie Adams had been very much loved.

Emmy and Lizzie hurried down the centre aisle to sit in the front row beside Dawn.

"Let's get this over with," Emmy said as she gave her friend a warm hug.

Lizzie squeezed Emmy's hand with her own and Dawn responded with a weak smile. The vicar seemed intent on recounting Maggie's long and eventful life, but Emmy's eyes were drawn to the photograph of her friend on the cover of the service pamphlet. The old woman's dear face smiled back at her, frozen in time, her eyes twinkling with her usual mystery.

It was only when the vicar started speaking about Maggie's love of stories and adventure that Emmy's chest began to tighten. A stinging in her nose and throat alerted her to the imminent arrival of tears and she dug inside her handbag for a tissue. She wiped her eyes quickly, breathing in and holding the breath for a ten count before expelling it through her mouth in what she hoped wasn't audible. Her head and the back of her neck prickled, and a shiver ran across her shoulders and down her spine. In her heightened state of sensitivity, she had the sudden uncomfortable feeling of being watched and she glanced around the church, afraid. *Jonathan?* But she dismissed the thought fast. This wasn't the same.

"I need to get some air," she whispered to Lizzie and Dawn, before rising to her feet in a clumsy fashion with her head and back bent to cause as little disruption as possible to the people behind.

The wind outside was a whip crack against her wet cheeks, and she bent her head away from its lashing sting, hugging herself for comfort as much as warmth. The sky had darkened to a moody grey since she'd been inside the church and fat drops of rain began to fall, smattering the concrete path and gravestones in tiny black splodges, watercolours blooming on a stone canvas. Emmy huddled in the arched entryway, peering through the deepening gloom with itchy eyes.

A movement in the tree-line at the far side of the churchyard caught her gaze and she shivered again, unable to shake the oppressive feeling that someone was watching her.

Pull yourself together, woman, there's nobody there.

I see you.

The two voices sounded in her head almost simultaneously and she took a sharp intake of breath. The first voice Emmy knew to be her own, but the second was one she hadn't heard for almost a year. Not until yesterday. A chill crept over her skin like wildfire, an icy grip burning at her throat.

Please don't let me be relapsing.

"Ems? You okay?" Lizzie's concerned face was all eyes as she slipped out of the church door.

Emmy forced a smile. There was no point in worrying Lizzie. Besides, it wasn't as if she would be able to do anything to help. No, the only thing Emmy could rely on now was her meds. Unhappy experience had taught her that the only way of silencing the voice were sedatives and rest. She gave herself a silent salutation of gratitude for having prepped her handbag for all eventualities that morning, but what she really needed now was a drink to take them with.

"I'm fine. Just got to me a bit back there, that's all," Emmy said, hitching the strap of her bag higher on her shoulder. "You wouldn't happen to have some water with you?"

Lizzie shook her head, the damp air lending a Pre-Raphaelite frizz to her bouncing black curls. "Sorry."

Emmy peered over Lizzie's shoulder through the doorway. "How long do you think is left?" Her mind performed a series of quick calculations. How long did she have before things reached critical mass?

"No idea. If it's anything like Maggie, it could go on forever," Lizzie said, shaking her head again, "But I do know you're not okay. You should go. I'll explain."

Emmy sighed, then squaring her shoulders she grabbed Lizzie by the hand and marched back over the threshold into the church. Not today, Satan.

THE REST of the service passed by in a haze of grief, emotion and mounting trepidation. The voice that had turned Emmy's blood to antifreeze was mercifully silent, yet she couldn't shake the unsettling feeling of being watched. Though she kept her head down for most of the time, her eyes darted with suspicion across the backs of her fellow mourners, like a nervous gazelle at a watering hole. She counted down the seconds until the final hymn was sung, then made quick and polite excuses before dashing off to find a shop to buy some water. Holy water, her mind said, and she railed against the notion. This was no holy business, but it was her salvation.

She twisted off the water bottle lid and popped a diazapam before leaving the shop, a hasty thanks for the assistant fleeing her lips. Then she darted back across the two-lane traffic to the church, skirting around grey, somber headstones, weathered and chipped like decaying teeth. It was no longer raining, and a weak sun played tag with skittish clouds. Emmy caught up with the throng still congregating outside the church and positioned herself between Lizzie and Dawn. There was nothing she could do now but hope the meds kicked in fast.

"It was a lovely service, thank you," Emmy said, shaking hands with the vicar.

Mrs Bath could always be relied upon to monopolise the conversation. Emmy let the older woman's well-meaning words wash over her, the slightly cracked timbre of old age both a balm and a reminder of all she had lost, and suddenly she found herself longing to hear Maggie's laugh one last time. She searched in her handbag for a tissue, rifling past her phone, purse, assorted scraps of paper and balled-up receipts, when she chanced upon a stiffer, thicker sheaf. Pulling it out she studied Maggie's letter, confusion clouding her head. She couldn't remember putting it in there. Then realisation hit her with the force of an oncoming train. Jonathan must have done it. This small kindness made a massive chink in her armour and she swallowed back the tightening in her throat and chest before she lost control completely.

"Excuse me," she whispered to Mrs Bath, placing a hand on the older lady's arm to get her attention, "I have to go."

Catching up with Dawn and Lizzie, Emmy hugged her friends and made her excuses. There was only one person she wanted–*needed*–right now. No sooner had she admitted it to herself did all her earlier cares and fears fall away.

It was like coming home.

Almost skipping past the gravestones, Emmy smiled as

the sun peeked out from behind a cloud. It bathed the churchyard in glorious, blinding light, illuminating the headstone directly in front of her so that the word 'DAL-GLIESH' stood out in relief. Emmy halted, her smile faltering, head cocked to one side. Dropping to her knees she ignored the damp, mossy ground and cleared away the grass and weeds that had grown up around the tablet. Half-hidden in the earth, it looked as if it had grown out of the ground rather than planted there, as if it had been there since time immemorial. Most of the lettering had been worn away to nothing but a mark that could have been an E or B was visible in front of the name Dalgliesh. Below this there were two dates: 1568 – 1624.

Emmy drew her eyebrows together as she considered the name. Fishing in her bag again, she took out her phone and quickly photographed the headstone, adjusting the brightness twice so that the lettering was clear. Then another flash of movement in the trees caught her eye and she straightened up, breathing hard, hair on the nape of her neck standing on end. Someone was there. She took a step towards the trees, away from the open path but a sudden whooshing in her head reminded her of the diazepam. Stifling a yawn with the back of her right hand, she held up the phone and took a quick snap of the scene.

"You don't frighten me," she said in a voice loud enough to carry. The action was exhausting. Her limbs were dead weights as she forced herself to turn away toward the exit. She got as far as the road before fear caught up with her, legs shaking uncontrollably. It wasn't far to the shop. She could make it.

The historic sights of Exeter, usually a source of comfort, passed by unnoticed until she reached Fore

Street and turned left to Stepcote Hill. The old, cobbled steps were wide and steep, and she swayed a little halfway down, but each step down took her closer to her goal. The Tudor façade of both the shop and her flat above in the overhanging eaves came into view before she got to the bottom and Emmy's heart sped up as she thought of Jonathan's searching blue eyes.

She didn't know what made her do it, maybe that same sense of foreboding that she'd experienced in the church (although it was somewhat diminished now thanks to the buzz from the drugs) but as she reached the bottom, she glanced back. A hooded figure dressed in black stood at the top of Stepcote Hill. Emmy couldn't see their face, but she had the unnerving certainty that they were watching her. Fear rising like bile in her throat, she turned away and took the last few steps into the shop at a near run, the tinkling of the old bell the last thing she heard.

CHAPTER 15

*S*oft sunlight sprinkling through the swaying leaves outside cast warm dappled shadows across the walls of Emmeline's room, illuminating her face as she slept. Jonathan was irresistibly reminded of Giorgonne's Sleeping Venus, which he'd seen in person on his first trip to Italy as a boy and more recently in one of the rare books downstairs. She looked lovely. Tendrils of her hair shimmered like spun gold, framing her delicate face. Her eyes and lips were closed. Her light rhythmic breathing filled his heart with overwhelming, choking relief. She could never know the fear he'd felt last night. The fear of losing her, a dread which had compelled him to stay awake all night, watching over her to ensure she was safe. That she still breathed.

He'd ached to touch her, of course. To hold her close and erase her woes with the gentlest of kisses. The longing in him so potent, it was almost all he could think about. Just the thought of the set of her lips, or the way a single smile could steal his breath from his very lungs made him almost wild with desire. But her safety was far more important than his yearning, so he'd done neither, immediately removing his hands from her body after carrying her upstairs and placing her in the bed.

She stirred, snuggling into the bedding before her eyes flew open a moment later.

Catching sight of him, she yanked the covers tights, wary eyes searching the room. "Why are you here?"

Jonathan heaved himself from the chair and moved to the door, hoping to avoid causing her further alarm. The way she had crumpled as she crossed the threshold of the shop yesterday, fear distorting her lovely features, had all but emasculated him. That he could not protect her when she needed him most was an arrow to his heart. Something very real had frightened her and if she hadn't passed out there and then, scaring him half to death, he would have done everything in his power to learn what it was. Now, she watched him, unsure and afraid and his spirits plummeted at the way she shrank from him.

"You asked me to stay with you," he said, widening his eyes, hopeful to invoke her memory.

"I did? Wait, what day is it?" She sat up in the bed, snatching for her magical, evil phone.

"It is Tuesday morning. The memorial was yesterday."

Emmy glanced at the phone and then back to him, brow furrowed. "How long have I been asleep?"

Jonathan grinned, "About sixteen hours. Did you sleep well?"

She stretched and yawned. "I *think* so. Wait a minute? How did I get here? Did you carry me?" A horrified look darkened her face and she peeked beneath the covers.

"Yes, and yes I left you fully robed. What kind of man

do you take me for?" His words were meant to be light-hearted, but he struggled to keep the edge out of them. *What kind of man indeed?* He knew he had no right to expect anything else. They barely knew each other and what little Emmeline did know, she'd learned from that hated Book. Was it any wonder her mind had immediately run to impropriety on his behalf after reading about all his exploits, his misogynistic old self?

Maggie was right when she'd called him a dinosaur. When she'd told him that one day a woman would come along to extinct the cad'osaurus out of him. For here she was. Emmeline. The woman he loved but would never deserve, no matter how gentlemanly his behaviour now. But even as he accepted this, the knowledge that she still doubted him crushed any remaining vestiges of hope he may have had to dust.

Emmy pulled a face and whipped off the bed clothes as if they scalded her. "I guess thank you is in order."

Swift vexation bloomed in Jonathan's gut like poison, and he struggled to put a lid on his temper before it could boil over. He might be able to accept that she would never feel the same way about him, but he wasn't going to put up with her attitude. For once in his long miserable life he'd done the right thing, and this was the gratitude he got for it? Biting back the barbed retort on his lips, he turned to the door.

"I shall take my leave. You know where to find me." He nodded to The Book lying next to her on the bed and left the room.

∾

EMMY DRESSED WITH EXTRA CARE, taking time to straighten her dark blonde hair and foregoing her usual make-up free countenance for a sweep of black mascara. Nervous embarrassment uncoiled in her stomach as the memory of yesterday's events returned. Had she really swooned in Jonathan's presence before passing out like a damsel in distress? What on earth must he think? Humph. Never mind what Jonathan thought, her own self-flagellation was more than enough. She made herself eat a bowl of cereal which had the taste and texture of wallpaper and paste, before swallowing it down with two cups of tea. Then she brushed her teeth twice, mounting trepidation tingling in her belly like a teenager getting ready for her first date.

Once downstairs, she flicked on only one lamp so that from the outside the store would appear dark and closed. There was no one about anyway, a cursory glance into the street confirmed. The tourists were still safely tucked up in their hotel beds. It was the first time she'd been grateful the shop was hidden down a city centre side street.

Sweeping her hair behind her ears, Emmy settled herself on the cushioned bench inside the phone box. Propping the door open with a heavy tome, she shoved a mismatched cushion behind her back and placed The Book that she'd been hugging to her chest down on her knees.

Why was this so difficult now? What had changed? Nothing.

Everything.

Opening The Book where she'd last read it, she took one last deep breath. She cringed inside with embarrassment at how easily she capitulated when the letters emerged and swirled around her. It was as if those same letters danced in her veins, his story now an integral part of her own. Then Jonathan's perfect form took shape, his weight filled the air, warming her from the inside, and time stood still as Emmy's eyes found his worried, yet hopeful expression.

Emmy was on her feet again, but Jonathan didn't make any move to join her. When he spoke his voice was gruff, uncertainty in his eyes. "Emmeline, I won't pressure you to tell me your woes, but I cannot pretend any longer. I am worried. Now, if you will excuse me, I've just found a good bit... I had to distract myself while waiting for you, somehow." He picked up a book from the shelf beside him and gave it his attention. *Lady Chatterley's Lover* again.

A thousand horses galloped in Emmy's chest. What was he doing? And why the sudden change of subject and mood?

"Oh, I see. Did you find anything interesting?" Her eyes darted from the book to his face.

"I should say so."

He smiled again, and it was so disarming that Emmy took a step backwards into the seat. She tumbled onto the bench with a kind of half laugh-half sob.

"We were going to make another video, do you recall?" He stepped closer to her, his own eyes never leaving Emmy's face.

"Yes... you still want to do that?"

"Of course," his smile faltered a little, "why would you assume differently?"

Emmy held out her hands, palms up and shrugged. "I don't know. I just thought..."

"You think too much, Emmeline."

It was true. She did worry and unpick every conversation, every expression. It was the curse of the mentally ill and anxious. Yet even before her diagnosis, she'd always overanalysed the nuances in people's speech and tells, looking for what made them tick, and why they chose the words they did. Perhaps that was why she loved all things literary, where characters' dialogue usually made sense, or their motivations were at least explained.

Real life people were far too complicated and complex to dissect and it was perhaps foolish of her to try.

Her chin rose a fraction. "You say that like it's a bad thing."

Jonathan laughed. "Not at all. I am simply trying to point out that you need to relax. If you will permit me, I would like to recite the sonnet I mentioned earlier. So, if you could oblige and find that cursed phone of yours rather than gawping at me like a trout on a hook, I would be most grateful."

Trout on a hook indeed! "I think you'll find that you're the fish out of water here," Emmy said on a laugh as she rummaged in her pocket for her phone.

"Ahh, there's the beastly contraption. Does it ever leave your side?" Jonathan took a step closer, a hunter stalking its prey.

Emmy let out a nervous giggle. "Do you want to do this or not? I have plenty of other things I can be doing instead of being insulted by you."

Jonathan's expression softened. "I am sorry. We'll begin, shall we?"

Emmy nodded, grateful for the distraction. Pressing record, she gave him a thumbs up with her free hand. Then Jonathan's deep voice filled the air, inching into the gaps and crannies between them, padding the cramped space, making the phone box even smaller than it had ever been before. The walls closed in, the books whispered their centuries of stories, and for a moment, Emmy was back in the shop on the night she'd found The Book. An echo of a caress she was yet to know prickled along her spine and the sound of her own breathing surprised her, coming in loud, ragged, gasps.

> *"Her face, crafted by nature's hand,*
> *Hast thou, my star-filled sky;*
> *Her strength, tethering me to the land*
> *With but one word that I may fly*
> *But from the knowledge of my past,*
> *And my crimes, I should find mercy*
> *Pray her forgiveness for all time lasts,*
> *And I cause her no controversy;*
> *Though Time is but a fickle mistress*
> *I fear her cruel cut nears,*
> *And thine faith turn to mistrust*
> *My sweet Emmeline, my bravest dear.*
> *Please take this as a fool's oath,*
> *That whatever may pass, thine will be enough."*

Time slowed, before standing still. Emmy blinked in disbelief as something that resembled strands of spun gold spilled from Jonathan's moving lips. The strands sparkled, catching the light from the chandelier, and his eyes glistened, reflecting glittery pinpoints like the first stars at twilight. Then the gold strands began twisting and dancing in the air between them, elongating and undulating into a beautiful cursive script. Some of the strands separated and reshaped into new words, and Emmy's eyes widened as she tried to read the words that were now forming. A soft, nervy laugh escaped her open mouth as the words 'Emmeline' and 'Strength' danced into view, and she reached out, but they disintegrated into gold-dust against her fingertips.

Jonathan eyes weren't on the phone. He was looking beyond it to her, and Emmy's skin tingled and tightened. Unmistakable desire swooped from her breasts to her throat and low down again to her groin. She sat very still, trying to absorb the words into her skin, but then his voice trailed off and the script faded into wispy, barely-there particles, until finally, it disappeared.

Emmy's finger wobbled as she pressed stop, releasing her held breath. Neither of them moved. What could she say to that? Everything seemed trite and insufficient.

"Thank you," she began, "No one has ever written anything about me before, certainly nothing that beautiful." And no one would ever write anything more beautiful ever again.

Jonathan's sudden movement caught her off guard as he came to sit beside her on the seat. "I meant every word." His eyes glowed with a wonderful lambency that made Emmy's knees weak and her throat constrict. It really wasn't fair. He was too good at this seduction thing. Even without the magical sparkly word stuff, he was irresistible. No wonder women happily tumbled into bed with him. Why wouldn't they? And why couldn't she?

She opened her mouth to speak, unsure what else to say but a beep from her mobile interrupted into the silence, and she almost hit the roof.

"You should see what that is. It could be important."

His eyes were too intense, and Emmy was glad for the moment of release.

A message indicated she had a voicemail from her solicitor. Hoping it was news about her share of the deposit on the London flat, Emmy stood, holding up a hand for Jonathan to wait. She quickly pressed call and listened, but any catching fire of excitement inside her soon crumbled to ashes as the solicitor's soporific voice informed of her of a complication with Maggie's will. Someone was contesting it. What? Why? And why wait until almost the last possible minute to say anything? Emmy's stomach flipped with nausea as she remembered asking Dawn and Lizzie weeks ago if she minded that Maggie had left the shop to her. *They wouldn't? Would they?*

Deeds Not Words.

Fighting a wave of bile rising in her throat, Emmy clicked off the voicemail call and in anger her finger swiped to the next message in the inbox. Her eyes scanned the text without interest at first but then her blood ran cold with terror. "Get out or watch it burn."

Fat tears sprang in her eyes before she could stop them. Her stomach somersaulted again, over and over. A sudden roaring in her ears made her cry out. This was too much. The tears began to fall in earnest, and then there was Jonathan. His arms enveloped her in a warm and all-encompassing embrace and Emmy sank into him, no longer caring about what he must think, only grateful he was there.

He held her, rocking her body while the sobs wracked through her, letting her cry it all out as she gave voice to her deepest fears. Maggie's death, the shop, Dan the Dickhead, the stranger, Maggie's will, and the latest threat. All of it came rushing out like an exorcism. Whether Jonathan understood, he didn't say, stroking her hair and hushing soft nothings into her ear. The only things Emmy didn't elaborate on were her illness and her feelings for Jonathan himself.

Sniffing and hiccupping into Jonathan's arms, Emmy fought to get her emotions under control. She'd be damned if she was going to play this damsel in distress role any longer. She unfolded herself from his embrace and got shakily to her feet, hunting in her pockets for a tissue. A large white handkerchief flapped into view next to her and she glanced up to see Jonathan gazing at her with was fast becoming his default worried look.

"Thanks," she said, taking the handkerchief from him and wiping at her sopping face. So much for that morning's mascara. Heaven knows what a train wreck she must look now.

"Sit down again. Please?" Jonathan was looking at her with a hopeful puppy dog expression, and Emmy let out a giggle that exploded into a hiccup. Unshed tears still itched at her eyes and Jonathan tugged her hand, pulling her back on to the narrow seat without waiting for an answer.

"You really have no idea how strong you are, do you? I am in *awe* of you. How have you managed to keep going with all this bottled up inside?" Jonathan's face searched Emmy's with that same wondrous lambency, reigniting the flames in Emmy's core that had been so unceremoniously extinguished by her waterworks. His words cut through the impending fresh batch of tears and she quivered as they filled spaces inside her that had for too long laid dormant.

Once again, she was put in mind of coming home, but this time it was of lighting fires in an empty house, filling it with warmth and light. He was so close she spotted a freckle on his lower lip she hadn't noticed before, and the thought of touching it, *tasting it*, made her a little delirious. *Well, a little more delirious anyway.* She smiled, and the movement dislodged a single tear nestled in her eyelashes. She made to dab at it with the hanky, but Jonathan was quicker. Taking it from her hands, he inched his head towards her, a hunger in his cerulean eyes.

"May I?"

Emmy nodded, a quick sharp yes, her held breath almost painful in her chest.

With almost untraceable gentleness, Jonathan cupped her face in his hands, swooping down to brush away the tear on her cheek with a cotton-soft kiss. Tremors like little earthquakes erupted throughout Emmy's body and she became perfectly still, making her breathing regular and shallow, ridding of her mind of everything but Jonathan and what he was doing right now. His lips traced across her cheeks, as if to erase the tears that had fallen there, landing as whispered caresses on her eyes, forehead, nose, before he drew back, gazing at her with undisguised adoration.

"Let me kiss you. Let me love you." Jonathan whispered, his voice velvet.

Kiss me? Love me? Yes, yes, a thousand time yes.

Emmy's mind tripped, dipped and swirled like a rollercoaster running dangerously close to the rails. *He's asking for permission?* Maybe the sixteenth century understood consent better than the twenty-first after all. A memory came to her. The time she'd begged her parents to take her on a Big Wheel at the fair. The little gondola had swayed when they reached the top and Emmy had looked down upon the very roof of the world, the view over everything breath-taking and daunting all at once. The whizz and whoosh of the whole carnival surrounded her, sweeping crescendos of blinding, bursting light and sound exploded like popping balloons full of rainbows, and she'd laughed and screamed as they fell back through time and space and ecstatic oblivion. Jonathan was asking to kiss her, and shock had jolted her lust-drunk mind into nostalgic melodrama.

Jonathan was waiting, his eyes now unsure, head titled to one side. "Is that a no, then?" He dropped his hands from her face a fraction.

"No. It's not a 'No'." Emmy said with a shy smile

"Thank you."

He flashed that brilliant smile again: Lord Jonathan Dalgliesh Weapon of Mass Seduction, leaving Emmy breathless, isolated on a barren speck of the world. The lone survivor of a devastating, yet beautiful and all-ravaging apocalypse. Cupping her face in his hands, he leaned towards her, sending thrills of delicious fission all over her body, the intensity of his gaze melting away any vague notions of resistance she may have still held. With almost unbearable leisureliness, Jonathan's mouth finally met Emmy's, and the world ended and started again, as she found a pocket of utopia in the soft, sweet sanctuary of his lips.

CHAPTER 16

*F*or a few precious and stolen moments (or it may have been several star-struck hours, or even a handful of sun-kissed lazy days) Emmy was the girl kissing a drop-dead gorgeous sixteenth century Tudor knight in a red telephone box as if it was the most natural thing in the world. And strangely enough, it was.

It felt so right.

He tasted like heaven, her own personal ambrosia cushioned by the warm, soft and delicious plumpness of his mouth. His hands gently held her cheeks, imprisoning her in an unyielding frame. A soft, guttural exclamation escaped from him as their lips closed and opened, meeting again, turning and twisting with the other's in a dance as old and erotic as life itself. One of his hands shifted from her face to grasp her hair at the nape of her neck, pulling her closer still, and Emmy gasped as his teeth grazed her lower lip. His kiss deepened into some-thing urgent and primeval, and Emmy's most sensitised zones stood to attention, her own hands now fisting in his glorious soft curls.

Jonathan pushed her back against the glass, pinioning her with his hips, his groin grinding and growing against her thighs. She could quite easily end up having fantastic bang-bang sex with Jonathan right here, right now, squashed together in this confined space. A wanton, needy part of her didn't care. *That* Emmy was already ripping a foil condom packet with her teeth, a hungry lioness tearing into the flesh of its prey. *This kiss!* She never wanted it to end.

But end it must. She had a shop to open. Untangling herself with considerable reluctance from Jonathan's embrace, Emmy pouted as she rose from the bench, straightening her clothes and hair, certain Jonathan would feel the heat pulsating off her skin. She avoided his eyes as she exited the booth and walked to the door, taking much longer than usual with the deadbolt and key in her shaking hands. Then she flipped on the rest of the lights and took a deep, bracing breath before she turned to face him. He was watching her, his blue eyes stormy, one hand rubbing the dark stubble on his chin. As she strode to the back shelves he caught her hand in his.

"As much as I desire to continue where we left off, I am even more worried for you now. Please tell me what the message said."

Emmy's heart, which moments earlier had been a stone skimming across the smooth shining surface of a lake, now sank to shadowy depths, shivers radiating from its epicentre in a rippled effect. She'd hoped he would have forgotten. Removing her mobile from her pocket she swiped the screen until she came to the text. Without saying a word, she swapped it for the hand Jonathan was still holding and moved away to fire up the computer and till. Once it came to life, she drummed her fingers on the countertop while she waited for the system to load. She was so focused on staring at the whirring little circle on the screen that Jonathan's growled utterance made her jump.

"Who sent this? Do you know?" He had left the phone box and was at the counter in two long-limbed strides, stormy eyes now positively thunderous.

"It's from a withheld number so I have no idea. Besides, it's probably kids messing around."

Jonathan slammed a fist on the desk. "Emmeline! I respect that you are a strong and independent woman, but I implore you to heed this warning. Too often lately have you brushed off these threats as if they are normal and to be expected. Now, as you know, I am unversed in your modern times, but I refuse to accept that society has deteriorated to the point of nonchalance in the face of coercion. It is simply unacceptable. Do you not have laws that forbid this kind of terror?"

Hearing her fears given voice, Emmy's shoulders sagged. She stopped drumming with her fingers and gave Jonathan her full attention.

"What do you want to hear from me?"

Jonathan took her hands in his and Emmy was surprised again by the warmth in them–another reminder that he was real. "I want you to stop pretending you're not afraid. I want you to show me that your happiness, your health–*your life*–mean as much to you as they do to me."

His words sent Emmy's heart into overdrive. On top of everything else that had happened lately, Jonathan's sudden declaration was almost too much to process. How easy would it be to allow him to take her in those strong arms and tell her that everything was going to be okay?

But fairytales didn't happen to people like her. When was the last time she'd read a romance novel which featured an MC with schizophrenia? Never, that's when. And if it didn't occur in the fantasy realm of Romance-landia, what hope was there in real life? Bitter experience had taught Emmy to count herself lucky to have any kind of 'normal' life. Schizophrenia was still horribly stigmatised and many sufferers had it much tougher than her, but she couldn't suppress the bubble of frustration that welled inside her when she considered how other mental health conditions had become more readily represented and accepted—not only in romance publishing, but by society as a whole.

No. The message was clear: YOU don't get to live happily ever after.

BESIDES, it was kind of moot anyway. No matter what magic had sent Jonathan spiralling into her life. Their kiss mattered little if he still wanted to return to his own time, if he wanted to leave her. So what point was there in pursuing it? It was exactly due to her own sense of self-preservation that she knew they couldn't go on like this, irrespective of how wonderful his kissing technique. Find the answer to his curse and let him go. It would be the hardest thing she'd ever done. She brought her fingers to her lips, unaware of the action until she caught Jonathan's scorching gaze, dropping her hand without hesitation. His kisses would not easily be forgotten.

"CAN I ASK YOU SOMETHING?" She was peering at him, shy now beneath her lashes.

Jonathan's mind was a battleground. He stared at Emmeline for an eternity, dizzy from the warring emotions competing for his attention. A part of him wanted to sing and shout with joy, to express his feelings in another sonnet or perhaps, a song. Kissing her had awakened something primeval in him and it seemed only fitting to now make her his muse. To create art and beauty from the pureness of her love. But another part was frustrated. Why wouldn't she allow him to take care of her? Could she not see how her apparent lack of concern for her safety was tearing him apart? He contemplated not allowing the change of subject without a fight. Then he sighed before running both hands through his hair.

"Anything," Jonathan replied, gazing at her with complete sincerity. It was imperative she trust him. How else would he convince her that breaking the curse no longer mattered? That she was the most important thing to him now? And that meant trusting her too.

Emmeline cleared her throat. "Earlier, you were pretty pissed off at me. And you were absolutely right to be. I behaved abominably. I'm sorry. You caught me unawares, that's all. I'm not used to being taken care of and I see now that's all you were doing, so thank you. But…I wanted to ask…why the sudden change of mood?"

Jonathan laughed. "I won't lie, I was annoyed, but it was as much with myself as it was you."

"I don't understand." Emmy replied, shaking her head.

He tucked one finger under her chin, tugging her to him, waiting until she had no choice but to look straight at him. "You make me want to be a better man, Emmeline."

Confusion clouded her eyes and it was a moment before she replied. "Thank you," she whispered, leaning in to meet his lips with her own with another long, lingering kiss.

It was a dream, he was sure. Any moment now he would wake up and this perfect fantasy which his subconscious had somehow conjured and brought to life in every tangible way, would be yanked cruelly from him and he'd be imprisoned inside the dark pages of his literary jail once more.

There was no way this beautiful, strong, incredible woman could be meant for one so underserving as him. But her lips continued to move with his, her hands crept up his back and into his hair, clutching at his curls and making his every nerve ending stand on end. A soft moan escaped her mouth and desire swept through him, wildfire pooling in his groin.

He never wanted to let her go. But there were things he needed to know, questions she'd neglected to answer about her safety, and it was with a considerable amount of reluctance that he broke their connection.

"Emmeline, will you please start taking these threats seriously?" he said, once his breathing had returned to normal.

She bit her lip and he very nearly reached for her again.

"Okay, I promise," she said in a small voice. Then, more forcefully, "I forgot, I found something yesterday that might be useful."

For a moment Jonathan considered taking her to task for changing the subject, *again*. But he let it go, vowing to tackle it at a later time. She got up and he relinquished his gentle grip on her hand with reluctance. She was safe here with him. He wouldn't allow anything to befall her. His chest constricted in alarm at the thought and he had to force the unwelcome images from his mind before they could unman him. She picked up the mobile phone from where she had left it next to the computer and wandered back to where he sat.

"I saw this headstone in the churchyard. It's got your name–well, surname–on it." Her fingers swiped across the screen three times in quick succession. "Maybe they're a relation of yours? I mean, Dalgliesh, it's not a very common surname, is it? Especially not around here."

Jonathan scrutinised the screen, hiding his surprise. "Interesting, but the timeline does not add up. I have–*had*– no relative with these dates of birth and death. I do not believe this to be anything more than a coincidence." Self-loathing rose like acid in his throat. His words contained no lie, yet he could not permit himself to feel good, not when there was still so much about him she did not–and could not –know.

Emmeline looked as if a retort waited on her lips, but her mobile rang before she could speak. Closing her eyes for a fraction of a second, she sighed louder than he had just moments before.

When she opened her eyes again she smiled, snatching his breath from his lungs like a master thief.

"Lizzie," she mouthed.

"Hey! I've got you on speaker," she said into the devilish device.

Then Lizzie's high-pitched voice filled the air, and Jonathan flinched. *What was this new sorcery?*

Lizzie didn't care for preamble. "Are you okay? I'm worried about you, you left so abruptly yesterday, and I know you weren't well. I can't begin to imagine what you went through with Dan but I'm here if you need me, Ems. Do you want me to come over? I'm off today. Actually, don't answer that. I'm on my way."

It was clear that Lizzie wasn't much concerned with punctuation either. Or breathing.

Emmeline turned her back on Jonathan, putting the phone to her ear so that he could no longer hear the conversation. Something Lizzie said as they finished the call must have been hilarious because Emmeline suddenly dissolved into uncontrollable giggles, clutching her ribs with one hand and the back of the chair behind the counter with the other. What was wrong here? How could she react like this? It was clear from Lizzie's words that something very serious was happening to Emmeline, yet she continued to behave as if she had not a care in the world. He had never met a more mercurial or fascinating woman and trying to understand her was becoming an obsession. She glanced up, eyes watering with mirth. Jonathan stared at her, grinding his teeth to keep his expression from stony.

Emmeline said goodbye to Lizzie and rearranged her face as she turned to look at him. "What's gotten into you?

You look like you've just sat on your sword." Her voice simmered with a merriment that threatened to boil over again.

"Well, let us examine why that could be, shall we?" Jonathan pounded the flagstones with temper-filled strides. "Perhaps I am vexed because you are in danger, and you are unable or unwilling to take it seriously. Or perhaps it is because you are driving me to the point of insanity with your 'I don't need anyone's help' act. I respect your strength and your need for privacy, but I wish I could convince you to trust me more. Perchance I need to earn that trust, however, in which case I put to you this argument: maybe the real reason for my vexation is because I find myself in the grip of confliction. On the one hand, I yearn to return to my time. It was my only goal for centuries—to be free of the shackles that bind me inside this Book, to rid myself of this half-life, this wretched existence. Yet, I am scared beyond measure of what should happen if I *am* freed, because that could mean leaving you, and I would rather live an eternity as half a man, if it meant I would be with you, than a full life without. For that would be no life at all."

Emmeline sucked in a short, sharp breath. She took a long time to speak. "Lizzie is coming. Will you stay... and meet her, I mean?"

She'd come to stand right in front him, halting him in his mission to wear a trench in the floor.

"If that is what you wish. I would say nothing could please me more, but I would be lying." His words dripped with indecency and it took all his self-control not to kiss her again, but then his voice softened. "She is a good friend, yes?"

"She's the best."

"Then why have you not entrusted her with all of your woes? Is that not what friends are for?" Jonathan cocked his head, disheveled curls falling over his forehead.

It was her turn to tread the floor.

"I don't know." It was a wholly unsatisfactory response and Jonathan was compelled to take her by the upper arms in a gentle but firm grip.

"Confide in Lizzie about what's going on, or I will. I cannot risk anything happening to you, Emmeline, and if I have to speak with your friend on your behalf to protect you, I will." He let her go with a shrug. "Now, do you want me to be here when Lizzie arrives, or would you prefer I give her the full magic show?"

Emmeline threw herself against him, taking his breath away.

"Stay, please!"

Lizzie arrived in her usual whirling dervish manner, like one of those crazy haired but cute, collectable trolls. She chattered non-stop about Maggie's memorial, Emmy's quick exit and both her and her husband Thom's work commitments. She'd flung her bag down on the floor beside the sofa, kicked off her ubiquitous six-inch stilettos and was currently reclined on the sofa, bare feet resting on the coffee table. When she'd paused long enough for Emmy to begin to tell her about everything that was happening, her normally bright smile faltered, and she began fidgeting with her hair and the cuffs of her blouse.

Three times she picked up her coffee cup only to discover it was already empty.

"And that's not all," Emmy said, hesitating. She'd just finished recounting her fear of relapsing. She jammed her hands in her jean pockets and took then out again almost straight away. Ugh, why couldn't someone make women's clothes with decent pockets? Then she shook her head and rolled her eyes. Someone was trying to coerce her into running away, someone else was contesting Maggie's will, business was quite literally all over the shop–it hadn't escaped her attention that there hadn't yet been a single customer that morning. Lizzie was looking at her with increasing concern, and Jonathan had just declared his love for her. Emmy's feelings for him hovered somewhere between wanting to jump his bones, retain her independence and begging him to take her away from it all, but she couldn't think about that now, so instead her mind was worrying about pockets.

At least her mind was quiet in one way today. The last thing she needed right now was an attack.

Jonathan squeezed her hand, reminding Emmy that she hadn't yet divulged the full nature of her illness to him. She let out a weary sigh and continued, "I've had messages too, threatening messages." So far, Emmy had been successful in circumnavigating the pointed looks Lizzie made in Jonathan's direction. While Lizzie hadn't come right out and asked, Emmy was certain it was eating her up inside not knowing who he was and why he and Emmy appeared to be so close. If Lizzie's eyebrows got any higher on her forehead, they'd have to send out a search party for them into the tangled forest of her hair.

"There was also a message painted all over the front of

the shop. A clear threat." Jonathan interjected, his own eyebrows lifting. He turned to Lizzie, "I have been attempting to convince Emmeline to report the incident. I had hoped that you might be able to persuade her."

This was the most Jonathan had said in Lizzie's presence and it was clear from her wide eyes and flushing cheeks that she was having a hard time taking him seriously and was affected by his looks as Emmy herself. Emmy smiled as she pictured what was going on in Lizzie's head right now. *Where on earth did you find this guy? Rent-a-Darcy?* Emmy leaned forward to grab her own cup. Taking a swig of coffee, she pondered what Lizzie's reaction would be when she told her the truth about Jonathan.

Lizzie was speaking again at last. "It's horrible, Ems, and Jonathan's right. You need to go to the police. I wish you'd told me before." Then she smacked herself upside the head, her eyes alive with sudden recognition. "You're the guy from Emmy's viral video, right? The guy she did the photoshoot with? I *knew* I'd seen you somewhere before! Is that how you met?"

"Not exactly, Liz, but yeah, he's the same guy." Emmy twisted herself around to address Jonathan, hoping to convey a message with her eyes before addressing Lizzie again. "You remember I told you about the strange man who appeared in the shop after I'd read Maggie's favourite book... how he was talking in riddles and he knew my name. And how I told you the next day... he appeared out of the book like magic. How we came back here and nothing happened? Well... you're looking at him."

Lizzie's mouth and eyes formed three perfect circles. Edvard Munch's 'The Scream' with Botticelli hair. She whisked her feet off the table and stood up in what was almost one fluid motion, before glaring down at Jonathan, chest heaving and hazel eyes furious. "I need a minute with my friend. Alone."

Jonathan didn't move. It was only when Emmy released her hand from his, did he turn his head around to regard her, doubt etched all over his face.

"It's fine. I'm okay. Wait in the back for a minute. Please?" Emmy rose to her feet while she spoke, signalling to Jonathan to follow. Jonathan said nothing and unfolding his tall frame from the settee with that long-legged elegance of his, stared at Emmy for a few seconds before striding to her side. He glanced over to Lizzie, then with a final meaningful look at Emmy and the gentlest of caresses along her cheek with the back of one finger, ducked under the low lintel and disappeared out of sight.

Lizzie was nonplussed. She stood up, hands on her slim hips. "What on earth is going on? I know you're sick and you can't help the things that your mind tells you are real, but this is me you're talking to."

"I knew you wouldn't understand, and I know it's hard to believe. I barely believed it myself the first time, and I'm still not one hundred percent I'm not dreaming, even now. But he's real, Liz. And I'm going to help him." Emmy gesticulated with her hands as she spoke, ignoring a tiny voice that asked if that last part was true.

What if he doesn't have to go back? What if he could stay forever?

"You're right, I don't understand," Lizzie said, her eyes filling with tears. "It's one thing to believe in Happily Ever After but another to find someone else to go along with the charade. He's using you, Emmy! And I'm scared that you can't see it. You're vulnerable and he's playing on that. I don't trust him. Let me help. Maybe we should call your doctor..."

Emmy let out a yelp of deep frustration. "No. This isn't poor, delusional Emmy and her twisted fantasies. This is real. No doctors, no nothing. Just let me show you. Please!"

But Lizzie wasn't listening. She was already halfway to the counter and as Emmy watched, horrified, she picked up Emmy's mobile and began scrolling through what must have been her contact list.

"Give me the phone."

"Ems, I can't just sit here and let you do this to yourself. What kind of friend would I be if I did nothing while you're obviously relapsing or having some other kind of breakdown? Let me call the doctor, please. You go lie down upstairs and I'll deal with him," she nodded towards the rear of the store.

"What do you mean, 'deal with him'? What are you going to do?" Emmy's voice was shrill.

Lizzie looked up from studying Emmy's mobile to answer in a matter of fact tone: "Tell him to take his sick and twisted games someplace else. And if he won't go, I'll call the police."

Emmy recoiled as her mind conjured up images of Jonathan trying to explain who he was to a bemused and impatient officer. She didn't reply, instead she strode past her friend to pick up The Book which she'd left in the phone booth. Fingers trembling as she rifled through the delicate pages, she stopped at a random point and took a deep breath. *So much for being able to handle everything on your own. Please let this work.* With another deep breath, she read aloud:

"That she is practised in the art of witchcraft, I am now certain, for it is not only her eyes that hold a special brand of magic. It dances from her fingers in devilish sparks. It is in the sound of her voice, soft and hypnotic, a siren call. If I don't resist, she will have me truly under her spell, and that, as the Queen's chief witch-hunter, I cannot permit."

As Emmy spoke, the room seemed to flatten and stretch, twisting inside itself as if time was speeding up, slowing down and finally standing still. Lizzie froze midway into her call with Doctor Harrison's secretary, her eyes wide and full of fear. Books flew off shelves and pages fluttered in a non-existent breeze. The scent of old vanilla intensified, and the lights dimmed and brightened and then dulled again, the motes glittering like silver and gold in the small shaft of light from the window. The eddy grew and swirled around them both and Lizzie shrieked, dropping the phone on to the counter, arms reaching out for Emmy like a drowning woman.

"What's happening?"

Suddenly, everything was calm again and the dust cloud bloomed into the now familiar thousands of sparkling letters, before taking the shape of a man Emmy had come to know and love.

"Hello again, Lady Elizabeth," Jonathan said, now standing in front of Emmy's stunned friend with a gentle smile as he performed a small bow.

CHAPTER 17

$\mathcal{I}$f Elizabeth Sorenson was anything, it was difficult to shock. Emmy wracked her memory for an occasion when she'd seen her best friend lost for words. She smiled inside. There really was a first time for everything.

Lizzie's mouth opened and closed, opened and closed, like a fish gasping for air. With a dazed look in her eyes, she removed her hand from Jonathan's light grip and walked with a drunken gait to the sofa. Once there, she crumpled down into it, muttering silent nothings to no one in particular. Emmy took one brief look at Jonathan before dashing up to her flat. She was down again in seconds, tripping on the narrow stairs in her hurry, water sloshing around inside its glass. She didn't like the idea of leaving Lizzie alone with Jonathan in that state. Who knew what she might do? She laughed to herself again as the irony hit her. It made a nice change to not be the unpredictable and unstable one in a room for once.

"Here," she pressed the glass into Lizzie's cold hands. "Drink it."

For once Lizzie did as she was told. She raised the glass to her lips and took a decent sip, then another, then she leaned forward and placed the water on the coffee table. Emmy watched her, anxious. Raking her friend's face for signs of shock. "Say something."

"Something," Lizzie whispered. Her eyes no longer chased unseen ghosts around the room, her breathing more regular. She was staring at Jonathan with dawning recognition, but then she fixed Emmy with her eyes, contrition written all over her face. "I'm so sorry, Ems. I mean, can you blame me? How? This can't be happening, right?" Her attention turned again to Jonathan who was still standing in the middle of the room, underneath the chandelier. Emmy would have liked to take his photo right then–the glow from the soft bulbs lit his seraphic face from above as if he were wearing a halo–but she didn't dare leave Lizzie.

"I apologise, Lady Elizabeth. I did not mean to alarm you." With slow, deliberate movements, Jonathan came to join them, perching on the arm of Maggie's chair as far from Lizzie as possible in the small seating area. "I cannot explain the magic to you, for I do not understand it myself. All I can tell you is that I was cursed by a witch many centuries ago to live inside a book–that book–and that I owe Emmeline my life for liberating me. I am not completely free. I must return to The Book every so often else I cannot take form. When you came here that day with Emmeline, something prevented me from revealing myself to you. It is clear to me how much you care for Emmeline and whilst I do not pretend to understand everything that you spoke of regarding her condition I have complete confidence in her choices. She read from The Book to summon me, knowing she could have simply called back me into the room instead. That told me a lot. As well intended your actions were, they also caused her considerable distress. Hence my revealing myself to you and not merely walking back through the shop."

Lizzie took another sip of water, her eyes narrowing. "So, you did intend to shock me?"

Jonathan laughed, a rich, musical sound that filled the shop with warmth. "I suppose I did. But my intentions were good for Emmeline's sake. My apologies."

"Well you did a bloody good job of it." It was Lizzie's turn to laugh. A nervous, hesitant titter so unlike her usual uncontrollable, childish giggling. "So... what now? You said you tried to get Emmy to go to the police, right?" Her head whipped between Emmy and Jonathan.

"Yes, but she won't listen to me." Jonathan answered at once.

"Ems, you know you've got to report it. And now, not later," Lizzie said, nodding her head with encouragement. "And about this thing with Maggie's will, maybe Dawn can look into that. I'm sure we can find out who's behind the standing."

Emmy nodded, distracted. Stretching her arms, she yawned. Why was everything so exhausting? Jonathan and Lizzie were right, of course, but all she wanted right now was to crawl into bed and forget about everything. Everything except Jonathan.

Rubbing her temples, she got up and moved to the door. No one had come through it in the two hours since she'd opened the shop. What difference would it make if she closed for a while and went to the police station to make a report? She was raising her left arm to slide the deadbolt across when a hurrying figure passing the window caught her attention, and an unwelcome chill crept up her back. But to her intense relief, it was just a young woman. No hooded figure in sight. The woman turned at the entrance to the shop and made to open the door. Head down while she'd been walking, the woman only looked up as she placed her hand on the door handle, jumping slightly when she saw Emmy stood on the other side of the glass.

Emmy recovered first, tugging the door open with a welcoming smile. Yesterday's clouds had gone, and wall-to-wall sunshine blazed in the sky. But the air was tempered by a cool breeze that swept over Emmy's skin, raising goose pimples on her arms.

"Good morning, lovely day out," Emmy said to the woman, "Sorry for startling you."

The woman smiled as she crossed the threshold, content to chat about the weather. Emmy glanced back to where Jonathan and Lizzie sat, now whispering together on the sofa. Lizzie giggled again but this time it was the full-on Lizzie Sorensen head back, throat exposed, belly laughter that Emmy knew so well. Jonathan was obviously exercising his bountiful charms. Examining herself for signs of the green-eyed monster, Emmy was surprised at the unexpected bolt of jealousy that shot through her. Frowning, she turned back to the customer, giving the woman the full benefit of her bookseller acumen.

The bell rang at least fifteen more times while Emmy was busy with the first lady and soon there was a respectable line of customers waiting for Emmy's help. A small group of teenagers huddled together, giggling as they cooed over some of the racier titles. It was obvious from their high-pitched laughter and nervous glances to the seating area they'd come to check out the Literary Lothario for themselves. Jonathan played his part with relish. He whispered something to Lizzie before disappearing upstairs and out of sight. The next thing Emmy knew, he was sauntering back down the staircase, wearing his old Tudor clothes again. As he began reciting sonnets and poetry from some of the books on the shelves, the waiting customers quickly gathered around him and several of the teens visibly swooned. One, a gangly boy of about fifteen, exchanged an impish grin with his friend before whipping out his mobile to record the scene.

Emmy tried to keep one eye on Jonathan's performance, drawn to him despite her conviction to give her full attention to her patrons. Lizzie joined her in serving the customers, who now clamoured to make their purchases. Juliet Landon's *The Mistress and The Merchant* was a popular choice. Emmy grinned and made a mental note to call her favourite supplier so she could restock it, fingers crossed it was still in print.

The shop brimmed with the kind of magic Emmy usually experienced reading a good romance novel. It was like getting a hug from a book, and if she could have embraced her customers, she would have done. As Emmy glanced over at Jonathan again, she was surprised to see he had left his moment in the spotlight. Instead, his eyes trailed over the figure of a man in a scruffy, oversized overcoat who was huddling in a corner near the door—right next to the bookcase Emmy had found The Book in.

Emmy continued hand selling and ringing up the

totals on the till, but her gaze never strayed far from Jonathan and his apparent interest in the other man. She told one of the teens the amount and while the girl rummaged in her purse to pay, Emmy grasped the opportunity to take a good sweeping look around the shop.

"Sorry to keep you all waiting," she called out over the throng who murmured in assent. She couldn't be sure what happened next because her view was blocked as the queue of waiting customers shifted to make way for the teenagers to pass on their way out of the store.

Emmy hailed a thank you to the teens who glanced back over, waving with hands now carrying bags full of books, and moon eyes for Jonathan. Happy customers, Emmy thought again, warmth spreading through her chest like sunlight. She chanced another look at Jonathan, hoping to share the moment with him, but he was now striding towards the cupboard door, beckoning to Lizzie with a couple of firm motions of his head in the direction of the back of the store. Lizzie must have understood the direction because she was out from behind the counter and dashing across the floor in a flash, her dark head a blur.

What on earth? But Emmy couldn't investigate further because a new customer needed her attention–a request for a rare London Bentley edition of Jane Austen's *Emma* would take some sourcing but could be a potential gold mine if she could find one for the right price. Emmy was copying down the customer's details when a commotion coming from behind her caught her attention. She whirled to find the source of the noise–the unmistakable sound of pages flapping and the thud of something solid dropping to the flagstones.

"Excuse me," she said to the customer, already halfway out of the nook behind the counter, but then she yelped as the man from earlier came barreling towards her, his expression one of pure terror. He stumbled and bumped into a table leg, almost sprawling on his face, but saved himself just in time. Two large, leather-bound books fell from the folds of his rumpled clothing and landed on the floor–one of them tenting open, spine side up. With another small, anguished yell he reached the door. Eyes eating up his face, he took one last terrified look back over his shoulder and tore out of the shop, legs wind-milling, arms semaphoring an s.o.s.

A startled tittering broke out among the crowd and a couple of pedestrians rubbernecked as the man sprinted away. Emmy suppressed a laugh and crossed to close the door. Then she turned to address her gawping clientele, gathering the would-be thief's books from the floor. The one that had landed awkwardly was in bad shape, its deli-cate spine snapped, a couple of foxed pages falling loose from their old-fashioned cotton binding. Emmy grimaced. If there was one thing she couldn't abide, it was mistreating books. They deserved respect.

"He must have just realised we're not Amazon," she said, cradling the broken book like a wounded animal as she sauntered back to the counter. Everyone chuckled in collective appreciation and Emmy placed the tomes on a shelf to deal with later. Then she retrieved the pen she'd tucked behind her ear during the disturbance to resume taking the *Emma* order.

Try as she might to concentrate on the needs of her customers, her fingers itched with impatience. Jonathan reappeared, striding across the floor with the self-possessed air of a model on a catwalk, a stark contrast to Lizzie's breathless, giddy face as she too rejoined them all in the main room. Emmy couldn't fail to miss the mirth now threatening to burst from Lizzie's lips, as she and Jonathan shared knowing twin nods.

Emmy should have been in high spirits, given the number of times she'd opened and closed the till by the end of the day, but her smiles grew less sincere, her replies less expansive as the queue of waiting customers dwindled. When she was finally serving the last customer, a sweet, little elderly gentleman in a tweed suit that smelled of mothballs, Emmy's thanks and goodbye were curt salutations she regretted the moment they left her lips. Picking up and replacing a couple of stray books on her way to the door, she turned the key in the lock with much more force than was necessary.

She needed answers—and food.

She hadn't eaten anything since breakfast. Sweeping her hair from her face, she pirouetted to find Jonathan and Lizzie watching her. Jonathan was back in his civvies, a pair of muscle- enhancing blue jeans and a deep burgundy Henley top which clung lovingly to his abs and chest. Taking his cue from the male models they'd seen on the marketing images inside Marks and Spencer, he'd opened the very top two buttons of the Henley and pushed the sleeves up to his elbows, so that a tantalising glimpse of chest hair and his hard forearms were on display. The twenty-first century had never looked so hot.

Before Emmy could even sit down, Lizzie exploded into the giggles she'd been trying to suppress, like a child desperate to perform in the school play, finally allowed to show off. "Oh, my days! I've never seen anyone run so fast. That was amazing!" Lizzie wiped away tears before they could ruin her perfect make-up. "Oh Ems! You should have seen it. His face!"

"Should have seen what?" It came out too loud, accusatory, so she tried again, directing a softer question at Jonathan. "Someone tell me what's going on, please?"

Jonathan's eyes danced with a different excitement to Lizzie's as he regarded Emmy with silent intensity. "I think we should let Lizzie explain," he said, not taking his eyes off Emmy, "She's desperate to tell you."

Emmy shuddered. *How does he do that?* How could he charge a look with such intimacy, such potency. It became all too easily to believe they were the only two people to exist in the whole wide world. The sensation of blood pooling low in her belly made her fidget where she stood, and she squeezed the muscles at the back of her thighs together, unable to relinquish his stare. Lizzie's voice seemed to come from far away, maybe even from another time.

"When you two lovebirds have quite finished!"

Flames licked at Emmy's cheeks and she ground her teeth, tearing herself from Jonathan's x-ray like scrutinisation with difficulty. Lizzie was rolling her eyes.

"Sorry," Emmy ducked her head. She moved to sit in Maggie's armchair, but Jonathan tugged at her hand, pulling her down on to his lap instead.

"Sit with me?" It was a question, not a command, and Emmy almost melted at the look of near desperation on Jonathan's face. How could she refuse? Making herself comfortable, she snuggled into him, unsurprised by the hardness of his thighs beneath the fabric of her jeans. His right hand rested on the seat next to her. Biting the inside of her lip, she placed her own on top of it, allowing her nails to scratch gently along his fingers. He flipped his palm over, and she clasped it between her own, before lifting his arm and depositing both of their hands, palms down, on her right thigh.

Hot, unbidden lust heated her pulse and she blushed in anticipation of where her imagination was leading her. *You're worse than those teenagers. Get a grip.* She could pretend if she had to. So, pressing her lips together, she faced Lizzie, who was enjoying watching their PDA with almost indecent amusement.

"So, you were busy serving that woman who came in first and it got quite crowded with those kids and everything." It was clear from her giddy tone how much fun Lizzie was having. Emmy had never seen her quite so animated. "Then that guy came in. Jonathan spotted him straight away. Said something wasn't right. So, Jonathan watched him, while I tried to help you serve. That's when he did it."

Emmy leaned forward, as much in interest at Lizzie's story as an attempt to control herself, for Jonathan was now trailing a light caress along her right thigh. His other arm was slung across the back of the sofa and his head was inclined towards Emmy's neck, his warm breath sending shivers racing into her scalp. He clearly had no desire to hear Lizzie's tale. Emmy shuddered, hoping her voice wouldn't give her away.

"Did what?"

Lizzie was in her element now. She jumped out of her chair and grinned with euphoria. "Stole a book. He tucked it inside his overcoat thinking no one had noticed. Then he shuffled off down the back there, presumably to steal more. That's when Jonathan stopped him."

Emmy arched her neck to look at Jonathan. "What did you do to him?"

What are you doing to me?

"Scared the absolute shit out of him, that's what!" Lizzie said, triumphant. "I got it on my phone. Look!"

And she produced a top of the range i-phone and fiddled with it for a second before clicking on the screen that now showed the back room of Emmy's shop. The bookcases housing authors W – Z resided there. The screen flicked into life and Emmy's eyes widened as she saw the scruffy man hovering near the tall bookshelves. He lifted his hand and almost imperceptibly, snatched a large book out of the row, stashing it inside his baggy coat. What happened next wouldn't be out of place in an old Hammer Horror movie.

A disembodied voice, that Emmy recognised to be Jonathan's even with the menacing chill he affected, spoke in an almost inaudible whisper. The invisible Jonathan must have been standing right beside Lizzie for the phone's microphone to pick it up. Then books started leaping from the shelves at random, the pages flying as they opened and closed around the man's face like a scene from *The Birds*. The shoplifter cried out and tried to bat away one of the nearest volumes knocking it to the floor where it landed with a thump. Screaming, he ran from the room and out of shot. Throughout it all, the raspy sound of someone trying to hold their breath provided a suitably spooky soundtrack, before the unseen director–clearly Lizzie–exploded into loud and delighted giggles, as the man ran past her. His death's head rictus face visible as he twisted to find the source of the laughter.

Lizzie was crying with laughter again, doubled over and clutching her sides. Emmy had to admit the clip was hilarious, but she joined in with her best friend's laughter a little too late. *What the hell is wrong with you?* Scared she already knew the answer, she didn't waste time probing the depth of her irritation and instead gave Jonathan a mock reproachful look.

It would have been a lot easier to pretend to be shocked by his behaviour if he wasn't still tracing small, circular featherlight motions along her right thigh, fingers edging higher and higher up her leg to her hip. Then his touch swept across the join where her leg met her body following the contour of her underwear, down and around to her backside, before working their way in the opposite direction towards the tops of her thighs. His expression was one of disinterest, but his husky breathing gave him away.

He shifted beneath her and a hardness that was separate to his muscular legs twitched against her behind. She gasped as pinpoints of desire burst low within her belly. Trying to regulate her own breathing, she stole a glance at Lizzie, but her friend was too busy re-watching the video to notice.

Leaning back, she cupped her palm around Jonathan's right ear. She almost gave in to the temptation to take his earlobe between her teeth but instead whispered, "Later," before fixing his blue eyes with her own. An unspoken promise passed between them and Emmy's libido went into overdrive as Jonathan responded with another nudge against her bottom.

Emmy stood up too fast, and all the blood that was pooling in ever-increasing momentum in her lower belly rushed to her head, and she swayed with dizziness. This was neither the time nor the place. They had things to do before…

"Can we go get this police report done? And grab food on the way? I'm starving."

Jonathan smirked as he stood up, manoeuvring out of Lizzie's line of sight as he adjusted his new jeans.

"I'll have to skip," Lizzie said, lifting her head. "I've got a million and one things I should be doing–and meeting your Tudor knight book boyfriend wasn't one of them. No offence." She added to Jonathan, who held up his hands signifying none was taken. She was stuffing her mobile away in her bag and was about to zip it up when Emmy spoke.

"Can you send me the video? I want to put it on Twitter. Oh, that reminds me, you went viral again and-oh my god, I think one of those kids must have put you on TikTok." She twisted to address Jonathan, showing him the reaction to their photoshoot on social media.

Jonathan raised one eyebrow. "*We* went viral," he said.

Only Jonathan could make going viral drip with suggestion. But Emmy had to admit that maybe he was right. She'd prepared herself for trolls and haters to make shitty comments about her weight, but to her intense delight and surprise, they hadn't really materialised. Ninety-nine percent of the tweets were positive and encouraging. Not that she really cared what other people thought, but it was nice to know that someone her shape and size could be accepted next to an Adonis like

Jonathan, and that such images could be powerful and inspiring to others.

Of course, the majority of the love stemmed from Twitter's Romancelandia community, who went wild for the cover re-creation, making suggestions and requests for future photoshoots, and inspired by Emmy and Jonathan's example, sharing their own cover reenactment photos.

Beaming, Emmy scrolled through the rest of the photos Dawn had sent and was about to turn off her phone when something important occurred to her. She regarded Lizzie again.

"I took a photo of this headstone I found at the church yesterday. Can you do some digging? See if you can find who it commemorates?"

"Course...You know, I'm sure I know that guy's face from somewhere. Can't think for the life of me where though. I can try to trace him too, if you like?" Lizzie removed her own phone from her enormous designer black handbag again and pressed on the screen three times. "Sent! Now, are you sure you're okay without me?"

"No, it's ok. Let the police deal with him, whoever he is. And I'm fine," Emmy said, a note of impatience creeping into her voice.

Lizzie's freckled face broke into a knowing smile as she looked between Emmy and Jonathan. "I know you are."

CHAPTER 18

*E*mmy was glad they'd had the foresight to grab a burger beforehand. But even the memory of Jonathan's wide-eyed mock horror as he experienced his first McDonald's wasn't enough to dull the banality of the reporting officer's questions. At one point, Emmy bordered on the verge of hysterical laughter when Jonathan, leaning back and swinging on an uncomfortable office chair like a schoolboy, had slammed both his feet and chair legs to the floor. The detective, who'd been asking them to give a description of the shoplifter, had just opened a modern e-fit facial recognition program on his computer. Jonathan's face was such a picture of incredulity, Emmy had to weld her lips together to prevent herself from dissolving into giggles.

Detective Griffiths, a short, squat young man who looked more like a schoolboy himself than a police officer, wasn't sure if the shoplifter and the threats were the same person, but he was "keeping an open mind all the same".

Emmy had the distinct impression the detective didn't

believe her about the threats. Having deleted the messages, there was no evidence but her and Jonathan's testimony–and it was clear from Detective Griffiths' reaction to the taller, attractive, but slightly odd other man, that he considered Jonathan an air headed model type. Narrowing her eyes, Emmy took in his young-old moon face, the ravages of teenage acne still visible in the pits and craters of his skin. She was used to being doubted herself, but having Jonathan's integrity questioned was an affront she wouldn't stand for.

"Will that be all?" Emmy said, unable to keep the impatience from her voice.

The detective stood, his own chair scraping along the floor with a metallic sound that clawed inside Emmy's skull. They all shook hands in perfunctory fashion and Emmy breathed with relief when she and Jonathan found themselves outside the Heavitree Road police station.

The room they'd sat in for the last hour had been stifling, little bigger than a cupboard and decorated as sympathetically. It was true, the detective had apologised for the surroundings, citing lack of availability, but the longer she been forced to sit with Jonathan, their arms almost touching in the cramped space, the more erratic her mind had become. She couldn't explain why this closeness affected her so, it was less intimate than how they had been with each other before, especially considering their earlier shenanigans at the shop. But she couldn't deny the building electricity that had buzzed between them every time they touched, or the sparks that seemed to fly from Jonathan's eyes each time he said her name.

Inside, Emmy had been sure it was Detective Griffiths'

demeanour putting her on edge. Now standing here with Jonathan with the weak autumn sun riding high over the chimney tops of the red brick Victorian houses on the opposite side of the road, Emmy's mind was clear. It was Jonathan. It was always Jonathan, and her heart began to race again as she thought of the unspoken assurances between them.

"Glad that's over with." She hoped to sound breezy, untroubled, but the crack in her voice gave her away.

Jonathan's eyes raked over her face. He brought a hand up as if to touch her, but then let it drop by his side again. "Can I ask you something?" he said at last.

"Sure," Emmy said, fingers fumbling the zip on her coat.

"Why did you tell them my address is the same as yours?"

Emmy blinked. This was the last thing she'd expected. "Well… because we had to tell them something and I didn't think 'inside a book' would go down well. Besides, it kind of *is* your address, isn't it?" She shifted her weight from foot to foot. Theirs had to be the oddest case of co-inhabitancy she'd ever heard of.

Jonathan nodded. "When you put it like that, I suppose you are correct. But does it not bother you? The improperness of it?"

"Improper? After what you were doing in the shop earlier?" Hot and cold shivers bloomed inside as the memory flashed through Emmy's mind.

"I rather enjoy being improper with you, Emmeline." Jonathan shot a salacious grin.

Emmy laughed again. "Let's go home." How could three little words be impregnated with such promise?

There was a pause while Jonathan simply looked at her, then he nodded.

"Home."

He fell in beside her as she turned toward the city centre but didn't make any attempt to hold her hand, so Emmy stuffed her own into the pockets of her coat. There was a crisper feel to the air of late that promised log fires, falling leaves and pumpkin spiced lattes. They walked in comparative silence, crossing over into the Princesshay shopping centre, although Jonathan halted every few yards or so to gasp in disbelief at some new-found delight of modern life. Each time this happened, Emmy would try not to roll her eyes, explain what the technology or innovation was for or how it worked, and Jonathan would shake his head, exclaiming it to be a marvel. They didn't talk about anything of consequence and the closer they got to the shop, the tenser Emmy's mood became.

As they passed the cathedral, cool now in its looming shadow, Emmy looked up at centuries-aged edifice. She'd only been inside once and that was almost fifteen years ago as part of a school trip. Checking her watch, she saw there was time.

"Do you want to go in? They do tours up to the roof. It's such a beautiful evening, it seems a shame to waste it."

Jonathan's bright blue eyes darkened like ink-flooded water as he regarded the spot where the cathedral's north tower broke the skyline, a castle in the clouds.

"You've been up there before, haven't you?" Emmy surmised.

Jonathan hesitated. Then he smiled. "No. But I know someone who has. I would be honoured to go with you now."

THE SMALL GROUP of tourists they'd joined was almost silent as they climbed the steep, narrow stone steps in the Cathedral's North Tower. The staircase was a tight corkscrew, curving upwards in an oppressive, dimly lit anti-clockwise spiral. Jonathan's left hand grasped the rough, thick rope that curled around the interior circular wall of the staircase. With his other hand, he gripped the handrail that was fixed to the outside wall. Every so many steps, the gloom would lift as they approached one of a dozen or so narrow rectangular windows carved into the stone like eyes. Then they'd pass the window and the shaft of sunlight would recede, plunging them into shadows again.

The group's chatter was nervous, punctuated by the steepness of the climb and after a few minutes, Jonathan had the unpleasant notion that they were going in a never-ending circle. He stole a look up at Emmeline who smiled in encouragement and the irony of his epiphany was not lost on him.

After several minutes, the light changed again, becoming brighter with each step, until at long last the guide announced they were finally at the top. He opened a heavy wooden door and Jonathan was hit in the face by a blast of cool air. Trailing Emmeline, he stepped out onto a small landing where the guide opened another door in the wall opposite which took them out on to the roof.

The wind whipped around him, gnawing at his cheeks and Emmeline snuggled into her light raincoat, zipping it up to her chin, her honey blonde locks whipping in the wind. She stopped and waited, her eyes finding his, and Jonathan's stomach tightened as the mysterious pull between them sparked again. The guide was saying something, but Jonathan couldn't hear it above the roaring in his ears.

Taking her hands in his, he led her to a corner of the roof away from the others, coming to a stop at a gap in the crenellations. They turned together to gaze out over the city, neither speaking, and Emmeline's mouth fell open as she took in the view. For a moment, even she was pushed to the rear of his mind as his eyes swept across the horizon from the Blackdown Hills in the far distance to the East, to the last of the day's diamond-dappled sun arrows bouncing off the River Exe and the estuary beyond. He tried to pick out Powderham Manor, but the vista was obscured by too many modern rooftops. Thinking about his family seat was a mistake and he fought to rid himself of the unwanted memories which had formed in his mind.

"It's beautiful," Emmeline said.

Jonathan took her by the shoulders, twisting her body to face his. Her eyes glowed with unfettered excitement and his breath caught in his chest as the air hummed around them.

"It's nothing compared to you." Jonathan said, hoping to impart his words with every ounce of sincerity in his being.

Lifting her chin with one finger, he leaned towards her. She was so close now, there was a fleck in her right eye he hadn't noticed before. A fire spot his mother would have called it, but he didn't want to think about his mother now. The wind that had been swirling since they'd arrived on the rooftop dispersed, and the air crackled with magic as Jonathan wrapped Emmeline in his arms and kissed her. Like he had never kissed anyone before.

Too soon the guide was telling them that it was time to start making the journey back down. He beckoned the group to him, and Jonathan released Emmy with the grace of a man who didn't appreciate the interruption. Emmy rocked back on her heels, dizzy and breathless. She smiled at Jonathan and shrugged.

"I guess we better do as we're told."

Jonathan's answering look was so suggestive, Emmy blushed. "I'd rather break the rules right now," he said, his voice husky. But he went along with her as she tugged his hand. They rejoined the group and the guide led them to a door identical to the first one but on the opposite side of the roof.

"We'll now go down a short flight of steps and make our way to the gallery above the nave. There you'll be able to see the great window over the West Entrance. Then we'll head over to the South Tower and begin the descent back down to earth."

There was a slight titter at that, and one of the group– a young man wearing a hoodie with the words 'The Paranormals' emblazoned in large letters above a cartoon of a ghostly figure–spoke. "That's what we've come to see." He nudged his companion, an older bearded man, in the ribs. The other man gave them all the benefit of a hirsute toothy grin.

"Ahh yes," the guide said with the briefest glances to the heavens, "the ghosts of the South Tower."

The group huddled closer, eager to hear more. The guide launched into the legend of the Exeter Cathedral ghosts: A priest and nun who had been sent to oversee the spiritual rebuilding of the Cathedral in the fourteenth century. Local legend had it that the nun and monk began a forbidden relationship, falling passionately in love.

"When it seemed that their time together must come to end, they committed suicide, and their spirits are said to haunt the tower in search of each other ever since." It was clear from the guide's voice that he held as much belief in this tale as he did flying pigs.

Jonathan stepped forward. "That is not entirely true. Martha Dewberry was no nun. She was a witch who placed a curse of extraordinary potency upon Father John. That they loved one another, I have no doubt. Yet the good monk was not of sound mind when he chose death."

The guide regarded Jonathan with misgiving. "Are you a local historian?"

"It is a subject I am versed in, yes" Jonathan said, flashing a wide smile. The rest of the group looked at Jonathan in a mix of appreciation and awe, and one woman stared at him with undisguised lust. Emmy wrapped an arm around his waist and pulled him close. The guide however didn't appear to be convinced and turned on his heel, leading them through the door and back down into the shadowy recesses.

The journey down the South Tower was–if possible–worse than the ascent. Darkness was encroaching outside, and the space was lit with a faint orange glow, which seemed to emanate from within the walls. The steps were narrower, and Emmy lost her footing at one point, a yelp escaping her lips as she clung to the rope. She stumbled into Jonathan's solid back–he was leading the way ahead of her this time. He turned at once, strong hands on her upper arms helping to set her back on to her feet, his expression so protective a heady rush of embarrassment and delight spread through her veins.

When at the bottom the guide pointed out a cat-sized hole cut into the base of a thick oak door, Jonathan's 'I told you so' smugness was almost too much to bear and Emmy punched him on the shoulder. He chased her giggling and shrieking through the cathedral, which earnt many reproachful glares from the other patrons and guide.

At last they reached the exit, laughing like children. As they burst out of the west door into the twilight Jonathan grabbed Emmy's fingers in his. He tugged her to him before picking her up and spinning her high in the air. Emmy shrieked again, hot, elated blood at boiling point. Then he fixed his arms around her waist, allowing her to slide along his body. Her stomach pressed into his chest, his mouth at her breasts, down, down, down she slid, until eventually their lips found each other.

Breaking apart without urgency, they walked arm in arm away from the cathedral, up the wide steps and across the Cathedral Green towards South Street. The city hummed with the late evening shoppers. Commuters fell into two groups: weary and shuffling their work-tired bodies onwards, or liberated and free, sprinting for their bus or train. Emmy had a smile for all. Even the harsh, danger-red of a fire engine blaring past them down Fore Street couldn't put a chink in her happiness. But moments later, as they turned into West Street, Emmy's world shattered.

CHAPTER 19

The fire engine was parked at an angle across the narrow street, front end encroaching into the small car park opposite the shop. People ran everywhere. Shouting and hollering only added to the chaos. The light on top of the engine was a nightmarish disco ball casting a weird blue glow over the darkening scene. Round and round the blue light went and Emmy's fragile, carefully cultivated grip on reality slipped several notches. Fire-fighters milled at the entrance of the shop and the acrid smell of smoke mixed with heady petrol hit Emmy's nostrils at the same moment she broke into a run.

"Emmeline, no!" Jonathan's voice seemed to be coming from both far away and from inside her head. Before she could take more than a few yards down the inclining street, he caught her from behind, clamping his arms around her.

Emmy fought but he was too strong. "Let me go! Breone's in there–and The Book!"

Jonathan released his vice-like hold but came to stand

in front of her. "Breone will be okay... and never mind about The Book." He swept his hair back. "You are more important than either. Now, if I let you go down there, do I have your word you won't attempt anything rash?" He was breathing hard, his eyes never leaving Emmy's face. Every two seconds they flashed a brighter blue than was possible without contact lenses.

Emmy couldn't speak. She nodded, swallowing back all the fears in her throat. She allowed Jonathan to take her hand and together they rushed to the makeshift barrier that had been placed in the road. A harried fire-fighter passed by them, unravelling a long hose and Emmy took her chance to call out to him.

"Hey! That's my shop. Have you seen my cat?"

The fireman glanced up and gave her a small, tight smile. "I can't say much right now, but we don't think it's as bad as it looks. I'll send the Chief over to you. Stay back behind the barrier."

Emmy nodded and waited. Jonathan's arms were wrapped around her again but this time they were a comfort rather than restrictive. One by one, the fire-fighters exited the shop and Emmy squeezed her eyes to try to see inside through the big window. But it was too dark to make anything out. There didn't seem to be a huge amount of damage to the exterior, a grey shadow eclipsed the glass in the door and the door itself was blackened around the bottom, some of the white paint blistered and peeling.

After what seemed like hours, the chief fire officer came to speak with them, the glasses on her wise owl-like face reflecting the streetlights which had illuminated minutes earlier.

"Assistant Chief Davies," she held out her hand and shook first Emmy's then Jonathan's with a practised double pump like a politician. "You'll be relieved to know no one was hurt. I'm sorry but we haven't seen a cat. We assume it must have gotten out before we got here. The damage is minimal. Mostly minor smoke and water damage which shouldn't take too long to disperse, and the door will need replacing. There's a scorched patch directly behind the door on the floor. It couldn't take hold because of the stone flooring, thank goodness. So many of these old Tudor buildings have oak floors. I'm afraid you won't be able to go in tonight, and possibly tomorrow. We have some more investigating to do and so will the police because it looks like arson."

"Arson?" Jonathan repeated before Emmy could reply.

Emmy's heart thudded. Who would want to do such a thing? She refused to believe someone wanted to destroy her shop. But then cold terror washed over her. The threats. The messages. Surely whoever it was didn't want her dead? That was ridiculous. She tried to think of all the questions she knew she should be asking but the chatter that had just begun in her head drove everything else from her mind. *Oh god, not now.* Rubbing her forehead, she turned to Jonathan.

"I need a drink. Please can you go and get something?" She pressed a five-pound note into his palm. To her surprise, he didn't hesitate.

"I won't be long." And he was gone, sprinting back up West Street with long strides. Emmy closed her eyes. She couldn't spare any time on the fact that she'd just let Jonathan loose in the big new city on his own. He'd be ok. He'd have to be.

She looked back at Chief Davies. "I have to take medication. It's quite urgent."

The other woman understood. "Do you need anything from inside? I can get someone to grab a few things for you."

Just Breone and The Book.

"No, I've got the meds I need here," she patted her handbag. Thank goodness she'd remembered to top up her 'out and about' supply. "Thank you though." The idea of a stranger going through her things gave Emmy almost as many chills as the thought of the arsonist, and as much as she wanted to ask them to bring her The Book, she couldn't bring herself to do it. How would they know which one for a start? If only she could be sure Breone was ok, she could concentrate on riding out this attack until Jonathan returned with a drink. She really ought to start carrying water.

As if on cue, Jonathan returned. Out of breath, he held out the bottle to Emmy before bending over, clutching his sides. Assistant Chief Davies gave them another nod and marched back to take charge of the scene.

"Thanks," she took it from him, untwisted the lid and swallowed two tiny white tablets in less than ten seconds. The unwelcome voices in her head competed with her own thoughts, but this was a battle Emmy was determined to win. She focused. Hard.

How was she going to pay for the damages? Yes, she could claim on the insurance but that could take weeks, months even. Was Breone curled up safe somewhere? Hopefully the threat of fire was enough to make her lazy moggy get off his arse for once and find an escape route. God, she was doing such a bad job of looking after

Maggie's shop and cat. Not to mention falling in love with Maggie's mystery man himself. And she really ought to make an appointment to see Doctor Harrison soon. Her attacks were occurring with alarming frequency.

Jonathan had recovered so she rested her head on his shoulder, glancing up at him again almost immediately. "How long have you got before…" But she couldn't make herself say it.

"Before I disappear?" His eyes were fixed on the sky. "Perhaps two, maybe three hours? I cannot say for certain."

Emmy gave a little stamp of her foot. "Then you must stay here, at the shop. You can't come with me tonight." Her throat was closing again. The impossibility of their situation paralysed Emmy's heart as if the arsonist had ripped it out of her chest and crushed it in front of her. "If you leave and later disappear, how can we be sure you'll be able to return again?"

"I'll wait until it is quiet and sneak back inside. Simple enough to do in my 'other' form. But none of that matters now. The only thing that I care about is that you are safe. Where will you go tonight?" He stroked her hair, catching a few tendrils between his fingers.

"Lizzie's, I guess. After I've dealt with Detective Griffiths." Emmy said rolling her eyes, as a police car carrying her least favourite copper arrived on the scene. "I know who I'd rather be spending my evening with."

Jonathan smiled again, but this time it was bittersweet. "I know, sweet Emmeline. It seems that whatever magic it was that brought us together, is now conspiring to keep us apart. Maybe we have upset the balance of the world and this is its way of restoring order?"

"I like the instability," Emmy said with heavy irony. "I better go see the charming Detective Griffiths. Stay here and stay safe and I'll come back for you tomorrow. And if you see Breone, give him a big hug from me."

And with that, she flattened herself against Jonathan's chest, kissing him with all the love and passion she could muster. A knot of terror twisted and tangled in her gut, leaving a scar of a possibility too frightening to imagine. But her imagination was not to be outdone. No matter how hard she tried to prevent her greatest fears from taking shape in her brain, no matter how much emotion she hoped to impart with her kisses, how deeply she wanted—no *needed*—him to understand how she felt, it wasn't enough. The unwanted notion came rushing in on a tidal wave of love, a tsunami of heartbreak. What if this was very last time she would see him?

LIZZIE PICKED her up from the police station, her usual exuberance replaced by a quiet attentiveness that made Emmy anxious, even with the diazepam. She would have preferred the too-loud scatterbrain. Tugging at her coat sleeves, she hunkered down in the car seat, paying scant attention to what her friend was saying. When they arrived at Lizzie's, Thom was waiting in the drive, one of the black and white kittens arching around his legs. *Netflix or Chill?* Emmy couldn't tell them apart and her heart plummeted as Breone's unknown fate struck her anew.

Once inside, Lizzie showed her straight to the guest bedroom even though Emmy had crashed there many times before. Thom trailed behind them not speaking. Tall and possessing a symmetrical yet nondescript face, one could be forgiven for assuming Thom Sorensen was a Danish sunglasses model, when in fact he hailed all the way from exotic Dawlish. A man of few words, he didn't hover. That was good. Lizzie on the other hand was going to be a different story.

"Oh, thank god you and Jonathan weren't in. Do the police have any idea who could have done it?"

Emmy perched on the edge of the bed, her fingers picking a nonexistent spec of fluff off the duvet. "They didn't really say. Just asked a lot of the same questions they'd asked this afternoon." She yawned, exaggerating the action with a theatrical stretch of her long arms and legs.

Lizzie took the hint. "I'll leave you be. Do you want a cuppa? Thom's going to go get a takeaway in a minute. I'll tell him to order you a sweet and sour chicken."

"I'd love one." Emmy didn't enjoy being rude to her friend but she didn't have energy to spare right now. As soon as Lizzie closed the door, she collapsed back on to the bed. The drugs in her system insisted she needed sleep, but Emmy fought them. She had to think.

For a few hours this afternoon she'd experienced a happiness she never thought she could feel again. Her heart mixed a potion of love, sorrow and desperation into her veins. How could one person be expected to cope with this avalanche of emotion? It was too much. Maggie, Breone, the shop, the fire, the arsonist, her illness, The Book. Jonathan.

Just when she thought she could start again. That maybe, just maybe, she'd be allowed to be happy, everything came crashing down on her in a perfect storm of emotion that left her hugging herself as if she was outside in a sudden downpour.

How could she have let herself think that she and Jonathan could ever be, when today's events with the fire only served to highlight the most obvious obstacle to their happiness? All the same worries she'd had yesterday after sharing their first kiss now hurtled back to her. She should be in Jonathan's arms now, kissing him, exploring his body in all the ways that made her tingle with delight. But because of who he was, where he'd come from, because of his curse, she couldn't. He wasn't real, and no number of stolen kisses at the top of Exeter Cathedral could change that.

If The Book had been destroyed in the fire, everything would be over and that wasn't a risk Emmy could take. Because the fire wasn't the cause, merely a symptom. It would be something else preventing them being together tomorrow. But how could she *not* risk it? He was her life now. Everything she did revolved around him. And then there was the small matter of what might happen if they did somehow break the spell—something they were no closer to achieving. Irrespective of Jonathan's declaration of wanting to stay with her, what if he couldn't? What if they were doomed to be torn apart, one way or another, after all?

Emmy clung to the hope of seeing Jonathan's face again tomorrow, grabbing it to her like a lifeline in a sea that rolled with wave after wave of seemingly unsurmountable problems. When Lizzie knocked on the door a minute later, Emmy didn't answer, for she was finally drifting into an uneasy, dream-filled sleep.

CHAPTER 20

*W*hen Emmy woke the next morning, it was to find a mug with a pink Post-It Note stuck to it on the chest of drawers by her head. She didn't own any Post-It Notes, pink or otherwise. Brow furrowed it was another two seconds before the events of the previous day caught up with her. She sat up too fast and her head whooshed. Three consecutive days popping sedatives wasn't something she was used to, and she didn't fancy making it a habit. Resting her head again on the pillows now propped up behind her, she reached out for the mug. Hot tea. Tearing off the note, she screwed up her still sleep-addled eyes to read the scrawl:

Gone to the library to do some research.

Help yourself to more tea, toast or whatever else takes your fancy.

Will call later, Lizzie x

Her mouth dried as she considered this small kindness. She'd have to apologise for how she'd acted last night. Lizzie would understand, she always did. But right now, Emmy had more pressing matters to attend to.

She made a quick phone call to ascertain whether she'd be allowed back into the shop that day, hushing the tiny part of her that hoped the answer would be no. It would be too easy to hide away. When she'd rung off, she grimaced as she got out of bed in the same rumpled clothes as yesterday (why had she been too embarrassed to let the fire service collect her belongings?) The faintest whiff of smoke permeated her sweater, jeans and hair, and she wrinkled her nose. Memories shuffled through her mind like cards, some more welcome than others. And today she was going to make some more, except these were the kind she'd rather forget.

The kittens sniffed around her as she pottered between the toaster and kettle in Lizzie and Thom's kitchen. Emmy smiled as she recalled the day she'd explained the true meaning of the saying "Netflix and Chill" to a naïve Lizzie, who'd gone on to insist that it was too late to rename the cats now. Other memories returned: nights out, holidays, school days; reading a poem she'd written as bridesmaid at Lizzie and Thom's wedding. It was preferable to fill her thoughts with happier times. She'd have to face reality soon enough.

She took the milk out the fridge and put it back again three times before realising she hadn't used it. Not tasting her breakfast, she chewed and swallowed then headed to the bathroom in search of mouthwash. It was going to be hard enough to do this in yesterday's knickers. There was no way she could say what she had to say today with dragon breath too.

A shaft of sunlight reflected off the glass frame

housing Lizzie's family tree illustration and Emmy paused in the hallway with a doleful smile. Lizzie was lucky to be able to trace her ancestry back so far. Ten generations of Burroughs leapt out of the drawing, as alive today through Lizzie as they were to the ink and paper ghosts of the past. Emmy touched the space where Lizzie had left room for her great, great, great something grandmother, careful not to leave a smudge on the glass. Emmy's only living relatives were her parents. Two of her grandparents had died before she'd even been born. But then eyes fell upon the space where Lizzie's late mother's name was inscribed, and Emmy's heart was filled with a pang of anguish for her friend and all that she'd lost at such a young age. She'd come this close to losing her own parents, but even so, she didn't think she couldn't truly understand how Lizzie must feel.

After a final scratch around each of the kittens' ears, Emmy slung her coat and bag over her shoulders and left the house, locking up with the spare key before hiding it under the chipped plant pot by the front door. Then she walked the few blocks to the bus stop, her heart breaking into lung-piercing splinters that took her breath away with every step.

The bus ride was short. Too short. Emmy alighted in Fore Street and began to wander down the pavement but changed her mind and spun around to take the more circuitous route down Stepcote Hill instead. She couldn't face retracing the steps she and Jonathan had taken back to the shop last night. At the top of the hill she halted as the image of the hooded figure watching her after Maggie's memorial service came flooding back. This was followed by the memory of flinging herself, terrified and confused, into Jonathan's arms.

Her powers of recall were determined to make this difficult no matter what route she took, so she hitched her bag higher on her shoulder and took a deep breath before heading down the sweeping stairway. Each step was the harbinger of another heart wrenching recollection and by the time she'd reached the pavement at the bottom, the fingers of her left hand were on her mouth again as Jonathan's kisses sifted through her mind. Turning left, she fixed her eyes on the door and finally, after what felt like forever, reentered her shop.

The sweet, pungent smell of smoke and petrol hit her first and she brought a hand up to her mouth again, breathing fast. Her stomach rolled, chest tightening. *Don't throw up, don't throw up, don't throw up.* Emmy closed her eyes and waited for the sensation to pass before venturing further into the shop, rooting herself to the spot, allowing all her happy memories of the old store to nurture her resolve. The shop was its own ecosystem and she was part of the flora and fauna here as much as the books, and she'd be damned before she let anyone tear it away from her. A ragged black circle on the floor by the door was the only charred blot on the landscape. She wouldn't try to remove it. It could stay as a reminder of all she'd nearly lost.

The silence was almost unbearable, so she called out two names, the second of which died on her lips as her eyes fell on the telephone box.

"Breone? Jonathan?"

There was a thud above her, and she held her breath, eyes wide as she watched the stairs. The muscles in her thighs fluttered as she waited, then she sagged with relief (or was it disappointment?) when the fat, squashed face of the ginger cat padded down the steps with zero sign of urgency. He sauntered towards her, tail swishing high like a pennant.

"Oh Breone." She scooped the cat up and carried him over to the sofa where she sank into the cushions without thinking. Burying her face in his fur, Emmy clung to him for warmth, knowing what she had to do. But first, she was going upstairs to freshen up.

Under the hot blast of the shower, she considered the option of 'just not doing it' but that was the coward's way out and wouldn't be fair to either herself or Jonathan. Washed and changed, she swept her hair into a messy bun and made her way back downstairs into the shop. The Book was in the same place Lizzie had left it yesterday. Reaching up to the shelf, she took it into her arms, cradling it with more care than ever. Then she returned to the sofa where Breone was now curled up, fast asleep, a fluffy orange striped scatter cushion.

Emmy closed her eyes after reading The Book, steeling her heart against what seeing his beautiful face would do to her resolve. The sound of impending doom echoed inside her head: dun-dun, dun-dun, dun-dun... Only when her mind was quiet did she open her eyes and look at Jonathan. Her meticulous planning hadn't worked. Her defensives collapsed.

"I can't do this anymore," she said in a cracked voice.

"Can't do what?" his words were gentle.

"This. Us." She gesticulated to them both. "It's too much. I fooled myself that it was enough, for you to be here like you are now and that it didn't matter you had to keep leaving. But I was lying. It's not enough. I can't live like this, knowing at any moment you might disappear and never come back. What if The Book had been destroyed yesterday? What would happen to you? You'd be stuck inside forever–or worse. I can't take that chance. It's killing me that I can't be with you fully, like I want to be–and on top of everything else that's happened lately, it's making me ill. *More* ill. I need stability, not this–this saga of never-ending angst. My heart might be strong enough to absorb the ups and downs, but my mind isn't."

Jonathan took three heavy, solemn footsteps away from her. When he turned back, Emmy gasped at the anguish in his eyes. "What are you saying, Emmeline? What do you wish me to do?"

Emmy got to her feet, arms wrapped her torso. "I don't know. All I know is that something's got to give because I don't have the strength to carry on like this. I can't stop whoever it is who wants to hurt me, I'm stuck with this pathetic excuse for a healthy mind and if I give up the shop, I'd be leaving you anyway." The tears came in earnest now, a tsunami of grief that laid waste to all in its path. Shaking, choking, Emmy longed to run to his arms and lose herself in him. But their predicament was hopeless, so she let her head fall and allowed herself to cry out all the pain and suffering that had built like a moat around her heart.

Jonathan was by her side in seconds, his big arms cocooning her with the comfort she desperately craved yet needed to reject. She tried to dislodge herself from his grasp, but he was too powerful. He held her, stroking her hair, murmuring in her ear, until she quit fighting and the final sobs wracked from her body.

"We need to talk, without interruption," he said, before spinning on his heel. He marched to the door, locked it, then returned to Emmy. Shepherding her to the staircase, he followed her up into the flat. Emmy didn't speak as he deposited her on a chair in the pokey lounge with extra care, as if she were a fragile porcelain doll that might break at any second. Emmy watched as Jonathan moved into the open plan kitchen, hesitant hands filling the kettle and switching it on, mistrust all over his face. Her heart fluttered a little at their domesticity and she caught it, stamping it into nothing before it could spread wings.

She had to give him credit. The tea wasn't bad considering it was his first attempt. She blew across her cup, giving herself time to get her thoughts in order. He was going to try to change her mind and she couldn't allow him—and all his endearing, tea-making sexy as hell ways—to distract her. The sight of Jonathan's uber masculine form now sitting in what was Maggie's chintz and doily festooned living room was both a shock and unintentionally funny. Jonathan however didn't appear to be perturbed by his surroundings. He picked up a floral-patterned cushion and lodged it behind his back. Clearly, he'd been here before, and he began speaking before Emmy was ready.

"I shall leave you today and not return. I cannot live with myself for being the cause of your distress or ill health, but before I go, I would like for us to speak with complete candour for once." His blue eyes blazed with a potent concoction of love and despondency, and Emmy replaced her cup on the small coffee table with shaking hands. Was she really going to let herself say goodbye to him?

"I have told you before how strong you are, how awed I am of you, but it is only now that I think I truly understand it myself. Please, tell me about your illness and the man who hurt you," he leaned forward, his hands that had been clasped in his lap now folding around Emmy's own. "If I am cursed to remain in The Book, then I would rather that curse be worthwhile. I cannot imagine anything of greater value than existing for eternity with my every thought being filled by every facet and detail about you. What would be the point in such anguish if it were not absolute? Tell me everything, please Emmeline."

Emmy's insides ached, even her bones seemed to cry out in pain. Sighing, she fixed him with a penetrating stare. "Okay, but I have one condition." If they were going to do this, they might as well do it properly. Maybe this would the best, most cathartic way of getting over him. Or maybe it would be the final straw that broke her.

"Name your price."

"You tell me everything about you, too."

There was no hesitation, no hint of deception in Jonathan's eyes as he replied: "Yes."

So, Emmy spoke. First telling Jonathan about Dan the Dickhead and how he had fooled her for so long. How she'd convinced herself that she loved him enough for them both and how when her symptoms had first manifested, he'd used the knowledge of her delicate grasp on reality to try to shame and trick her. How he'd taken the broken jigsaw puzzle of her mind and scattered it to the wind.

There are still pieces missing.

"You know, he almost had *me* convinced at one point," Emmy twisted the corners of her mouth into a semblance of a smile. "Of course, the sicker I became, the easier it was for him to cheat. My hallucinations gave him the perfect alibi. And the worst part was that he managed to convince everyone else of it too. My parents, work colleagues, Lizzie. I tried to tell them that it wasn't me, that I knew what I'd seen: the text messages, the receipts in his pockets for hotel rooms and champagne. The emails from "work" planning business trips. And then there was my writing... When we first met, Dan was super encouraging about it. He'd ask to read everything, even though I'd tell him it wasn't finished, and he was always ready to brainstorm plot bunnies and characters with me."

Emmy drew her knees up to her chest and she took a sip of tea before continuing.

"But something changed around twelve months after we'd moved in together. He no longer had time to read and started making odd remarks about my writing being a waste of time. That's when I should have realised, and maybe if my mind hadn't chosen that time to break, I might have put two and two together.

"Over the next few months, my grip on what was real slipped to frightening lows. I became convinced people were following me and talking about me at work. I couldn't watch television or listen to the radio because I was sure there were other voices in the background telling me awful things, like I was fat and ugly, or I couldn't write, and that I didn't deserve to live. During this time, Dan cheated on me with at least seven different women that I know of. There were probably many more. Then I caught him in bed with a work colleague and even then, he tried to tell me I was hallucinating. That night, I sent my boss a new chapter from my book. I guess all my psychoses must have started to creep into my writing because she told me later that it was some scary shit. I don't know, I've blacked it out. I do remember I tried to kill myself that same night, however." Emmy's voice cracked on the last sentence. She had to keep going. Push on through. Don't think about how it made you feel at the time. Don't think about how it makes you feel now. Don't think. Just speak.

Teach us to care and not to care.

Jonathan had moved from the seat opposite her to the arm of Emmy's chair. He scooped her into his arms, neither of them saying anything, and held her for several moments. When he let her go, Emmy avoided looking at his face, trying to remain numb so she could finish telling her tale.

"That's when they sectioned me—we have laws now that mean you can be taken to a secure hospital for your own good, so you don't hurt yourself. But the worst of it was that nobody would believe me about Dan. Nobody except Maggie. They all said it was just another symptom of my illness. He pretended to be the dutiful partner when I was released—oh, he was good, I'll give him that." She let out a hollow laugh at this and for a moment paused, lost with her memories.

"I remember how he charmed my mum, even through the fog of drugs I had to take during those first few weeks. But then he tried it on with someone from my work, only he didn't know she worked with me. The day I confronted him and heard him confess to everything was both the best and worst day of my life. Even then, he tried to blame me, but I'd had enough. My mind was tougher, and I could differentiate between reality and fantasy. I went back to work. My parents flew home to New Zealand and the doctors were happy with my progress. I kicked him out and haven't had a major hallucination since...until these last few weeks.

"I have schizophrenia, Jonathan," Emmy said, her voice now stronger, no longer faltering the way she had throughout the retelling of the Dan the Dickhead episode. That's what she liked to think of it as, a moment in her life, like her teenage obsession for *Twilight*. Monumental and all-encompassing while it lasted, but she was a different person now. Or at least it had been. Now recent events had brought it all crashing back. "It's an illness of the mind, a mental illness. It means I sometimes hear and see things that aren't real, but my brain convinces me that they are. And sometimes I get panic attacks because I'm scared of what I might see or do. It's hard not being in control of your own thoughts."

She got up and went to stare out of the window, tugging her sweater cuffs down around her wrists. A pale, yellow sun was a pearl caught in a net of clouds. Her stomach, which had been knotted with queasiness for most of the morning, untwisted. This was the most she'd spoken to anyone about her illness and her past, even more so than Maggie. She leaned against the window, the glass cool on her forehead. But Maggie had wanted Emmy to find The Book, so she could meet Jonathan. Maybe it was him she was meant to be telling after all. But what use was it if she couldn't write? Because surely that was the key to breaking Jonathan's curse? She had to write–or rewrite–The Book, and the very thought of it made her skin itch and her heart turn over with terror.

She'd once seen an internet meme about Kintsungi,

the Japanese art of repairing broken pottery by filling the cracks with gold. The belief was that when an object suffers great damage, rather than cover up its broken history or throw it away, the flaw adds unique value. Making it more beautiful and something new. Emmy couldn't imagine ever being able to repair her broken pieces.

Jonathan moved to stand behind her, and Emmy sensed he wanted to hold her again.

"Emmeline."

He didn't speak again so she had no choice but to turn and look at him. A small jolt of surprise kicked her in the stomach when she registered the tears in his eyes.

"Why do you not believe me when I tell you how strong you are?" He whispered.

"I'm not strong." Emmy lifted her chin. "If I was, my mind wouldn't be able to play tricks on me so easily."

He swept his hair from his forehead, a two-handed sweep. She'd pissed him off, she could tell.

"I am not educated in these matters. In fact, I wager most people would know more about illnesses of the mind than I do, given that in my time, mania and hysteria were things to be feared. Hearing voices was surely a sign of witchcraft," he held up a hand as Emmy made to interrupt, "but, I am not a fool... You may not be a witch, but you are the strongest person I have ever met. I see it in your eyes when you think you cannot endure another setback, another challenge. There's a mettle inside of you that burns brighter than the forging of any sword in a furnace. It glows even though you do not know it, like a beacon in the dark. You have a never surrender spirit that both captivates and intimidates me."

He dropped to his knees at her feet, clasping her hands in his own. "It was never my intention to hurt you, Emmeline. God knows you've been hurt enough."

Emmy took her hands away and gripped the back of his head, running her fingers through his curls as she pulled his face to her stomach. Then she laughed despite how her heart was tearing into two. "You finally said it."

"What?" Jonathan cocked his head to one side, looking up at her.

"I'm not a witch."

She laughed again, and he joined her. The sound released the tension in the room like someone letting gas out of an overinflated balloon.

"I just explained how much you intimidate me and that is what you picked up on?" Jonathan's answering grin was tender as he stood up, reaching out to tweak her on the nose. "What am I going to do with you?"

Emmy's own smile was filled with bittersweet emotion. Stick to the plan. That's all she had to do. Swallowing, she brushed past him and headed to the kitchen to refill their mugs. When she was done, he was sitting in Maggie's armchair again, his jaw set, eyes stormy.

"Your turn." Emmy prompted.

CHAPTER 21

"*I* come from a long line of witch-hunters, but you won't have read about my family in any book. This was long before Matthew Hopkins declared himself Witchfinder General, you understand. Yes, I have studied this subject, trying to educate myself about issues I only knew one side of. I was on, what people would now call, 'The Wrong Side of History' I believe. Witchfinders were paid handsomely for their services. After my seventh birthday, my father began taking me with him on witch-hunts. You cannot begin to imagine how exhilarating this was for a young boy. I saw things you would not believe, things that would shock and scandalise you. Things no boy should have. One of these being the trial and execution of my own mother for witchcraft..."

His voice trailed off and it was a moment before he resumed, his mind haunted by the ghosts of his past. "My childhood was bereft of strong female role models. As far as my father was concerned women were categorised into three groups: young, old and witches. The first two, he further distinguished in that old meant undesirable. I am sure I do not have to spell out what being young classed a woman as."

He stood up, restlessness and shame powering his footsteps. "I am not proud of it. My father was not an honourable man, and for the first twenty-eight years of my life, I was his duplicate. I was young and easily brain-washed. I remember feeling more emotion when he told me how my great, great grandfather was killed by a witch in a nunnery than I had during my mother's trial. That's how indoctrinated I was. I aspired to be just like them, these brilliant, popular, cruel and ultimately unattainable men whom I hero-worshipped. When my father also died by a witch's hand, my world was destroyed. I inherited the title, land and status as respected nobility, but none of it mattered to me. I was consumed with rage, a need to avenge their deaths by killing any who practiced witch-craft once and for all, and I took up my father's mantle as chief witch-hunter with relish. Often arbitrary in my own accusations, I did not wait for proof of guilt. I have lived with the knowledge of this shame for centuries. Nothing I can do can atone for my crimes."

"It was Martha wasn't it? The witch who killed your great-grandfather? The one who pretended to be a nun in the cathedral." Emmy's voice was level with under-standing.

Jonathan halted. "Yes, it was she. My great, great grandfather tracked her across the county from Dartmoor and thought he had her cornered, but she was more powerful than he gave her credit for. There was once a time when I did not care for the nuances of humanity. Back then I was convinced that was only good versus evil.

It was only much later that I learned that witches are just like everyone else and there are degrees of light and shade within witchcraft in all its forms. A great many of the "good" kind were hunted and killed simply for practicing arts such as midwifery and healing. But you must understand, it was a time of great mistrust and suspicion. Non-witches were also often falsely accused–some would claim to hear voices. All met the same watery fate." His eyes shot up at Emmy's answering flinch. The knowledge that he was yet again the cause of her suffering was a sword to his gut, twisting and pinning him with guilt and shame. He hurried on before the anguish in her eyes could pierce his steadfastness.

"Martha, however, was consumed with the worship of the devil. She'd disguised herself as a nun and took refuge in a nunnery in Barnstaple. After appearing to get away with killing my great great grandfather, she grew in confidence, accepting a summons to return to Exeter to oversee the Cathedral works. This was where she met Father John. My father chose to believe she had killed herself because she knew he was coming for her, but years later I realised that it was John's love that both saved and condemned her. For him she repented and found God. I have never forgotten her final words before she flung herself from the tower. 'I am whole now'."

"You were there?" Emmy breathed. "That's why you knew so much about her yesterday. Why didn't you tell me? I would never have suggested we go there if I'd known."

"No, I was but a babe in arms. But my father was. Anyway, it is many years long since departed and forgotten. Time is not only a great healer it also aids in the blurring of memories and I have had a lot of it to do my penance. Exeter Cathedral is no more a source of distress for me than any other building. But I digress." Jonathan came to sit again. "You remember I told you about Lady Catherine?"

Emmy nodded, pouting.

Jonathan threw his head back as his laughter filled the room, relief rising in waves that he'd successfully navigated one of the most dangerous territories of his past terrain. "You *are* jealous! Do not deny it. I sensed it yesterday too when Lizzie was telling you about what happened with the thief."

Emmy's cheeks shot pink like the sting from a whip and her eyes fell. Jonathan's mirth was short-lived as he took in her despondency.

"I am sorry, Emmeline. I would have never hurt you." Jonathan cupped her hands in his, eyes no longer glittering.

"I know," Emmy said, and the words wrapped around his heart, daring him to believe they could be true. She removed her hands from his and settled into her chair, picking up a cushion and hugging it like a shield. "You were saying–about Lady Catherine?"

Jonathan sighed and raked his hair.

"Lady Catherine and I… it was complicated. Like I told you, her husband was moving to overthrow Queen Elizabeth and there were whispers that he was consorting with witches. More than whispers. I think Lady Catherine saw me as her way out. She used me as much as I did her. Believe me when I say there were no broken hearts in our relationship. The one thing I came to regret about our affair was the night we caught up with her husband, for that was the night I first encountered the witch who damned me to this." His speech was alive with his past now, rather than haunted by it. "At least, I used to regret it."

Emmy's normally bright eyes ransacked his face, misery swimming in their depths. She was trying to hide it, but Jonathan sensed her sadness. At least his tale was almost over, and he could put an end to her suffering.

"The witch we found him with was young and alluring. She escaped our clutches that night because none of my party, including myself, realised what she was. But something about her called to me," he glanced up suddenly, steely determination in his eyes, "it wasn't love, if that's what you're thinking, although I confess to feeling lustful in her presence. She was, as I said, very attractive. Moreover, she had a magnetic quality that compelled me to her. As if fate, destiny—whatever you wish to call it—intervened. I searched for her again, alone this time, my quest taking me into the passages below the city. It was only after I found her... after I'd slept with her and scorned her proclamation of love, did I learn she was a witch."

His voice grew stronger and he gripped Emmy's fingers between his own.

"I am not proud of it. I *was* my father's son, after all, but something in me changed that night. When she used her magic on me, I didn't see it coming. I was too self-absorbed, too wrapped up in myself to understand what my rejection did to her until it was too late. I shall never forget the look in her eyes as she wrote the words to damn me to eternity in limbo. The hurt I had inflicted pierced me like no blade ever could. If I could escape, I swore to myself I would never hunt witches again and do everything in my power to protect them, and anyone accused of the craft."

He was suddenly on his knees before her, tears glistening in his eyes.

"You have to know though, Emmeline, I am reformed, long-since changed and repentant. I thought I'd learned all there was to know about my mistakes. I thought I'd done enough these past five hundred years to atone, but then I met you and my whole earth shifted on its axis anew. I was so afraid of falling for you, afraid that I would lose myself and my desire to be free, but what I didn't understand was…I was already lost. And in finding you I found myself again. My humanity. You became my shining star. Your compassion, my new compass."

The tears began to flow then, and Jonathan let them, each one a demon drawn from tortured soul as poison from a wound. Each saltwater drop imbued with his story and history. It was an exorcism. Soon there would be nothing left of him but an empty shell, a hollow where a once proud man had stood. But he welcomed it. Because he would be nothing without Emmeline anyway. Nothing but her mattered anymore.

"You are my true North, Emmeline. My South, East and West. And even if you should recoil from me, from all that I have done, as I fully expect you to, I shall remain eternally grateful for the time we have had together. For the chance to have loved you and been loved by you, even just for a short while. I will treasure it and keep it with me forever."

∼

THERE WAS silence after Jonathan finished speaking, punctuated only by the ticking of the antique clock on the windowsill and Breone's loud purring, for he had skulked into the room unnoticed by either of them. Emmy lifted herself up out of the chair and padded over to the cat to stroke him, examining her reaction to Jonathan's tale, his confession to being a Witchfinder and the dark history surrounding his family. Her dream made sense now, as did that unsettling feeling of rage she'd experienced when she'd discovered him reading her words. She scrutinised herself for signs of the same emotion. She should be repulsed by all he had done, and yes, a part of her was. She tried to qualify her knowledge of the Jonathan she knew—the good Jonathan who only ever tried to please her and take care of her, the Jonathan whom Maggie had befriended—with frightening images of the man he'd described. Her mind rebelled at the idea of such a correlation. There was too much good in him now, surely? It was so clear. The number of times he'd put her needs before his own, helping her with the shop, the photoshoot and videos, his sonnet. Those couldn't be the actions of a bad person. It was an over-simplification to see him in such black and white terms. *Of course* he held some morally grey areas inside, just as she herself wasn't an angel. Just as it was with every human on earth. Because what are human beings but living sacks of contradiction and conflict wrapped in an elastic skin? But something deep inside, deep down in the truth of her marrow knew he was a changed man—and a kind one too at his core.

Those things should count.

Then there was also the matter of his curse and how he had suffered since—with good reason most would agree, including Jonathan himself. But how long is too long a penance? How much atoning can one make before their sins are forgiven?

Emmy didn't have the answers to these questions and so instead, her thoughts shifted to something else Jonathan had said. His insistence that she was jealous. Was she so transparent? After all the probing of her feelings, the times she'd convinced herself that she didn't care who Jonathan talked to, who he laughed with. Was this to be *her* curse? The final burden bestowed upon her by Dan's infidelity? Would she ever trust again? It was a moot point anyway because Jonathan was leaving and there would be no one else she wanted to trust. Not after him.

"You must be hungry, Lazybones," she said, picking up the cat who went floppy in her arms, purring louder still. He was definitely losing weight. At least she hadn't failed at everything.

She placed Breone on the kitchen tiles, while hunting in the cupboard for his food. It seemed like a lifetime ago that she'd found The Book and her thoughts at the time returned to her now. *Who was Lord Jonathan Dalgliesh, and could he live up to Fitzwilliam Darcy and Henry De Tamble?* Well, now she had her answers. A man who had seen and done many terrible things. A frightened and isolated boy who idolised his brutal father. A deeply loyal, supremely arrogant, yet conflicted soul, who had come to learn the error of his ways? Emmy's mood at the impossibility of their situation blackened further.

Their love was a faulty firework that had sputtered, choked and died before it could explode into life. Its mangled, charred remains lay smoking on the scorched ground of her heart. Jonathan was far from perfect boyfriend material–book or otherwise, and Emmy suddenly realised she couldn't begin to despise him for the man he'd once been. Not when she loved the man he now was.

She hadn't heard him move and started when he appeared behind her.

"So, now we know everything there is to know about each other. This is when we are to part." Jonathan's voice was thick with emotion.

Emmy's chest heaved with sudden, silent sobs. "I guess so. I'll never forget you." She took a step closer to him. She could do this. She had to. Even if it meant not knowing what it would feel like to lie in his arms, to kiss him again, Even if it tore her apart from the inside.

Jonathan's smile was his most tender yet and Emmy's already fragile heart pulverised to nothing. Like dust, she thought in delirium.

"Goodbye, my sweet, strong Lady Emmeline," Jonathan said, picking up her hand one last time and brushing his lips against her skin with the gentlest of kisses. Almost immediately, he began to fade, time slowed and the air in the room decompressed so that Emmy sucked for breath. He was evaporating into nothing and soon, even the dust would be gone.

"Jonathan, wait!"

CHAPTER 22

*a*s Jonathan's form swam back into being, the tautness in Emmy's chest released and she gulped down huge breaths as if she'd been suffocating. Jonathan looked at her, a wary hope etched upon his beautiful features.

Was she really going to say this? Biting her lip, Emmy spoke, "I know I said we should end this...but...wouldn't it make more sense to–you know–do it properly before we call it quits?" Hot, nervous energy flooded her cheeks and chest, amongst other places, and she turned to fuss Breone.

Jonathan only stared at her, his face giving away nothing.

"Aren't you in the slightest bit *curious*?"

"About?"

"What it's *like* in 21st century?"

"I'm confused. Are we not *in* the 21st century?" His pupils dilated a fraction and a ghost of a smile fleeted across his lips.

Emmy's heart rate doubled. "I don't mean us, well no, actually I do." Why was this so difficult? She was a strong, independent woman, wasn't she? She should be able to do this. It was only a word. She took a deep breath and said in a low voice, "I mean...sex."

Please don't make me spell it out.

"What are you saying, Emmeline?" Jonathan finally asked, one eyebrow raised in roguish fashion.

Yup, you're making me spell it out.

She gulped again and spluttered, "Make love to me?" Emmy didn't know what to do with her hands, first bringing them up to cover her face, fingers splayed as if she was watching a scary movie, before pressing them together in front of her nose and mouth in an attitude of prayer. Then she dropped them to her side, fingertips circling around her thumbnails. Jonathan was taking a long time to speak. Too long.

With not just one but a double two-handed sweep of his wavy hair, Jonathan opened his mouth to speak, closed it again and then took one step closer to her.

"By Christ, Emmy. What do you want from me?"

"You," Emmy said in a small voice. "I just want you."

"But you want me for what, one time? I suppose I do have it coming. Nothing like a bit of divine retribution to teach the scoundrel a lesson."

Emmy threw her hands up in agitation, shaking her head. "No! I didn't mean it like that. Although it is funny if you think about it. Don't pretend being used is hurtful after what you told me about Lady Catherine. After everything I've read."

Jonathan's face darkened. "Lady Catherine was different. We both wanted something from each other."

"And you and I don't?" Emmy raised her chin in defiance.

"I only want to love you."

Emmy's retort died on her lips. She laughed, soft and hesitant in the silence that followed. "I think we want the same thing."

Jonathan took another step nearer and Emmy's heart which had flatlined just moments before, restarted with a jump.

"Then why are we arguing?" he asked, a glow burning in his eyes, dying embers coming back to life.

"I don't know." A single tear tracked down Emmy's cheek and she melted as Jonathan's fingers swept it away.

"Then stop crying and come here."

Emmy sniffled, collapsing on to his chest with a laugh that turned into a sob. Jonathan's arms embraced her more tightly than ever and as she looked up into his eyes, he smiled.

"Can I just check something?" His voice was soothing, but there was a note in it that spoke of unfulfilled promises.

Emmy nodded into the concave space at his throat, her fingers entwined in the dark hair there.

"You aren't planning to have your wicked way with my body and cast me aside after all then?"

The bubble of laughter that escaped Emmy's mouth echoed in the shivers that ran through her body. "No, I'm not going to cast you anywhere," she said. "But I am going to have my wicked way with you."

She stretched up to kiss him, and all her earlier conviction evaporated. As if she could give this–*him*–up so easily. An indescribable rush of love, desire and need swept through her and she tugged his hand, urging him to follow her into the bedroom. Once there, they broke apart, glancing at each other for an endless moment, the bed now between them. Jonathan was the first to speak.

"Are you sure you want to do this? he asked.

Emmy nodded. Big nods. "Hell yes."

Jonathan's sexy smile sent Emmy's lust into overdrive. With agonising slowness, he closed the distance. When he reached her he trailed one slow finger along her cheek, across her lips and down over the smooth expanse of skin above her breasts. Paralysed by the power of her need, Emmy could only watch as he dipped his head to leave barely-there kisses on her mouth and heaving chest, retracing the path his finger had made moments before.

Desperation sent a delicious kick to her belly and she grabbed fistfuls of his glorious curls, pulling his head back up to her lips. Their kisses deepened. Thrills of delight and agony burst like firecrackers beneath her skin. Her knees buckled as his hands cradled her breasts, brushing at her nipples through the fabric of her clothes, which hardened almost instantly at his touch. With busy fingers they both worked fast to lift her sweater over her head, before unbuttoning her blouse, removing her bra, jeans and underwear. Pride in her body settled over her as she stood in front of him naked, liberated and uninhibited, waiting for his reaction. When it came, it didn't disappoint. She'd never felt this powerful, this in control. That she could have this kind of effect on him sent her mind spiralling into orbit, drunk on its powerful aphrodisiac.

"You are so beautiful. So strong." Jonathan said, his voice soft and awed. "And to answer your question, when it comes to you, Emmeline, I'm curious about *everything.*

Every smile, every kiss. Every breath-taking, meandering, glorious curve of your body *and* your mind. I'm greedy and I want to lose myself in *all* of you."

He began to undress, and Emmy resisted the urge to assist him. She'd dreamed of this moment too many times to waste it now. Standing back, her mouth went dry as he removed his shirt and jeans. When he got to his briefs, she murmured in appreciation as the completeness of his masculine beauty was finally revealed. Then she couldn't control herself any longer and flung her body at his. Pushing him back on to the bed, she answered his lazy smile with one of her own as she climbed on to his lap, her hands exploring every inch of his washboard abs and hard, hairy chest.

"Hold on," Emmy said, leaning across him to the small chest of drawers beside her bed. She rummaged around inside the top drawer for a moment before her hand emerged again clutching a small box. Jonathan's eyebrows drew together as Emmy removed the condom from the foil packet. Then, as understanding dawned, his eyes widened in wonder.

"I think *I* better do this," Emmy giggled.

"Be my guest," Jonathan replied, his voice husky.

The way he lay completely still, a look of pure worship on his face as he watched her roll the condom down. It was the single most erotic thing Emmy had ever seen.

When she was done, he leaned forward and kissed her, trailing whisper soft lips on her neck and throat. She cried out as first his fingers and then warm mouth closed around her nipples. The gentleness with which he touched her was both perfect and infuriating and Emmy's self-control balanced on a knife edge.

He must have sensed her restlessness because his kisses became more urgent. Emmy responded by grinding herself against him. His head inched down her body with each brush of his lips. Her breasts, kiss. Stomach, kiss. Down, down until he buried his face at the apex of her thighs, kissing, caressing, licking and teasing until she arched off the bed, calling his name.

Sinking on to him was like slipping into a memory half-forgotten, a story yet to be told or a lifetime yet to be lived. His eyes held hers, hands and lips extra gentle. Time slowed, spinning, deepening. There was the heady scent of vanilla, the smoothness of his skin, the hard tautness of his naked body, completely real and moving beneath her, with her, inside her. Their breathing raced, muscles clenching–quickening. Jonathan whispered her name in reverence and silent tears stole from Emmy's eyes, as the fragmented pieces of her heart began to fuse together. T

The joins where she was once broken, now glistening with words engraved in gold.

FROM THE SECOND he had first laid eyes on the beautiful young woman through the leaded window of Adams' Antique Books, to their first gold-dust kiss downstairs beneath the chandelier, to moments earlier when Emmeline had removed her clothing, revealing every delicious curve of her generous body, Jonathan Dalgliesh had been convinced he was dreaming. There was no way, no possible twist of fate, which would mean that this vision could be meant for him. It was too fantastical, too miraculous to even contemplate. He was unworthy. And so, he had refused to believe in miracles, even as one happened upon him.

Yet, here she was, naked and glorious, riding him with unbridled abandon. Her eyes were closed, but small gasps of delight escaped her generous lips. Lips which only moments earlier had sheathed his cock like a velvet scabbard. Her spectacular breasts swung heavy in his face, and he clasped the nipple of one between his teeth, reveling as it hardened in response. Granted, Emmeline's surprise request that he take her to bed had caused a blade of panic to flash across his thoughts, tightening his chest with uncomfortable, unfathomable knots. He could barely acknowledge the fear which threatened to unman him, but he made himself face it.

What if - after all this time - his traitorous cock refused to stand? What if he failed to satisfy her?

It was this last question which terrified him most. Not the possibility of humiliation, but the idea that he might disappoint Emmeline, when pleasing her was the only thing he had longed for and dreamed of for weeks now.

But his fears had been without merit. Maybe it was the magic he sensed whenever in her presence, or perhaps it was simply Emmeline herself, but something about kissing her, about the smooth expanse of her skin, of losing himself in her cries as she came to pieces around his fingers and tongue, made him feel as if he could accomplish anything. That maddening veil, which usually shrouded his existence outside of The Book, had evaporated into nothing at her faintest touch, and he wanted nothing more now than to wallow in her wetness, drink in her delicious rose garden perfume and luxuriate in every inch of her pillow plump softness. He had never felt this alive, not even *before*. It was as if there was enough of her to breathe life for two.

She moaned now and opened her eyes, pushing down on him with even more urgency. If only they could stay like this forever. For the first time in five centuries, Jonathan felt the hand of Time shift in its inexorable hold upon him and the knots in his chest unraveled in tandem with the tightening of Emmeline's orgasm around his cock, his own undoing following immediately in response. Where once he had felt as if he was drowning in days, now it was her engulfing him, and he gladly let it.

"Jonathan! I–"

The sound of his name on her lips tipped him over the edge and he slammed into her, his fingers clutching handfuls of her fleshy buttocks. With one last effort, he lifted his hips to meet hers and then gasped, collapsing against her in beautiful, devastating, sweet relief.

"Emmeline Walker," he whispered, breathing ragged and choking back tears as he cupped his hands around her darling face and forced her to look at him, "I know I will never be worthy of your love and I do not begin to understand your curiosity in me, however grateful I am for it, but I must tell you: I love you. You have given me hope again. I don't know how it's possible, but you make this cursed man feel like the luckiest man alive."

IT WAS three hours later when their conversation grew into something more than softly muttered exclamations and words. They'd made love again twice, each time more tender than the last and Emmy had drifted into a slumber of exhausted yet satisfied bliss, her head nestled in the crook of Jonathan's arm. She traced lazy circles in the hair on his chest, a strange and bewildering contentment washing over her. Had she ever been this happy? The sinking sun cast lengthening shadows across the room, and she lifted her hand to a shaft of sunlight where thousands of particles glittered and whirled. If she could bottle time, this would be the moment she'd choose.

But time was a luxury she didn't have. Whatever magic had brought them together, a sixth sense told Emmy that this bliss couldn't last, not unless they could find the answers first.

Time.

Indefatigable, unrelenting, unforgiving Time was all around them. She felt it in the spaces between her heartbeats, sometimes luxurious, slow and unwinding, but then frantic and portentous. Each second that ticked by was a harbinger of whatever fate awaited them. They'd wasted too much of it already and they were no closer to discovering the answer to Jonathan's curse. Granted, there had been distractions aplenty, but Emmy couldn't shake the nagging doubt she was missing something obvious. She pouted as she unfurled herself from Jonathan's arms and threw back the covers.

"I was enjoying that," Jonathan said with a lazy drawl.

"Hmmm, me too, but we've got things to do."

Jonathan raised one eyebrow. "We?"

Emmy grinned. "Yes, we. Now get up." She whipped the duvet off him revealing his glorious nakedness. A now familiar warmth bloomed deep within her belly, an echo of the orgasms that had washed over her in delicious waves only minutes earlier, and it took every ounce of restraint she could muster not to climb astride him again.

She headed to the kitchen, occupying herself with mundane tasks as she allowed her mind to wander. The ginger tom purred a grateful reply as she set extra biscuits down, his orange bottle brush tail curling around her legs. Then she dressed before joining Jonathan in the lounge, carrying two steaming mugs of tea. He was sitting on the couch, a small magazine wrapped between one finger and thumb, a closed expression on his features.

"Tea?" She didn't want to ask him what was wrong and focused instead on setting his mug down on the table without spilling it. What if he'd changed his mind? But then she shook herself. Declarations of love and good—no, *great* sex weren't going to tear down all the walls she'd built around herself. Stuff like that only happened in books and movies. That wouldn't be fair to either of them, but allowing herself to accept Jonathan's love for what it was had at least breached her defences. Whatever was bothering him, she needed to know, and she would deal with it.

"Everything okay?" She asked, sounding a lot braver than she felt.

Jonathan turned his face to her and at once his cloudy gaze cleared, his eyes as blue and wide as a Cornish sky. "Yes, forgive me. I was lost with my thoughts." He reached for Emmy's hand, tugging her down next to him on the small chintzy sofa.

"About?"

"Not about us, if that is what you are asking. Of one thing I have never been more certain. That you can still love me after everything you know is more than I deserve," Jonathan said, as he ran a finger along Emmy's jawline.

Emmy snatched her eyes from his, unable to bear his intensity. She cupped her mug in both hands and blew across the top of the steaming liquid, watching the surface eddy. "Then, what?"

Jonathan laughed. A deep, throaty sound that filled the room. "You are not going to allow me off the hook, are you?"

Emmy took a large swig of tea and immediately regretted it. The boiling liquid stung her tongue and mouth and she spat it back into the mug almost choking. Eyes watering with pain, she slammed the mug back down on the coffee table, sloshing tea everywhere.

"Shit!"

She sprang to her feet and dashed into the kitchen for a cloth. Avoiding Jonathan's eyes, she began mopping up the rapidly increasing lake of tea that was now spilling on to the rug. Only when Jonathan's hand close around her own, did Emmy look up at him again.

"Sit. Please?"

Emmy gave in, scrunching up the now sodden cloth and depositing it on the table. She got to her feet again and walked around the table to sit in the chair opposite. What on earth was wrong with her? *Don't answer that.*

Jonathan opened his mouth and closed it again. It was strange to see him so hesitant and unsure, he was usually so self-composed. Finally, he began to speak.

"I was not entirely truthful with you a moment ago, when I said I was not contemplating us," he said, his voice low. Emmy's stomach twisted in pain. *Here it comes.*

"For too long I was preoccupied with the desire to

return to my own time, but I am not sure what my time is anymore. My memories are clouded with shadows of the past. The weight of the man I was, of centuries of wrong-doing, presses upon my now. He is a spectre who haunts my every waking hour. Even if there was no future for me here, even if you rejected me as I am fully expecting you to at any moment, I should not wish to return to being *that* person."

Jonathan was on his feet again and Emmy let him walk. After a few moments, she spoke.

"But I don't understand. What does this have to do with us?" Her voice caught on the last word and she glanced away from him again, her throat dry. Her mind's eye pictured the black shadows where the smoke damaged walls met the whitewash walls and wooden beams downstairs. Suddenly, the smell from the fire assaulted her senses again. She could taste petrol and smoke on her lips. Perhaps Jonathan sensed her despondency because he was by her side again, his lips tender on her skin, kissing away her fears.

He cupped her face in both hands and whispered, "Because, my darling Emmeline, as I have already explained, I could not go back now. For that would mean leaving you. You, the bravest, most selfless person I have ever known, who freely offers her love to one such as myself."

"I'm not brave." Emmy frowned.

Jonathan smiled, shaking his dark head. "After everything you've suffered, to still be willing to open your heart to another is brave. Hope is an act of bravery. Loving someone is an act of bravery."

He bent to kiss her softy before straightening up again.

"So, you see, my love, you have captured me with your bravery, which presents us with a new problem. One that means we may have little time left together."

"What do you mean?" Emmy's heart thundered.

Jonathan let his hands fall from Emmy's face. "The Book, Emmeline. If you were to continue reading at such a pace." He fixed her with his gaze.

"The story might end?" Emmy's voice was a whisper. Her heart skipped then resumed pounding. "What do we do?"

"Maybe you have to stop reading."

"But then you won't be able to appear." Emmy stood up, hands on her hips. "That's unacceptable... What if I just reread parts I've already seen? Would that affect you?"

"I don't know."

Emmy shook her head with vehemence. "We'll just have to figure this bloody curse out." A ghost of an idea had formed in her mind, and she pounced on it.

Jonathan wasn't listening. Instead, he'd picked up the magazine again and was peering at it with curiosity. It was one of those free local magazines that came through the door every now and then, filled with the usual mix of local interest pieces, adverts and gardening tips. The cover was emblazoned with a bright orange pumpkin carved with a Jack O'lantern face.

"Hallowe'en?"

Emmy looked up. "Yeah, I take it you know what that is?"

Jonathan's face darkened. "Hallowe'en was a time when communities came together to build great fires to ward off evil spirits. It wasn't a celebration as such, but it was steeped in tradition. Of course, some would use it as an excuse for merriment. I should have been at one such burning the night I was cursed, but I was young and foolish, and went witch-hunting instead. Tell me about it today."

Emmy studied him for a moment before deciding he did really want to know. "It's probably quite different to what you remember. The history of it comes from the festival of Samhain, a Celtic tradition, but Halloween today is its bastardised American offspring. You know, ghosts and ghouls and all things that go bump in the night. Now, it's more commercial than traditional and people still use it as an excuse to get pissed." Emmy rolled her eyes. "Kids go trick or treating, which is where they dress up and knock on doors for treats. It used to be that they would play a trick if you didn't comply but that's died out, thankfully. Mostly it's an over commercialised holiday, steeped in old and odd tradition."

"Ghosts, you say?"

"Yeah, why?" Emmy sat forward, picking up the magazine.

"You know how easy it was to scare that thief yesterday? We've done romance novels–and most agreeable that was too." Jonathan's eyes danced with scandalous humour. "How would you feel about a Halloween event?"

Emmy stood up, her mouth dropping open as her mind considered the possibilities. "A Haunting at the Bookshop? You'd be happy to do that?"

"I don't see why not. It could be fun." Jonathan grinned, pulling her down into his lap and kissing the tip of her nose.

Emmy gave a little shake of her head. "There's no time. Halloween's in two weeks, we'd never get it organised."

"What is there to organise?" Jonathan shrugged. "Stick that video Lizzie sent you on Twitter with a notice saying there will be more ghostly goings on and people will come in droves. If there is one thing that I am sure of, it is that the supernatural always draws a crowd. The only thing *you* need to do is sell lots of books. Leave the rest to me."

Emmy had to admit he might have a point and set about crafting a suitably spooky Tweet. She turned her face to him again, finger hovering over the send button.

"But… you've done so much already. It feels wrong, especially when I can't help free you." She disentangled herself from his embrace, the warmth in her chest abating.

"Emmeline," Jonathan breathed as he enveloped her in his arms again, "You already have."

He kissed her, and as he covered her with his body, Emmy's heart was gripped with a conviction she'd never felt before. She had to find the answer now and she had an idea where to look at last. The ending of The Book.

CHAPTER 23

1568

*M*y plan is fraught with danger, but something compels me to go alone. I slip away from the bonfire unseen. The crackles and hisses send shivers through my skin and I fight to keep my mind on the task in hand. Magdelene. I cannot explain the hold she has over me. Something about this mysterious young woman calls to me. Destiny? Fate? I cannot say. Yet all I know is that my mind has been consumed by her ever since we first encountered her with Lord Somerset. Of course, given his proclivity for consorting with known witches, we immediately suspected her, but she surprisingly passed the tests.*

I make the entrance to the tunnel with good time, the whoops and cheers from the bonfire far behind in the distance now. With one last check that I have not been followed, I lower myself into the dark gap, thankful I had the foresight to bring a torch. I have to stoop most of the way and twice bile rises in my throat as the stench becomes overpowering. Grasping a handkerchief to my mouth, I grimace and keep going. It will not be long now before the tunnel opens up into the chamber where I know she will be waiting for me. How I know this, I cannot say.

After a few minutes, the darkness begins to lift, and my legs almost turn back. But she compels me onward once more and the next moment relief floods my veins as her beautiful face comes into sight.

"I knew you would come," she says in a voice so sweet, she must have stolen it from an angel.

Her white blonde hair emanates a soft glow like a halo and her blue eyes dance in the flame from my torch, sparkling like icicles. She moves toward me, padding gently like a cat, disrobing as she comes, until she stands before me naked and ethereal. My chest tightens, and I whimper as she places my hand upon her breast, her upturned face now inches from mine.

HER CRIES still echoing around the chamber, I climb off her. I yank on my hose, unpleasant over the slick sheen of sweat on my skin, but I pay no heed. There is still time to get back to the bonfire and the festivities if I hurry. My head is clearer than it has been in days and as I chance a look at Magdelene again, I shake myself. Yes, she is young and beautiful, but there is nothing special about her and certainly nothing ethereal.

"Are you leaving so soon?" Her face is pained, and I turn away, saying nothing.

"Look at me, Jonathan, please. I love you," Magdelene says at last.

Her pleas bounce off me and before I can stop myself, I laugh, releasing all the pent-up tension and confusion I'd felt this past week. Her face falls and changes, distorting into something monstrous that rips the laughter from my throat as a scream.

Dawning realisation grips me with an icy hand. That she is practised in the art of witchcraft, I am now certain, for it is not only her eyes that hold a special brand of magic. It dances from her fingers in devilish sparks. It is in the sound of her voice, soft and hypnotic, a siren call. If I don't resist, she will have me truly under her spell, and that, as the Queen's chief witch-hunter, I cannot permit. But I have been bewitched by her all week and now the enchantment has suddenly worn off after our lovemaking. I stumble backwards, scrambling on my behind for the way out, tearing the flesh of my hands on the rough floor. But Magdelene is quicker.

Drawing herself up to her full height, she looms over me, casting deformed shadows on the walls. My throat closes over, every nerve ending on fire.

"Deceiver!" she cries, conjuring a large leather-bound book from the air, mumbling a chant I can't decipher. Her voice grows louder and louder until the words ring from the roof of the chamber. Her curse is the last thing I hear before my world disappears and my beating heart ceases.

Bound by word
Bound by paper
A life captive
Bound forever
Bound in flesh

Bound in blood
Gaol eternal
Bound to book"

~

2018

EMMY SNAPPED The Book closed with a gasp. What was it? A prophecy? A grimoire? How many shocks could one person take? Perhaps this is what it felt like to have your heart jump-started with a defibrillator. An ominous sense of finality crept up on her as she examined her feelings about Jonathan and Magdelene, the witch who'd cursed him. It had been a mistake to read the final page, but a part of her had known this was coming all along. Still, she had to be sure now.

"Jonathan!"

Silence. The air didn't change, the dust didn't swirl. Emmy's heart began to race. Slamming The Book down, she leapt out of her seat and called his name again.

"Jonathan, where are you?" Panic stung her like a million angry bees. She fought back a river of rising bile, spinning this way and that, eyes searching every dark corner. For one dizzying moment, her head swooned so badly, she feared another fainting fit.

"Emmeline," a gruff voice whispered behind her.

She spun, and her relief was complete. She ran to him, but pulled up short when the horrible, terrible truth caught up with her overwrought senses. The Jonathan that stood before her now was almost transparent. The letters and words that made his form no longer glistened under the lights. Instead, they were dull, wispy and fading fast, as if someone unseen was erasing them from history. He hovered between life in her world and certain death in his own. With a sob, Emmy reached up to stroke his dear face, her earlier shock about his story with the witch, Magdelene, now all-but forgotten, but her hand fell through air. It was like trying to touch smoke.

"What's happening to you?" She struggled to speak between harsh breaths.

"I don't have much time. I do not think I will be able to return." Jonathan said through obvious pain as he faded further still. His eyes widened in horror, a man witnessing his own demise, before forcefully fixing on hers.

"Emmeline, I lov-

Then he was gone.

Shock and heartache threatened to shut down Emmy's body. She couldn't give in to it. If she allowed herself to capitulate for even a second, she wouldn't be able to go on any longer. *Keep moving, keep busy.*

Wisdom is caring yet remaining immovable with our words.
Deeds Not Words.

Words Are *Deeds.*

Wisdom is caring yet remaining immovable with our words.
Be still.

Deeds Not Words.

Words Are *Deeds.*

Be still-

"No!" Emmy screamed. She tore round the shop, yanking books from shelves, letting them fall to the floor. A rage she'd never known consumed her and she flipped the coffee table, screeching again. None of it mattered now. Running to the bookcase she'd first found The Book in, she clawed at the shelves, scattering books and ripping pages. Her fingers gripped the edge of the top shelf and before she could stop herself, she brought the whole towering structure crashing down in a cloud of dust.

Her heart pounding and eyes wide, she held her breath.

What have I done?

But before she could castigate herself further, her attention was captured by an old oak door which had been hidden behind the shelves. Breathing fast, she tried the handle, but it was either locked or too stiffened with age to move. A movement at her feet startled her and she clutched her thundering chest. In a blur of ginger fur, the slimmed-down Breone meowed once before streaking through a small hole cut into the bottom of the door.

The key!

Emmy sprinted to the counter and pulled out the drawer, scrambling through pots, pens, and bits of paper, searching for the small rusty key she'd found in Breone's bell. At last her fingers had it, wedged into a corner at the back of the drawer. With gritted teeth, she tugged as hard as she could, finally pulling it free.

She stood in front of the door again, the antique key now clasped between thumb and two fingers. Swallowing, she waited until her hand was still before placing the key in the dusty lock and turning it.

A loud click reverberated through the shop, a haunting echo in time.

CHAPTER 24

*O*pening the door was surprisingly easy. Emmy had been prepared to put her back into it, but it flew inwards with the gentlest of nudges. Cold air swirled around her feet and she took out her phone to light the way. Peering into the gloom, a spiral stone staircase was revealed, and Emmy was forcefully reminded of her trip to the cathedral with Jonathan. Taking a steadying breath, she tiptoed down the narrow steps, one hand flat on the wall to balance herself. The darkness intensified after ten or so steps and an icy finger of fear ran a sharp nail down her spine.

Straightening her shoulders, Emmy pushed the sensation away and continued. Thick cold air brought the skin on her arms out in goosebumps and her nostrils flared as an unpleasant dampness wafted up to meet her.

Finally, the steps levelled out. Squinting in the dim light from the phone, Emmy could make out a fluffy ginger tail a few yards in front of her.

"Breone." She hurried over the cat, who purred in

reply before dashing off again. This time Emmy was faster, and she chased after him, into a large chamber filled with a radiant light.

"Hello Emmeline."

Emmy's heart stopped. Deep down she'd known all along who she would find here but to have her suspicions confirmed was mind-blowing.

Maggie.

Or should she call her Magdelene? Except it wasn't the Maggie Emmy knew. This woman was the Maggie from her dream: a YA fantasy queen Maggie, youthful, luminous and beautiful, but her blue eyes held that same devilish spark. Emmy stared in disbelief as the young woman glowed and pulsated with the strange inner light of an apparition. Then grief and anger took over.

"Why didn't you tell me?" She spat, taking a step forward. "I trusted you! Why didn't you confide in me about Jonathan, about yourself? I'm not some pawn for you to play a sick chess game with."

Maggie's face fell. "Oh, Emmeline. It wasn't like tha'. It wasn't like tha' at all."

She held out her arms, but Emmy folded her own over her chest and stood her ground. "No? What was it like then?"

Young Maggie turned away and walked over to Breone. The cat rose up on his hind legs and the familiar stranger smiled, scooping him into her arms.

"You've probably guessed by now he's an excellent mouser," she said, stroking his fur. "Or he used to be at least. When the cathedral retired him, he found his way to me through the tunnels. I think we put each other to good use. I am relieved to see he's lost some from around the middle. Gettin' a bit fat, weren't you, Bre?" She added, snuggling his battered face.

Impatience billowed in Emmy's gut. "Maggie. I don't care about how you got Breone, I want to know about you... and Jonathan." Saying his name was too much and she pressed her lips together, breathing hard through her nose.

Maggie settled Breone back down on the stone floor. When she looked at Emmy again it was with centuries worth of torment.

"I didn't mean for any of it to happen. I was in love with him, you see. I thought I was in love enough for the both of us. But he didn't love me. Back then he didn't have love in his heart for anyone. I bewitched him to make him fall in love with me." Maggie whispered, smiling sadly. "Yes, it is possible to make someone fall in love, but there's always a price to pay, as my grandmother, Martha, found out. This was powerful magick that I shouldn't have tampered with. Of course, once he'd taken what he wanted from me–thanks to the spell I'd put on him, of course–the enchantment broke.

She ran a hand over her eyes, seemingly lost in thought and for a moment the cavern was silent bar the growing whispers in Emmy's head. Then the clouds disappeared from Maggie's expression and she continued.

"I did not handle his rejection well. That was my second mistake. I cursed him and, as you now know, that curse was a lot more effective than my Love Spell. It was the most powerful spell I ever cast, so powerful in fact, that it rebounded on me, grantin' me with long life. Whether I wanted it or not."

Maggie paused again and each beat of silence clanged

inside Emmy's mind like a portent of doom. Her chest was starting to tighten, and the whispers were growing into a rushing in her ears. She held out one hand to prevent the older woman from going on, but Maggie didn't notice. It was as if she was exorcising something from deep within herself.

"I regretted it almost immediately. Not because of myself, you understand, but because of the half-life I'd condemned Jonathan to. Now some might say that as witch hunter and womanizer he had it comin', but who am I to make that call? No, it was an abuse of my power and from that moment on I did everything I could to reverse the spell, but my magick was never the same again. It was no use. Jonathan despised me at first, of course—and quite rightly too—but over time, we struck an accord, which eventually became a dear, dear friendship. And, as I'm sure you've discovered, he's not the man he once was."

Emmy's shoulders sagged, and she leant against the damp curved wall of the chamber for support. "I don't understand what any of this has to do with me though."

Maggie's eyes widened, tears gathering at their corners. "Because you, my darling Emmeline, are the most wonderful, most powerful Word Witch I have ever known."

Emmy was upright again almost immediately. "Oh, don't you start. I am *not* a witch."

"There are many types of magic and many types of witches, Emmy. Some are born into the gift. Some learn their craft over many years. Some can disguise it from others. But you? You have a special magic."

"Ugh, please don't even think about saying it's because

I hear voices because so help me, Maggie…" Emmy hands fisted at her sides, thunder and lightning crashing in her head.

Maggie looked astonished. "Goodness, no. I wasn't goin' to say anything about your illness. It's nothing to do with tha'. It's *writin'*. *Words.* There's a reason why I suggested your parents name you Emmeline. Deeds Not Words, remember? But for us Word Witches it's the opposite, Words *Are* Deeds. Well, not quite the opposite, more like *words can be as powerful as deeds.* Words have the power to change the world. Words are how laws are written, how treaties are documented. Words start and end wars. And romance writin' is the most powerful magic of all. We're supposed to create love and peace but making a Happily Ever After, it's the hardest thing to do because you have to truly mean it." Maggie's blue eyes blazed as she fixed Emmy with the full force of her five hundred plus years.

"Now, I know I said that it's impossible to make someone fall in love with you without repercussions, but I have a feeling that if you wrote a Love Spell, it might just work."

Emmy had to count to ten before she could reply. Her head pounded and her stomach lurched. The voices, for once, however, seemed to have ceased their incessant whispering and that gave her the strength she needed to say what she had to say.

"It was you, wasn't it? Making all those magical, unexplained things happen like the telephone ringing and my university notes appearing again? You did all that." She took a step closer to the other woman, pointing one finger at her as she did so. "You had no right to manipulate me like that."

Maggie titled her head and gave Emmy a benign smile.

"No Emmy. That was all you."

Emmy let out a sound that was somewhere between a sigh and scream. "What do you mean it was me?"

"I told you," Maggie said, "You're the most powerful witch I've ever known. Magick always needs an outlet and for you, it's in your words. But it creeps out in other ways too."

Emmy had had enough.

"Jonathan is dying. It's probably too late already," she gulped, a sudden grip of grief and denial threatening to derail her. "And if you think I can write him back to life, your mind is even more messed up than mine. You know I can't write, not anymore. Not after what happened with Dan. And as for your hocus pocus bullshit, you can stick it. What do *you* know about love? You just admitted you put a spell on someone to make them love you–and it didn't work! I've had enough of this. I'm going back to London. Someone is contesting your will. Did you know that too? Someone is after the deeds to the shop and no words of happily ever after are going to make them go away. This is real life, *my* life, not a fairytale." She tuned on her heel and made for the stairs.

"Emmeline, wait! It is possible I have a livin' relative. I am sorry I did not tell you before, but I had a baby. Jonathan's baby. I gave her away, but I know she grew up and was happy with children and grandchildren of her own. I lost trace of her descendants a couple of generations back but there's a definite chance her–*my*–bloodline is still alive today. But even if I had known that such person or persons existed, I still wouldn't have left the shop to them because I always meant for you to have it."

This was too much. Tears blurring her vision, Emmy stumbled away from Maggie, who was no longer a beautiful and powerful queen, but now a rather sad and pathetic looking old woman, fading fast. Breone scampered up to Emmy's heels and she grabbed for him, grasping him to her.

"Goodbye Maggie."

With a hole in her chest where her heart should be, Emmy and Breone climbed back up the stone steps and into the light.

~

SHIVERS WRACKED Emmy's body as she stepped through the door back into the shop. She clung to Breone's soft warmth. Why didn't Maggie tell her? Or Jonathan? So much for their heart to heart the other night. So much for telling each other everything. Overcome with the same sense of creeping loneliness and depression she'd had after the drama with Dan and the way he'd turned even her own family against her, Emmy sank to the floor. Putting her head between her knees, she cried and cried. Was there no one she could trust?

"Emmy?"

She looked up into Lizzie's anxious face. Her friend crouched down in front her and pulled her in tight, not saying anything. Emmy cried out all the pain and suffering in her heart and after a while, the tears began to slow. She sniffled and wiped at her soaking face.

"Your jacket," she moaned, pointing the damp patch she'd left on Lizzie's shoulder.

Lizzie shrugged. "Never mind that, it'll dry out. What's going on, Ems?"

Emmy searched for a way to explain without her having to go through it all again. She opened her mouth and closed it twice before finally saying, "Whoever is contesting the will can have it. I'm going back to London."

Lizzie's eyes widened. "Oh, Ems." She drew her in for another hug. "When I got here and saw all the chaos, I thought something terrible had happened. I called Dawn because I was too chicken to go through that door on my own. She'll be here any minute. I'm so sorry."

Emmy rested her head on Lizzie's shoulder. There was something she needed to do but the thought of it made her skin crawl.

"It's not your fault," she removed herself from Lizzie's embrace and pushed up off the floor. Straightening her clothes, she fixed Lizzie with her eyes. "Any chance of a cuppa?"

Lizzie held out her hands, an invitation for Emmy to help her up. "Sure. Emmy?" she glanced back as she reached the stairs to Emmy's flat, "I know I wasn't always there for you with Dan, but I'm here for you now."

Emmy's heart turned over with love for her friend. It was exactly the kind of unconditional support she needed right now. "Thanks Liz."

She waited until the door closed upstairs before tiptoeing to the flipped over coffee table. Reaching under it, Emmy retrieved The Book, not caring about the words she read. When nothing happened, she threw it back to the floor. She dashed away fresh tears with the back of her hand and sauntered across to Breone who was curled up on the counter. Her phone beeped. Dawn had left a voicemail, but the line was too full of interference for Emmy to understand much more than: *"It's li... trust..."*

Emmy chucked her mobile on to the counter and was about to fuss Breone's head when a scrap of paper sticking out from under his fur caught her eye. She slid it out from beneath him and gave a short, humourless laugh. To say she felt empty inside would be a lie because that would imply that she had an inside, when the reality was that she was numb. It was as if she'd ceased to exist and her body was running on autopilot. With zero interest and in a monotonous voice she read aloud the spell she'd written weeks ago:

"Free from paper
Free from words
A life released
Time re-turned
Freed in flesh
Freed in blood
Life eternal
Rewrite the book"

IT WASN'T QUITE the same compressing sensation she'd become used to, but something happened, like a faint glitch or rip in time. Life flooded back into her body. She was suddenly aware of how fast her heart was beating, how loud her breathing sounded in the silence. Jonathan's faint outline appeared before her, and she didn't know whether to laugh or cry, settling for a strange hybrid of the two.

"Why didn't you tell me? You promised to tell me everything?" She worked hard to keep the accusatory tone from her voice, but the pain of his betrayal was too raw. A solitary tear escaped her eyes, like a prisoner, free at last, but broken.

A tiny muscle in his cheek pulsed; the heart of a small, cornered animal. His face was haggard, aging fast before her eyes and he spoke with great effort.

"I am more sorry than you will ever know. I promised myself I would never hurt you, thinking that by keeping the secrets of my past from you, I was protecting you. I was deeply ashamed of who I was, petrified that you would read about my exploits and want nothing more to do with me. But it was folly...." He drifted for a moment. "From the moment we met, it is you who has been protecting me. I thought that I could shield you from further pain by defending your memories of Maggie. The number of times when I told you how strong you are, yet I didn't trust that strength enough to confide in you. You remember I told you what Maggie said? She was right. You *are* magic, Emmeline. I only wish I'd believed in it sooner."

Emmy's determination to take him to task, which had been wavering during his speech, returned at the mention of Maggie.

"But what about your child? The one you had with Maggie? Didn't you think I needed to know *that* at least? And don't pretend you don't know what I'm on about. You knew what that name on the headstone meant the other day. Don't deny it."

"I don't. I am sorry, Emmeline. You're right, you did surprise me with the news about the grave. But Maggie swore to me she had lost the child. When you suggested the possibility that I might have had an heir, I was too shocked to admit the truth. The likelihood of it being mine and Maggie's seemed too outlandish. Not to mention the strong probability that any heir of mine is long since dead, as I myself should be. I was wrong to keep this from you, but I truly did not believe the grave and I to be connected." Jonathan's voice became weaker with every passing second, but he took a deep breath and rallied once more.

"Maggie's curse did more than imprison me inside The Book −it meddled with time. Perhaps Time has decided to redress the balance."

"I completely agree." Lizzie's loud voice rang out from behind Emmy, making her jump. She was studying her fingernails, an almost bored expression on her face. Except for her eyes, which glittered with a strange kind of excitement.

The sudden charged atmosphere sent a cold shiver through Emmy's scalp. What was going on?

"You know how long I've spent researching my family tree, Ems. It was so frustrating because there was always this gap whenever I got to finding out who my great-great- great- something grandmother was. I searched for years, unable to unearth any information about her, but I knew that she was important to me. Perhaps it was a sixth sense or something. Then you unlocked the mystery for me when you showed me that headstone." Lizzie smiled and smacked herself on the forehead. "Of course! The answer was staring me in the face all along."

Her heels clicked on the floor as she paced between them, the sound echoing inside Emmy's skull with sick foreboding.

Lizzie turned to Jonathan.

"You're right. Maggie hid the baby from you, but she gave her up to protect her from you and your witch-hunting pals. So, you did have an heir. Her name was Loretta and she was my missing link. The records didn't show her because Maggie never officially registered her birth. But she's my ancestor, as is Maggie and as are you. And now a descendant from yours and Maggie's sordid little tryst is the last thing you're going to see before you die."

Lizzie raised her hand and began writing on the air with her finger, whispering under her breath. Shock and confusion rooted Emmy to the spot. Before she could come to her senses, a series of sparkling letters appeared at the tip of Lizzie's finger as if she was using a giant invisible sharpie to write on to nothing with. Breone hissed from the counter, jolting Emmy out of her reverie and she lunged at Lizzie as the word "Erased" hovered between them. Jonathan moaned and collapsed to the floor.

"Jonathan!"

No, no no! This can't be happening? Not Lizzie!

After everything they'd been through. Working at the shop together and their shared love for Maggie. Birthdays, holidays. Drunken nights out and hungover mornings. How Lizzie had helped her pick up the shattered pieces of her life after Dan. How Emmy had been a bridesmaid at Lizzie and Thom's wedding and Lizzie had asked her to read out a poem she'd written especially for the occasion. Staying at hers last night after the fire. And what about just now when she said she'd always be there? Nothing made sense anymore. It was as if someone had taken the story of Emmy's life and turned it into a fairy-tale, but instead of handsome princes and happy ever afters, they'd rewritten it as a waking nightmare haunted by wicked witches and poisoned words.

And her best friend forever Lizzie was the chief antagonist.

The knowledge that all the people she'd trusted most in the world, first Dan, then Maggie and Jonathan, and now Lizzie, had all deceived her was almost too big a heartbreak for Emmy's already battered soul to bear. Maybe there was something fundamentally wrong with her? Why would everyone she loved keep betraying her like this?

Yet, even as she asked herself these questions, she still couldn't bring herself to believe the worst about her friend. Her head and heart both fought to reject the idea, to force it out before it could take root and twist into something too grotesque to be denied. Maybe she was dreaming, and she'd wake up soon. But the seconds ticked by, and the ticking from the grandfather clock resounded in her head with unmistakable portent. She had to try to reach out to her. To get her best friend back.

Emmy shook her head rigorously. "Lizzie, what's happening? I don't understand."

Lizzie smiled, but her face was no longer a Lizzie Emmy recognised. Distorted and wild, her expression was one of undisguised spite and Emmy shivered.

"I knew about him," she jerked her dark head at Jonathan, "years ago. I saw him disappear after talking to

Maggie when I was sixteen. You know, on the day I came to see her about coming to work her with you here? But she never trusted me, not even when I looked after her when she got ill. It was always Emmy this and Emmy that. Where were *you* then? Too busy with your new life in London to care, that's where. Why wasn't I ever good enough, special enough? Nothing I did seemed to matter. And what did I get in return? A musty old copy of Vanity Fair."

Emmy backed away, willing herself to wake up. Thackery's novel had always been Lizzie's favourite, and that musty old copy was a rare edition, worth thousands. "That's not true. Maggie was so proud of you. Look at everything you've achieved. Maggie used to call me every time you were on telly to make sure I knew to watch."

But Lizzie spat back. "You were always her favourite, Emmy. You must have realised that. Why else would she leave the shop to you and you alone? But you couldn't just go back to London, could you? It would have been so much easier that way. No matter. I overheard what she told you just now about witchcraft and writing, but what she failed to mention is that *I'm* her flesh and blood so this shop and everything in it is rightfully *mine*." She looked at Emmy like she would a bug under microscope.

"Pretending to be surprised when you told me about Jonathan wasn't easy, but I had to try to get rid of him somehow. I could see he was the only thing stopping you from leaving. And that day when I came back here with you and you read The Book, I had to hide my true self from him. That was some of the most difficult magic I've ever attempted, but like Maggie said, it comes in many forms. I just happen to be very good at concealment.

What I didn't know was *why* I'm a witch, but thanks to your and Maggie's little heart-to-heart just now, all my questions have been answered." She paced around the shop as she spoke, pausing every now and then to run a long, lacquered fingernail along the spine of a book.

Then she stopped and turned to face Emmy again, an unidentifiable expression on her face. "Another thing I've always excelled at is my ability to transport my readers to another time and place. You're not the *only* writer here, Emmy. So, now it's your turn. No one's going to question me when I call your doctor telling her you've lost your mind again. *Oh, it was so tragic. She just lost it and I couldn't do anything to stop her. Poor Emmy...*Ready to spend the rest of your miserable little life locked inside your own fucked-up head?"

Emmy's eyes darted right and left, searching for something to defend herself with, proof at last if she needed it of her non-witch status. And even though a tiny part of her was ready to welcome the release, it was only now, at the end of everything did she understand how much she loved Jonathan. How nothing he'd done in his past mattered. If he truly was dying, there didn't seem much point in carrying on. Her biggest fear now was that Lizzie would curse her to a lifetime of her illness. The thought made her blood freeze.

But her fight for survival kicked in when a sudden ginger blur crossed her vision. Breone, leaping into action with the vigour of a much younger animal, flung himself off a tall bookcase and was now clawing at Lizzie's hands and face. She shrieked and pushed him aside.

Oh no you don't! Emmy launched herself at Lizzie, mentally thanking her mum for blessing her with an overwhelming height and weight advantage. Easily over-powered, Lizzie stumbled and tripped, backing into a tall bookcase, which wobbled before toppling over. Lizzie darted out from underneath the falling shelves, but then screamed as it pinned her by the ankle.

A breathless Dawn came clattering through the door and Emmy whirled to learn what had caused this latest commotion. But her attention was immediately captured by the sight of Jonathan, crumpled on the floor. A page torn from an old book, crushed into a ball.

"Goodbye, sweet, strong Emmeline. I will always love you."

His voice was barely a whisper, but it echoed in Emmy's head as if he'd yelled it. She rushed to where he lay. He reached for her; one arm outstretched to eternity. Fingertips disintegrating into nothing as he spoke. Then his hand and arm, his whole body dissolving before her very eyes. Not just disappearing into letters as he usually did, but completely, irrevocably. As if he'd been erased from all existence.

Ink and paper.

Blood and dust.

Emmy scrambled across the floor to retrieve The Book from where she'd dropped it earlier, riffling through the pages, tears leaking from her eyes.

But it was too late, Lizzie's spell had wiped The Book blank. Jonathan disappeared and Emmy's world ended.

CHAPTER 25

$\mathcal{T}$he café where Emmy chose to meet Dawn was crowded. This was good. She hated being alone. That's when memories haunted her like wraiths, whispering moribund messages of all she had lost, taunting her with visions of a future with Jonathan at the bookshop that could never be. She sipped at her coffee, envy flaring across her chest like a struck match at the normality of the people around her. Two weeks had passed since that fateful night. The longest two weeks of Emmy's life.

Dawn appeared a few moments later, hovering over the table as if unsure whether to hug Emmy or not. Emmy made the decision and got up out of her seat, wrapping her arms around the shorter woman.

"Congratulations! When do you start?"

"End of next month. I want to get settled in Sacramento first so I'm heading over a few weeks early. Check out the apartment they've set up for me, that kind of thing." Dawn's eyes were bright and watchful. "Mum's throwing a 'Well Done for Passing Your Exams slash Leaving Party' Saturday after next, and one person who definitely won't be there is Mark. I broke it off for good this time. It's girls all the way for me from now on." She paused for a moment before adding, "I'll understand if you don't make it." They took their seats and Dawn lowered her voice.

"Lizzie confessed. Thom too. Of course, she didn't tell them about the witchcraft stuff, just the phone calls and arson shit. I still can't believe she did it." Dawn was wearing her bracelets again, which jingled as she rubbed her temples. Her cropped hair was now bleached white blonde.

"But why? I still don't understand..." Emmy's voice trailed off. Chances were she'd never understand.

Dawn rummaged in her bag and brought out a file. She opened it and removed a sheet of paper, upon which was a photocopy of a sepia-toned photograph. The print was grainy, and it was clear that the photo it had been made from had suffered damage here and there. A group of women smiled at the camera, their panelled coats, long skirts and oversized hats all indicators of a bygone era. Each woman had a sash slung across her body like ammo, the legend 'Votes for Women' clear to read. In the middle of the group stood a petite lady with fair hair, a mischievous glint dancing in the depths of her light-coloured eyes.

"The police found this photo at Lizzie's, along with a load of other stuff about her and the shop. Lizzie is convinced it's of Maggie. Somehow, she traced that headstone you found back to her and Jonathan. As far as my friend can tell, Lizzie considers herself the rightful owner of Adams' Antique Books."

Dawn gave a little shrug. "We can't be sure if she actually *is* a descendant of Maggie's–the records aren't clear–it's possible but not probable. But in Lizzie's mind, that headstone and her own investigations into her family tree were all the proof she needed. Add to that the fact that Thom's family seat owns the estate and the lease, and you can see where the prosecution case for motive is coming from. They think it's an insurance job, but they'll probably add coercion and endangerment charges too if they trace those dodgy calls and texts you got back to them."

Dawn's friend worked for the CPS. Emmy swallowed. She didn't want to hear any more, but Dawn wasn't finished.

"Remember the shoplifter?"

Emmy's head snapped up from a napkin she was tearing between her fingers. "What about him?"

Dawn sighed. "He was working for Lizzie and Thom. The police think they paid him to follow you around and make the calls. We know him, from school. Billy Westbrook. Remember him? Well, Billy changed his name to William Jones. Let's just say he's no stranger to the Exeter constabulary. They'll be calling you in a few days. They want to make sure they've got enough to charge Lizzie and Thom because it looks like Thom's lawyer is setting up Billy to take the fall."

Billy Westbrook? Emmy had had to refute his advances once in fifth year. Still, it was hard to reconcile the chubby-cheeked Billy from school with the shaven haired scruffy and hooded man who'd hounded her for weeks. She took another sip of her coffee but pulled a face at its bitter aftertaste. Her phone told her she had three hours before the train to Paddington.

"Will you come back with me before I go? I've got to pick up a few things." *And there's something I'd rather not do on my own.*

Dawn smiled in reply, placing her hand over Emmy's. "Of course."

The tears came then and Emmy let them, grateful to her friend for allowing her the luxury of release without fuss or reproach. When she was under control again, she sniffed and looked up into Dawn's cat eyes, ever-patient.

"I fully expect to open a newspaper soon and see your name in an article about some massive US human rights case. I'm gonna miss you so much," Emmy said, her voice catching on a sob.

Dawn smiled her wise beyond years smile. "Promise you'll come and see me in Cali, Em. You can't expect me to do this endless hot girl summer thing all on my own!"

"I promise!"

Emmy laughed despite herself as Dawn swept a pair of oversize sunnies on to her beautiful face before linking arms with her friend as they left the cafe.

THE SCENE inside the shop was exactly how Emmy had left it on the night she'd los–since that night. She couldn't bring herself to think his name. Her grief was so raw, an open, septic wound, and any meditation on the whats and whys of what had happened only infected it further. She'd stayed at a hotel ever since, the only belongings she'd taken with her were a change of clothing and Breone. She and Dawn had made a detour back to her room to pick the cat up and they now stood silently on the threshold, looking through the half glass door.

Like Alice, Emmy thought a little deliriously. She fought it. She'd had enough of this particular Wonderland to last her a lifetime. The heady scent of vanilla was a wrecking ball to her self-control as she'd opened the door, daring her to gag. She pressed her lips together and breathed through her nose, trying to prevent the smell from resurrecting all her suppressed memories. But it was if someone had opened a flicker book inside her brain. Images of herself and Jonathan and everything that had happened in the last few months played inside her mind like a silent movie.

Willing herself to take on the detached state her meds sometimes gave her, Emmy drifted and pretended it was happening to someone else. Yes, that was it. She could be an unseen bystander, watching from the sidelines. Gripping Dawn's arm for support, she stepped further into the store, the sound of her heels echoing on the flagstones. Her eyes fell upon a small pile of magazines on the counter. It was the same issue that Jonathan had been reading. Halloween. She clasped the top copy to her breast, belatedly remembering that today was the last day of October and their plan for A Haunting at The Bookshop. None of it mattered anymore and she let the magazine fall from her fingers to the floor, where it landed with a soft thud.

She turned to Dawn, who was watching her with concern-loaded eyes.

"Will you wait here for a minute?" Her voice was steady. Good.

The other woman nodded, relinquishing her grip on Emmy's fingers.

This was something Emmy needed to do without an audience, but she didn't want to go alone. So she freed Breone from his carrier and held him to her, burrowing her face in his ginger fur for a second. With a final glance at Dawn who smiled in encouragement, she headed through the oak door and picked her way down the dark steps, using her phone again to light the way.

When she got to the chamber, her heart was so loud in her ears, she had to pause for a moment and remember to breathe. Fearing an attack, she grounded herself against Breone's warm reality and as the anxiety passed, the tightness in her chest loosened.

The chamber was empty. No longer filled with radiance from the ghost of Maggie. She'd expected as much, but that didn't stop Emmy from speaking to the walls as if Maggie could hear her.

"I forgive you. I forgive you both," She said. Whether she meant Maggie and Jonathan, or Maggie and Lizzie, she wasn't entirely sure. Her voice echoed back to her and a sudden breeze wafted across the tiny hairs on her arms. She whirled, searching for the source, as Breone leapt from her arms and scampered away into the darkness.

"Breone!"

Emmy huffed as she charged after him down another tunnel. The cat didn't respond to her calls, instead, he remained a few yards ahead of her no matter how fast she ran to keep up with him. The tunnel seemed to go on forever, and after a few minutes, the air changed again, becoming noticeably warmer and brighter. The path ahead started to incline, and Emmy's sides hurt as she struggled to keep up with her runaway moggy. He came to a sudden stop at a set of stone steps, identical to the ones he and Emmy had only moments ago descended.

Looking back at Emmy, he meowed, before climbing the steps with pace, his muscular little body leaping with the kind of grace only felines possessed. Emmy was nowhere near as lithe and when she got to the top of the staircase, she was panting hard. Breone scratched at the wooden door, his back arching.

Emmy was pleased to find she hadn't completely lost her sense of wonder and she tried the handle. Locked. Fishing in her pocket, she brought out the key from the other night, before sticking it straight into the lock and turning it. Her mind raced. What was behind this door? She had an idea. A blast of cool air hit her in the face as the door swung open and Emmy found herself in another room, this one with a higher ceiling and another door ahead. But this door was barricaded by several large wooden planks. Emmy rushed over and began pounding her fists on it as hard as she could on the blockade.

"Hey! Is there anyone there? Can anyone hear me?"

Breone shot into a gap in the wooden boards, slinking through a hole in the base of the door and out of sight.

"Breone!" Emmy yelled. Her hands hurt, and her throat was hoarse from shouting, but she didn't stop trying.

After what seemed like forever, a confused voice answered her calls and Emmy sank to the floor in relief. Several hours later, the door was finally breached, and Emmy drew in a ragged breath before stepping over the threshold into the echoey South Tower of Exeter Cathedral.

2019

THE LITTLE SHOP teemed with life. Excited chatter bubbled around the walls as tourists and customers craned their necks to get a glimpse of the now famous tunnel entrance. Emmy's discovery of the hidden passage had been the tip of the iceberg and subsequent expeditions had uncovered a labyrinth of previously lost tunnels. The old bell over the door rang in harmony with the till as crowds flocked to the shop, now the final stop on the Exeter Underground Passages tour. Much to her bemusement, Emmy herself had become something of a reluctant local celebrity. Almost eleven months had passed since she'd discovered the chamber and as Emmy took down the details for another large order, she was surprised to see that tomorrow would be September again.

As she served another happy customer, warmth spread through Emmy's chest telling her she'd made the right choice. This was home. She was as much a part of the books and dust as Maggie had been. Moving away from the counter she nodded to herself as she looked around the store. Her right hand moved instinctively to massage her breastbone but then she let it fall again. It was always going to hurt, but Maggie was still here, in the books and the dust and—most importantly—inside her heart. Emmy closed her eyes for a moment expecting to hear the older woman's voice but for once, her mind was silent.

After all the stress, Emmy's condition was finally stable. Twice monthly visits with her psychiatrist and a change in medication had helped, but Emmy knew it was more than that. She still occasionally heard the voices, but she was better equipped to cope with them now. A strength she never knew she had had given her the courage to stay. Yes, she'd been broken, but broken didn't equal weakness.

There was strength and beauty in scars.

She'd taken a course in Japanese Kintsungi–a gift to herself–and the first pot she'd made took pride of place on a shelf behind the counter next to her treasured copy of *Practical Magic*, her trophy from the Spellcasters competition, and a photo of Maggie. You didn't throw things out just because they were smashed. You sealed the pieces back together with gold and made something new and unique. You let those joins show, put them on display, for they were the glue that created new from old. Emmy didn't need fixing. She was strong enough already. And if she could handle the mess life had thrown at her in the last two years, she could survive anything.

Wisdom is caring yet remaining immovable with our words. Be still.

Breone was asleep on Maggie's favourite chair, purring happily. Most of his days were spent enjoying inordinate amount of fuss from customers and chasing Netflix and Chill, whom Emmy had adopted, around the store's many nooks and crannies. The only blot on Emmy's perfect landscape was Lizzie and Thom's trial two months earlier, when they had been convicted with coercion, arson and attempted fraud and sentenced to almost six years each.

Well, not quite the only one.

Late at night, when the tourists had gone back to their hotels, Emmy sat hunched over her laptop, tapping at the keyboard, a bird pecking at non-existent grain. A strange tingling in her fingers burned as she typed. But with each wave of euphoria, each time she let herself dare to believe, her hopes were ultimately dashed. The fields where once she'd grown an abundance of words, now fallow. Wasting away to dust.

Yet here she was once more, attempting to weave magic with words. Maggie's insistence that Emmy was a Word Witch had lit a fire inside her soul that couldn't be extinguished. Her shoulders and back ached with tension, eyes ached from staring at the screen. For too long the discarded manuscripts had piled up, and each was a paper cut to her heart. Maybe she was right all along. Maybe Maggie had been wrong and she wasn't a witch after all. But if not, at least she could say she finally believed in herself and that *this* book was the most honest, most sincere thing she'd ever written.

Words *Are* Deeds

It was true, words did have power, but they weren't something to be afraid of. And she'd allowed her fear of the voices and what they might say to stand in her way for too long. Of course, the voices would never completely go away, but they were at least now under control. Her illness would always be a part of her, but it didn't define her. It didn't mean that she had to be imprisoned by the voices, not anymore. Not now she'd found her own voice, her own words. The irony of that epiphany hadn't been lost on her. Just the fact that she was writing again was something to cheer. And Leticia wanted to publish it! That was definitely worth celebrating.

But it wasn't enough. Pressing save on the edited, completed manuscript, she closed her eyes, praying with every fibre of her being that this time the spell would work.

Please, let this be The One.

Because just like reading, writing was imbued with that same page-turning, one more chapter quality. Weaving one word after another, until they made a sentence, a paragraph, a story, a tapestry. A life. Just one more chapter. There was a lifetime of infinite promises wrapped up in those four little words.

Just one more chapter…

Nothing.

The sound the laptop made as Emmy snapped it shut was the final nail in the coffin of her heart.

~

2020

"Congratulations, Emmy!"

A champagne cork popped, and someone shrieked. Dawn passed Emmy a glass with a grin.

"Don't worry, it's sparkling apple juice," she whispered. "So, how does it feel to be a published author?"

Published author. Emmy turned the words over in her head, testing the weight and shape of them with her mind. In truth, it hardly seemed real that she would find herself here now. Not only a writer but also the owner of one of the most successful independent bookshops in the country. She glanced at the expectant faces, waiting for her to read a passage from *How to Write A ~~Perfect~~ Book Boyfriend: A Love Spell*. All her Happy Ever After Publishing friends were here, including, of course Leticia–former boss and now her editor. The older woman waved at her from across the room where she was currently charming Emmy's parents, who–like Dawn– had flown in especially for the launch party.

"Honestly? It's a bit weird," Emmy confessed to Dawn in an equally conspiratorial whisper, "but I think I'm okay with weird." She would never be able to repay her friend for convincing her to stay, but at least she'd been able to replace the smashed studio lights.

"I know you are," Dawn said as she hugged Emmy. "Now if you'll excuse me, there's a snack over there with my name on it.

Emmy laughed as she watched Dawn slink across the bookshop, weaving in and out of the throng until she came to a stop in front of a young woman with geek-girl glasses and curly brown hair. Stacey? Sarah? Something like that. She worked for the local newspaper, that much Emmy could remember.

Jenny from the HEA marketing department was coming to the end of her speech and Emmy's stomach did a series of slow somersaults. She took a deep breath and turned to take in the giant blown up image of her book cover. It was a simple design. Her name and the book title in a striking white font overlaid across a close-up image of a square jawed Adonis in Tudor period costume. The art department had done their best, but the cover model was no Jonathan. Inhaling once more, she stepped forward to soft applause. Opening The *New* Book at her favourite spot, she looked up and began to read.

How to Write A ~~Perfect~~ Book Boyfriend: A Love Spell

Write what you know. That's what they say. But how do you know what you know? I'm not talking about two plus two equals four, I mean the good stuff, the stuff they never teach you in school. The life-lessons you can only learn by laying bare your soul until Knowledge impales you like the headlamp on a train, running you over with the full force of its wisdom and experience until you can feel it illuminating your soul, marinating in your marrow. Only then will your tears be made, not of salt, but Knowledge. Only then will you bleed Knowledge. For Knowledge is power. And Knowledge can only be attained by failing. We try and fail every day. I've messed up so many times, I've lost track. And that's not to say I'm now a fountain of all Knowledge because that's far from the truth. But what I do know is that everything I ever learned came from words. From communicating with others, from listening and learning, from reading and writing and attempting to make sense of the words in my heart and head.

I am a Word Witch and this is my story.

Once you start to see the world as a book that we're all writing our words in, life starts making more sense. The words we use every day have power. There are those who believe the universe is made up of atoms and dust but look closer and you might just see that it's words that bind us all. Words are magic. They exist at the edges time and space, weaving in and out of our lives in an inescapable, irresistible thread. Sometimes the threads become entangled and we make a mess, and our arteries and veins become too knotted, preventing Knowledge from entering our hearts. But occasionally, our words will create something so beautiful, so precious, and so worth fighting for, the letters them-

selves glisten on our paper-thin souls imprinted there in gold.

That's you, Jonathan. You are my Knowledge. You helped me find my own precious words–my voice– and for that, I will always love you.

EMMY DROVE the deadbolt home and set the alarm. The launch had been a resounding success. Leticia's excited chatter was still ringing in her ears. Sensing it was safe to come out again, the two younger cats appeared from their hiding places to join Breone on the counter. For a moment, the only sounds were their purring and Emmy's low humming as she cleared away glasses and plates ready for tomorrow.

A crackle of static made her drop the glass she was holding. It fell to the flagstones and shattered into a thousand wicked pieces, glinting like diamonds. The air flattened and compressed as she bent to retrieve it, crushing Emmy's ribs inside her chest. Dust bloomed and glistened and a sudden whooshing was followed by the unmistakable sound of hundreds of pages rifling in the air.

Emmy's eyes widened as book after book after book flew from the shelves, the words from them springing loose and glittering like stars, just like Jonathan's sonnet had done. Hot tears of excitement began to stream down her face, and she rose to her feet hardly daring to believe. A ringing echoed through the shop and Emmy turned to the telephone in the red box. She crept towards it, watching as the handset vibrated in its cradle, the noise growing louder and louder until Emmy was convinced it was ringing inside her head. She mashed her hands to her ears, heart now in her throat.

Please, not another relapse.

Then silence fell, as if the shop could understand her thoughts. Even Maggie's old grandfather clock stopped its incessant ticking. Breone appeared at Emmy's side. Emmy had just stretched out an arm to him when the bell over the door tinkled. It was the sound of coming home.

Jonathan.

No longer merely a shadow of a man made up of letters and dust, this Jonathan was real and whole. His face shone with life, eyes sparkling under the chandelier, cheeks flushed with excitement. Emmy's heart flatlined and restarted. Before she knew it, she was running to him, but her legs wouldn't move fast enough. For once it was her body that had broken and not her mind, which was racing ahead and already imagining being in his arms. Breathless, she came to a stop inches from him, not ready to believe he was real but unable to deny every nerve now standing on end screaming at her inside that he was. A tiny pulse beat in his neck. He needed a shave and a new network of wrinkles crinkled at the corners of his incomparable eyes as he smiled. For what seemed like an eternity, neither spoke.

"Emmeline," Jonathan breathed. He stared at the blow up of *How to Write The Perfect Book Boyfriend* cover art, delight written all over his face. "You did it!"

Emmy swallowed, trying to lubricate her mouth and throat which suddenly felt like she'd been wandering for days in a desert. "I-I...Is it really you?" It was all she could manage. Her fingers itched with longing and she crossed her arms in front of her chest to stop from reaching for him.

"It's me. I'm here, and I'm never leaving you again." Jonathan's voice cracked on the final sentence, but he cleared his throat and continued, holding up one palm when Emmy moved to interrupt. "I had centuries to prepare a speech for this moment but now it is here I find myself lost for words. You took them all from me and made them anew. You wrote me into your soul where lie all things strong and magical. So, Lady Emmeline, if you'll permit it, let me tell you a story of mine own."

"Go on," Emmy nodded in encouragement.

"Once upon a time, there was the most beautiful, most incredibly strong and powerful Word Witch called Emmeline, who, if she'll allow it, will be loved forever and ever by me," Jonathan said.

Emmy laughed and entwined her arms around his neck, pulling him close. "I'll allow it," she said, "but only if you shut up and kiss me."

Their lips met and the love of a billion Happily Ever Afters exploded inside Emmy's heart. But this wasn't The End. It was only...

The Beginning

ACKNOWLEDGMENTS

I've dreamed about writing the acknowledgements for my debut novel for so long now, I'm unsure where to begin and I'm certain I'm going to mess them up and/or forget someone. Huge apologies if I do. I can only point to a cocktail of euphoria, disbelief, imposter syndrome, and chronic pain & ADHD-induced brain fog as the culprit mixologists.

Firstly, I want to thank Brittany and James at Violet Gaze Press for taking a chance on me with this story and these characters, and for being so kind, understanding and undemanding of me as both an author and a person. As far as I know, mine is the first Romance novel which features an MC with schizophrenia, and I will be forever grateful to Brittany for immediately understanding my motivation for writing it, and for not shying away from a mental illness which is still heavily stigmatised and misunderstood. Your dedication to diverse and inclusive Romance, and unwavering support and belief in both me and Emmy have been both my rock and inspiration. I cannot thank you enough for helping me bring her story to life.

Which leads me to my editor, Ali Williams. Ali already knows how grateful I am for her brilliant insights, wealth of Romantic fiction knowledge and general excited flailing, but I want her to know that she's also my oracle and Word Witch extraordinaire!

Huge thanks to Najla Qamber and the whole team at Qamber Designs for creating the cover of my dreams. I can't stop looking at it! It's like seeing my characters come to life, which is extremely meta. Art imitating art, or something like that.

To the wonderful Violet Gaze Press family: I love you all. You make me want to be a better writer. #VGPStrong 12

To Shari Conyer, who was there at *The Book Boyfriend*'s beginning. To Tami Croft, who's strength and spirit inspires me every day, just like Emmy. And to Rhian Smith, who really *was* there at the beginning of it all, back when I was a wide-eyed teenager with big dreams and a heart full of love stories. Your encouragement has never waivered and I'm lucky to have you in my life. I love you awesome ladies!

To some of my favourite people and fellow writers including (but not limited to) Emma Finlayson-Palmer; Lorna Claire Riley; Anne Boyere; Anna Orridge; Laura McKendrick (thank you especially for your early help re sensitivity); Kiley Dunbar, Lizzie Carr, Mellisa Welliver, Poppy Dale, and Christy Kate McKenzie for being just *lovely*; Sandy Barker, Lucy Morris, Lucy Keeling, Sally Calder, Lucy Mitchell, Rebecca Duval, Leonie Mack, and everyone involved in UKRomChat past and present; my DISCO buddies Linda Corbett, Denise Sutherland, Helen Barell, and Katie Kenzie; Ellie Lock (Brrrdupp! Brrrdupp!); Stuart White; Emma Dykes and TWP ("Just write the f*cking book!"); all the incredibly talented and wonderfully generous peeps in VWG; and just ALL my lovely friends & followers on social media who - for reasons best known to yourselves - enjoy my special brand of Romance chat, strident activism and absurd nonsense. Thank you all for your support and friendship over the years.

Thanks to industry peeps including (but again not limited to) Sarah, Jo and the whole team at Writers HQ; Elane and Sarah at IAmInPrint; Alison May; Imogen Howsen; Janet Gover; my NWS readers and bursary sponsor; Jeni Chappelle, Maria Tureaud, Katie McCoach, Miranda Darrow & the whole RevPit team; Stephanie Carty; Sara-Jade Virtue & BaTC; Savvy Authors; Authors for Oz; Luanne G Smith; Choc Lit; and anyone and everyone who has supported me over the years, either via generous feedback and critique or in some other professional capacity.

I want to give a quick shout out to two of my favourite famous men: Henry Cavill and Jack Savoretti for being the twin inspirations (twinspiration?) behind MY FAVOURITE BOOK BOYFRIEND EVER™, with an extra thanks to Jack for consistently singing songs to write romance to. Seriously, if you're struggling to write a sex scene, bang on some Jack (fnarr fnarr) and the words will be pouring out of you in no time!

This brings me to some of the most important people of all: Romance writers and readers. It's no secret that I wrote this book – my love letter to our beautiful, hopeful genre - for you all, and I hope you love it as much as I do. Thank you for inspiring me with your stories and words of hope, heart and HEAs. Irrespective of gender, or whether you are a writer, reader or both, you are all Word

Witches, and I feel blessed to be able to share just a sprinkle of your magic.

Writing this story has been a true labour of love and there were many times when I thought I would never finish even a first draft. In recent years, I've faced new challenges with my health, both physical and mental. Living with chronic health conditions like CRPS and ADHD isn't easy, but I know myself better than ever now. I understand what I'm capable of and I've learnt to accept my limitations. There are far too many of you to thank for helping me on this leg (pun intended) of my journey but please know, I appreciate every single one of you.

But this book isn't about me. It's about the power of words and about voices not usually heard. About including people who don't normally get to read *their* stories in the pages of a Romance novel, the chance to see someone like them living, loving and being loved in return, and having their own well-deserved Happily Ever After too.

Last but by no means least, I want to thank my wonderful family.

To Kieron: husband, rock and better man than a million, trillion book boyfriends, I love you. "You've got to promise not to stop when I say when".

To my beautiful children, Charlie and Jesse: I'm so proud of the two amazing, kind, talented, funny, and caring young men you're growing up to be. I love you *most*.

To Mum and Dad, you've always supported my dreams and I can't thank you enough for always being there.

To Grandma, for always asking how my writing is

going and inspiring one of my favourite characters in this novel.

And to all my other friends and family, thank you.

But most of all, I want to thank my brother, Phil, who deserves the universe and more! *The Book Boyfriend* wouldn't exist without you.

Thank you all,

Jeanna x

P.S. I did it! I wrote, edited, revised, submitted, revised, submitted, revised, submitted and (eventually)... PUBLISHED THE F*CKING BOOK!!!

JEANNA LOUISE SKINNER

Jeanna Louise Skinner writes romance with a sprinkling of magic. Her debut novel *The Book Boyfriend* is out in 2021 and she is working on a prequel. She has CRPS and ADHD and is one of the co-founders of the RNA DISCO Chapter, for members with disabilities and chronic health conditions. She's also the co-creator of @UKRomChat, a Romance-centric live Twitter chat, which was nominated for the RNA Media Star Award in 2019 and 2020. She lives in Devon with her husband, their two children and a cat who sounds like a goat.

facebook.com/jeannalouiseskinner
twitter.com/JeannaLStars
instagram.com/JeannaLStars

Printed in Great Britain
by Amazon